PRAI

MARIO ACEVEDO

"Decidedly good, unclean, unwholesome fun."
Baltimore Sun

"Raymond Chandler could never have imagined an L.A. like this where hard-boiled, private-eye vampires fight crime, as well as commit a few during lunch breaks. . . . The mean streets have never been meaner—or stranger—and the result is a high-speed, well-crafted romp through the forests of the night."
Booklist

"[Acevedo] manages to update vampire lore in clever and imaginative ways."
El Paso Times

"Deliciously unique. A smooth combination of Anne Rice and Michael Connelly, with a generous portion of Dave Barry. Loaded with thrills, sex, violence, and laughs."
J.A. Konrath, author of *Bloody Mary*

"My built-in garlic factor usually puts me off vampire books, but Mario Acevedo has come up with such a fascinating character—Iraq war veteran Felix Gomez, who is a private detective as well as a vampire—that I was won over."
Chicago Tribune

"Vampire P.I. Felix Gomez is irresistibly entertaining."
Rick Riordan, Edgar® Award-winning author of *Mission Road*

By Mario Acevedo

The Adventures of Felix Gomez

THE UNDEAD KAMA SUTRA
X-RATED BLOODSUCKERS
THE NYMPHOS OF ROCKY FLATS

And forthcoming in trade paperback

JAILBAIT ZOMBIE

ATTENTION: ORGANIZATIONS AND CORPORATIONS
Most Eos paperbacks are available at special quantity discounts for
bulk purchases for sales promotions, premiums, or fund raising.
For information, please call or write:

**Special Markets Department, HarperCollins Publishers,
10 East 53rd Street, New York, New York 10022-5299.
Telephone: (212) 207-7528.   Fax: (212) 207-7222.**

THE
UNDEAD KAMA SUTRA

MARIO ACEVEDO

An Imprint of HarperCollinsPublishers

This book is a work of fiction. The characters, incidents, and dialogue are drawn from the author's imagination and are not to be construed as real. Any resemblance to actual events or persons, living or dead, is entirely coincidental.

EOS
An Imprint of HarperCollins*Publishers*
10 East 53rd Street
New York, New York 10022-5299

Copyright © 2008 by Mario Acevedo
Excerpt from *Jailbait Zombie* copyright © 2009 by Mario Acevedo
Cover art by Will Staehle
ISBN 978-0-06-166746-6
www.eosbooks.com

All rights reserved. No part of this book may be used or reproduced in any manner whatsoever without written permission, except in the case of brief quotations embodied in critical articles and reviews. For more information, address Eos, an Imprint of HarperCollins Publishers.

First Eos paperback printing: November 2008
First Eos trade paperback printing: March 2008

HarperCollins® and Eos® are registered trademarks of Harper-Collins Publishers.

Printed in the U.S.A.

10 9 8 7 6 5 4 3 2 1

If you purchased this book without a cover, you should be aware that this book is stolen property. It was reported as "unsold and destroyed" to the publisher, and neither the author nor the publisher has received any payment for this "stripped book."

*To the memory of my parents
and my sister, Laura*

Acknowledgments

THANKS TO the crew at HarperCollins: my editor Diana Gill, her assistant Emily Krump, publicist Gretchen Crary, and publisher Rene Alegria. A special appreciation to my agent, Scott Hoffman, of Folio Literary Management, LLC, and to the Peter Miller Literary and Film Management, Inc. To CJ Lyons for the tour of Hilton Head Island and not feeding me to the alligators. I wouldn't have gotten this far without the support of my critique group, Rocky Mountain Fiction Writers, the Lighthouse Writers Workshop, Mystery Writers of America, and El Centro Su Teatro. I owe much to the friendship and advice of Erika Paterson and Eric Matelski. Lastly, where would I be without the crank comments from my family? Tia Angelica, Sylvia, Armando, Janet, my sons Alex and Emil, and Uncle Sam and Tia Alma. Happy fanging everyone.

CHAPTER 1

F IND HIM," the alien said. "Find the man who killed me."

I sat on the alien's bed. We were on the second floor of a cheap motel in Sarasota, Florida. To get up the stairs I had to get past three hookers, their pimp, and a blind man selling pot—for medicinal purposes only, of course.

Gilbert Odin, or, rather, the alien who masqueraded as my abducted and long-deceased friend from college, lay on his back. His jaundiced eyes looked ready to pop from their sockets. His slender body stretched the length of the mattress and his wing tips hung over the end. Iridescent blood pumped from the wound on his chest, stained his clothes, and pooled on the bedcovers. It looked like maple syrup mixed with motor oil. The stench of his charred flesh and his natural reek of boiled cabbage would've watered the eyes of a buzzard.

I cradled in my lap the space blaster I'd found on the floor—I'd almost tripped over the thing when I entered.

Odin wheezed and gasped. His mustache arched across the top of the flattened oval of his mouth. Every faltering breath pumped more of that thick, shimmering blood from the hole in his torso. The puncture looked like someone had impaled him with a white-hot length of rebar. A black ring of burned flesh surrounded the thumb-sized opening.

Odin was dying and there was nothing I could do to help him. No use dialing 911. What could I say? "Send help. I'm a vampire and need an ambulance for an extraterrestrial dying from a ray-gun blast."

"Felix." Odin's hand touched my leg. "Find Goodman."

"Goodman who?"

I'd barraged Odin with questions since I'd been here. An hour ago I was cruising south on I-75 when he called my cell phone. He asked for help, gave directions to this squalid motel along the North Trail Corridor, and hung up.

Question one. How did he get my number?

Question two. How did he know I was in Florida?

Question three. Why me?

He hadn't answered these or any of my other questions. All Odin did was roll his eyes, squirm on the bed, and bleed.

The lights were out and the room was as dark as the night sky outside. I had removed my contacts to unmask the mirrorlike retinas—the *tapetum lucidum*—in my eyes and use vampire vision.

As a supernatural, I could see the auras of the psychic energy fields that surrounded all living creatures. The color of these auras corresponded to our chakras—our spiritual centers and the level of our psychic awareness. Humans had a red aura, the first and lowest chakra, which centered on manifestation in the material plane. Vampires, orange aura, the second chakra, connection from the material to the spiritual. Aliens, third and yellow, for transformation. To what?

Judging from what I know about aliens, I wouldn't regard them as more evolved or spiritually developed than vampires.

Auras can display our emotions more clearly than facial expressions. Since humans are blind to psychic energy, this gives us vampires the advantage when we pump them for information.

Odin coughed. His aura faded to a diluted piss-yellow color. The penumbra of his psychic shroud tightened around his body.

The last I'd seen of Odin was years ago, after he'd hired me to investigate an outbreak of nymphomania at the Rocky Flats Nuclear Weapons Plant in Colorado. He knew the nymphomania was caused by a special isotope of red mercury leaking from a UFO the government had squirreled away, but he hadn't bothered to fill me in. I had to uncover that on my own.

Odin might exist on a higher psychic plane but he was still a liar. Something else Odin hadn't told me was that he was an alien impostor and what he really wanted was a prototype psychotronic device other aliens had brought to Earth in violation of their intergalactic law. The psychotronic device was to test controlling humans by using psychic energy.

Screw that. We vampires didn't need competition from extraterrestrials. So I had destroyed the device and had left Gilbert Odin the Alien with the mutual understanding that our identities would remain secret.

Now he was back, and dying.

Odin reached for the nightstand beside the bed. His aura brightened as he struggled against death.

I stood and faced him.

Odin hooked his fingers over the drawer pull and opened the drawer. He groped inside and withdrew a letter-sized envelope.

"Take me here," he whispered. His thumb rubbed against

numbers scrawled over the front of the envelope. Smears of his blood stained the corners.

I took the envelope. It was heavy and contained something thick. The numbers on the front read:

27.25 82.46

"What do these mean?" I asked.

"Just take me there," he said. "Help me get home." Odin turned his head toward me. The skin hung from around his eyes like he was starting to peel. "I have a family."

I had considered a Mrs. Gilbert Odin and larvae Odins on another planet. Hope they stayed there. "You miss them?" I tried to sound sympathetic.

"Are you kidding?" Odin gasped. "That's why I took this job." He chuckled, *snork, snork, snork.*

I opened the envelope. It contained hundred-dollar bills in a wad thicker than my index finger. "What is this? About twenty thousand bucks, right? For what?"

Odin turned his head back toward the ceiling. The loose flesh sagged from his skull as if he was deflating. Odin had told me he had gone through cosmetic surgery to blend into human society. With his body shutting down, the alterations were disintegrating.

He aimed a crooked finger. His fingernail fell off and left a purple splotch on his skin. "For you."

"Why?"

Odin smacked his lips and worked his tongue out of his mouth. It flopped on his chin and rolled down his cheek to land quivering on the bedspread.

Yuck. I hoped the tongue didn't sprout eyes and legs and start walking on its own.

"Find Goodman." I guess Odin didn't need a tongue to talk. The voice sounded like a trio of drunks were in his throat. He had mentioned having a trifurcated speaking passage.

"Did Goodman do this to you? With this?" I held up the blaster. The gun had a housing the size of a large orange, with knobs sticking out the top and rear. Despite its size, the blaster felt light in my hand. The back of the housing had hieroglyphics around the circumference. A pointed barrel made of glass-like material stuck out the front. The grip and trigger seemed improvised for a humanoid hand.

"Goodman," Odin repeated. His aura faded to a faint glow around his body.

Goodman who? This damn alien was loony enough the first time I'd seen him. Now, so close to death, his delirium made him incomprehensible.

I slapped the envelope against the nightstand. "You want my services, then help me. Who is Goodman? You said, 'Find the man.' He's not an alien? He shot you with a blaster. This one? Where did he get it?"

Odin waved me close. I leaned over him and worried that he might spit a body part at me.

He whispered: "Find Goodman."

What a mess. A dying extraterrestrial doing God knows what mischief on Earth. Mix that up with an assassin using an alien ray gun. But if I turned Odin away, what business did I have being a vampire private detective? Problem was, I kept getting cases that made me feel like Moses standing at the Red Sea.

"Okay, Gilbert. I'm in."

"One more thing," he whispered again.

What was he suckering me into? "What is it?"

"Save the Earth women."

I should've expected this. An even bigger mess. "Save the Earth women from what?"

"No more questions." Odin touched my face. "Tag, you're it."

His hand dropped—literally, it fell off his wrist and thumped on the floor. His aura faded to nothing.

Gilbert Odin, the alien impostor, was dead.

And I had to find the one who killed him.

CHAPTER
2

I HAD A dead alien on my hands and twenty thousand in hundred-dollar bills. I could ditch Odin and take the money, but his final words had hooked me.

"Save the Earth women."

Given Odin's extraterrestrial origins, the ray gun, and the mysterious gruesomeness of his death, I knew he wasn't asking that I save the Earth women from bad hair days. Someone had killed Odin to get him out of the way.

I'd come from my home in Denver, Colorado, to southern Florida. I was on vacation and after a different mystery. Over the last few months I had collected random pages from a manuscript called *The Undead Kama Sutra*.

My sole vampire client had mentioned the manuscript in passing. He said the myth was that this *Kama Sutra* could adjust a vampire's psychic energy and turbocharge our supernatural recuperative powers. I hear a lot of crazy things in my business, and blew it off. Later the vampire brought fourteen grainy photocopied pages of the manuscript. He told me they'd been copied from a private collection in London. Or Frankfurt. He wasn't sure.

This *Kama Sutra* showed vampires in various poses, acrobatic couplings with other vampires or humans. The captions were handwritten in English, with additional notes scribbled in Greek and Sanskrit.

I found other references to this particular *Kama Sutra* on the Internet, either posted on blogs or in academic treatises. What piqued my interest, besides the interesting erotic and graphic drawings, were the allusions that sex in these poses was psychically therapeutic. But the captions were incomplete, and from what I deduced, the trick was performing sex using the proper technique in the right sequence and for the correct duration. Each cycle of poses referenced a chakra and the ailment it was meant to cure.

We vampires know how disturbances in our psychic energy field can alter our health and humor. The disturbance that most got to us was keeping a daylight schedule, and the usual remedy for the "sunlight blahs" was an extended nap in a coffin.

An entry in one blog mentioned the name of someone researching this *Kama Sutra*: Carmen Arellano. I knew a Carmen Arellano; she was the head of the Denver *nidus,* Latin for "nest." Figures: if anyone was studying an erotic manuscript, it would be her.

The blog went on to say that this Carmen was in Florida, and the last I heard from the Carmen I knew was that she was also in Florida.

I had called her and voice mail picked up. Carmen's message said she was in Key West working on her "tan." I'd bet a cooler full of arterial type-A negative that these two Carmens were the same vampire. I left word to expect me and began my road trip to Florida in my Cadillac.

Was it possible that sex was psychic therapy? I couldn't dismiss the idea as ancient bunk.

An impossible story? Hell, I'm a vampire and am sitting shivah with a visitor from another planet. Tell me again what's impossible. If this preternatural *Kama Sutra* was authentic, it was worth exploring to make it easier for us vampires to exist in a more crowded and suspicious human world.

Now I had two mysteries to solve. This one and Odin's.

I gathered Odin and all of his loose parts into the center of the bedcovers. I bundled him and folded the edges of the blanket to keep his blood from leaving a trail.

His funk stuck to my clothes and I doubted I could get them smelling fresh again. What would his stink do to the trunk of my Cadillac? I extended a talon and cut the thick plastic cover off the mattress. Standard issue for a business that rented rooms in fifteen-minute increments. I wrapped him in the clear plastic. Later I'd cinch the cover tight with duct tape. That should do it for now, since I wasn't going to keep him in the trunk of my car longer than tonight.

The two Benjamins I left on the dresser should pay for the room and the bedcovers. I put on my sunglasses to hide my eyes, though wearing sunglasses or contacts prevented me from using vampire vision.

Odin's corpse had deteriorated enough that I could carry him under one arm. I palmed the blaster with my other hand and shoved the gun into the front of my trousers. This weapon might come in handy, especially since I'd left all my firepower back in my desk in Denver.

Outside, the second shift of hookers prowled the curb alongside North Tamiami Trail, the main drag in this part of Sarasota. They strutted on stiletto heels around discarded hip flasks and bottles of malt liquor.

I carried Odin down the stairs. The plastic wrap slipped loose and something dribbled from the bundle. Four of his toes bounced like grapes against the steps. I swept them with my foot into a patch of weeds under the balcony. Good thing it wasn't something from between his legs. After folding his corpse into the trunk of my Cadillac, I secured the plastic bundle with a roll of duct tape I had stashed next to the spare tire.

None of the hookers showed any interest. Considering this neighborhood, a whale could fall out of the sky and flatten the motel, but no one would admit to seeing a thing.

I drove off and stopped a few blocks away to examine the envelope with the money. What did the numbers on the front mean?

A phone? Radio frequency? Internet address?

Odin had said, "Take me here."

So these numbers must be a place. Were they map coordinates?

I got a road map, checked the margins, and read the tic marks for latitude and longitude. If these were coordinates, the spot was three miles west of Bradenton Beach in the Gulf of Mexico.

The map didn't show any islands out there, only water. Would I be taking Odin to meet a boat? I'd check it out. If no one showed up, I could dump him into the water.

I flipped the envelope over, took out the money, and looked inside. No other instructions. So when was Odin to be delivered?

My call then. Tonight. *Before* he stinks up my car.

I stopped in a local sporting goods store, bought their cheapest GPS unit, and headed toward the beach. The clouds settled low and reflected the amber haze of the street lamps. A drizzle misted my windshield. Drops splashed against my car and became heavier by the minute. By the time I crossed from Cortes to Bradenton Beach, the downpour had chased everyone indoors. I parked close to the marina on the eastern side of the island, facing Sarasota Bay.

I carried Odin to the beach and left him along the water's edge. From the deserted marina, I borrowed a Wave Runner, and returned to fetch the body.

I draped the bundle over the rear of the seat, secured his

body with bungee cords, and fastened the GPS to the handlebars with duct tape. To use my night vision, I removed my sunglasses. Heading south around the island, under the bridge, then west through the wet gloom into the Gulf of Mexico, I followed the direction indicators to the coordinates I had programmed into the GPS.

The rain felt hard as ball bearings and stung my skin. My hair lay plastered against my forehead. My soggy clothes flapped from my limbs. The chill was uncomfortable and made me look forward to a hot cup of coffee and A-negative. Behind me, the glow of civilization faded on the eastern horizon. The distance marker on the GPS counted the meters to the coordinates.

One thousand. One hundred. Fifty. Twenty-five.

I rolled the throttle to idle.

The Wave Runner drifted forward.

Ten meters. Five meters. At zero, the arrow turned into an X.

The Wave Runner stopped and bobbed on the waves. I gave Odin's corpse a mule kick. "Get up. We're here."

Waves slapped the fiberglass hull. Rain puddled in the crevasses of Odin's plastic shroud.

The surface of the water shimmered with the beat of the raindrops. The shimmer took on a metallic sheen and I realized this was from hundreds of little fish leaping from the water. The sheen became pink from the tiny red fish auras.

I looked over the side of the Wave Runner into the murky water. What made them behave like this?

The Wave Runner's engine stalled. Suddenly an electric charge pulsed through the seat, up my spine, and into my arms and head. My limbs buzzed like the tines of a tuning fork. Glowing blue rings from St. Elmo's fire curled around my wrists and ankles. The hair lifted from my scalp. My *kundalini noir*—that black serpent of energy residing in every vampire instead of a heart—coiled in panic. Get out of here.

My hands and feet stayed put. All around, the little fish floated lifelessly in the water.

The Wave Runner rocked backward. Something huge rose from the water in front of me.

CHAPTER
3

A SMOOTH, PEWTER-GRAY hump the width of a tennis court rose from the sea. My Wave Runner slipped backward on the water cascading from an enormous rim surrounding the hump.

The object lifted clear of the sea, then hovered noiselessly about fifty feet before me. It had a spherical body bisected by a wide disk.

A flying saucer. A UFO. One straight from the late-night drive-in movies. Those guys with the cheesy special effects had it right all along.

Odin had asked for my help in finding his assassin. Why didn't he ask these aliens? Unless this UFO was robotic . . . or was this more of the scheming among the aliens? Odin had told me that extraterrestrials had to keep their visits secret because Earth was under quarantine, which was why he'd hired me before.

Odin also asked that I save the Earth women. But from what, exactly?

The grip of the blaster poked against my belly but I remained paralyzed. Not that the gun would do me much good. The crew of this ship certainly had more dangerous weapons, and if they wanted me dead, they could've disintegrated me already.

A hatch about a meter square opened in the belly of the sphere and a faint beam of light fixed upon my craft. Rain sparkled in the light, like confetti. The bundle holding Odin's remains started to vibrate. The Wave Runner swung around as if its back end had been snagged by an invisible hook.

The bundle strained against the bungee cords. The Wave Runner surged toward the hatch.

The bungee cords tore loose. Odin's bundle sproinged from the seat and levitated for a moment before floating toward the hatch. The bundle rotated and went headfirst into the UFO. The hatch closed.

The electric charge disappeared. My limbs relaxed. The fish in the water came to life again and fluttered away.

The UFO remained still for a moment. The rain eased and stars appeared in the black patches behind a gray mist above. The UFO rose silently and headed into the sky.

Sayonara, Gilbert Odin.

When the UFO was a speck in the mist, I reached to my waist and pulled out the blaster. Whoever shot Odin had used an alien weapon, maybe this one. I examined the knobs and the strange markings.

The rain stopped abruptly.

I looked up. The UFO loomed directly over me.

Startled, I shrank against the seat. Why had they returned? To abduct and probe me? My sphincter tightened.

I readied to dive into the water. The electric pulse returned and my limbs were paralyzed as before.

The hatch opened again and the beam of light focused on me. The blaster trembled in my hand.

A voice spoke from the light, a feminine voice, calm yet stern—like a warning from a librarian. "Let go of the weapon."

I released my grip. The blaster floated upward through the hatch.

"Thank you." The beam vanished. My muscles relaxed. The hatch closed and the UFO rose to zoom upward through the sky. Rain pelted me again.

I'd been hoping the ray gun would even the odds when I found Odin's killer. Not anymore.

I grasped the handles of the Wave Runner and wondered if it would start again. Thankfully, the engine coughed to life and burbled the water. I swung the Wave Runner east and cranked the throttle full-open.

A half-mile from shore, a couple of fighter jets screeched in my direction. They roared above, two F-16s armed with air-to-air missiles. As they zoomed past, strobe lights blinking, the auras of the pilots looked like crimson smears against the darkness.

The jets pitched upward on the trajectory of the UFO. If the fighters were after the saucer, good luck. Odin's intergalactic hearse was probably on the other side of the moon by now.

The jets disappeared into the clouds and it was just me and my questions. Didn't the Air Force debunk UFOs? How would they explain this? Lie, of course.

I returned the Wave Runner to its slip. So far I had the name Goodman, a murder using an alien blaster, UFOs, and a warning to save the Earth women. As far as leads, I had next to bupkus.

The cawing of a crow echoed through the misty darkness.

A crow? What was a crow doing out in such a cold, wet night?

To find me.

The crow meant the Araneum—which translated into

"spiderweb" in Latin and was the formal name for the world-wide network of vampires formed to protect us from exter-mination by humans—wanted me for a job. The Araneum used crows as messengers, and why else would that bird be here?

I felt my shoulders sag. I didn't need more work; I was on vacation.

A small red aura gave away the crow's position, where it sat tucked along the bottom of a shack, trying its best to stay out of the rain. The crow cawed again, an irritated squawk of discomfort.

"Shut up, you feathered bastard. I didn't ask for you to come around." The crow never brought good news, like I was needed in Cancún to rub sunscreen on horny coeds.

I approached, my wet shoes crunching the sand and bro-ken shells covering the beach. I wondered what the Ara-neum wanted at this hour. The crow kept its small black head drawn into its shoulders to conserve warmth. This bird didn't seem pleased to be out here, either. To the Araneum, it didn't make a difference if you were a vampire or a crow. Duty called.

The crow turned its shivering head toward me and blinked. It struggled to stand, as if its joints had rusted, and then walked toward me in a stiff-legged limp. A shiny metal capsule was clipped to its left leg.

I picked up the crow. Its wet feathers crinkled. The small, warm body trembled. I tucked the crow's torso under my armpit. The bird squirmed and I clamped my arm to keep it still. I unclipped the capsule, a tube made of filigreed plati-num and gold, with a ruby-encrusted cap.

I hunched over to protect the capsule from the rain.

The Araneum used swatches of vampire skin as notepa-per, a precaution to maintain secrecy, since the skin would burst into flame when exposed to sunlight. Rumor was the patch of skin came from a condemned vampire. But it was dark and raining. What about exposure to water?

I shook raindrops from the capsule and unscrewed the cap. The odor of rancid meat burst out like a fart. Yep, vampire hide. I extended a talon from my index finger and used the long, narrow tip to draw out the contents.

Surprisingly, there were two items inside: a folded square of onionskin-like parchment—the vampire skin—and a piece of newsprint.

The parchment unfolded to the size of the palm of my hand. A message was written in ornate calligraphy, in brown ink—dried blood? It read:

Our esteemed Felix Gomez,
The vampire underworld has a new threat, the extra-terrestrials. Because of your experience with the aliens, we have chosen you to investigate this threat. Under no circumstances are you to allow yourself or any other vampire to be compromised by these extra-terrestrials.

What did the Araneum mean, "compromised"? Captured? Exposed as a supernatural? How could that happen? Any other vampire? What other vampire? And what about "these extraterrestrials"? The only ones I knew just left Earth. Why was the Araneum passing this information now, *after* I'd sent the alien Gilbert Odin on his way? If this was so damn important, why didn't the Araneum alert me sooner?

We expect your usual thoroughness. Your investigation is to be kept confidential.
Report when completed.
Araneum

Report when completed what? Thoroughness at what? Who was I supposed to blab the investigation to? Talk radio? The Araneum knew more about this threat than I did. Why were they so stingy with information?

Rain trickled down my face and splashed onto the parchment, smearing the ink. No poof into flames.

I slipped the crow from under my armpit. It blinked and snorted indignantly.

I waved the parchment in front of its beak. "Okay, wise guy, if there's no sunlight, what's to keep this from getting into the wrong hands?"

Snapping faster than a mousetrap, the crow snatched the parchment from my fingers and the swatch of vampire skin disappeared down its throat. The crow swallowed, looked at me, then burped smoke.

I waved away the foul-smelling puff. "Next time give a warning."

The crow chirped, sounding like "Ha, ha."

I gave it a shake. "If you got anything coming out your butt, keep it to yourself."

I unfolded the newsprint, an article about a charter airplane, a Cessna Caravan, that had crashed last week near San Diego, killing all seven aboard. What did that have to do with the aliens? Obviously the article was a clue, but for what? Okay, I am a detective but a little help was always appreciated.

Raindrops soaked the newsprint. I wadded it into a soggy ball, which I offered to the crow. "Might help with your heartburn."

The crow squirmed, indicating that it wanted to be let go. I pushed the wad of newsprint into the capsule, screwed the cap back on, and clipped it to the crow's leg.

I set the crow on the sand. It shivered and remained still for a moment before starting to limp away. I expected the crow to leap upward but it didn't, instead continuing on its trek through the rain.

A pair of headlights crossed over the bridge from the mainland. When I looked back at the beach, the crow was gone.

I returned to my Cadillac. I had my orders.

CHAPTER
4

I SPENT THE next two nights in Fort Myers, in a proper hotel more upscale than the Sarasota pit where Odin had died. I didn't feel like sharing a place with bedbugs or hookers.

Trouble waited for me, so I needed to regroup and refresh. As a vampire, I could only last so long on a human daylight schedule before turning into a cranky and dull-minded insomniac. I had to stay sharp. The best way was a long nap in a coffin but I didn't bring one. Too bad I couldn't try a routine of poses from *The Undead Kama Sutra* to help realign my chakras.

I went online and checked the classifieds at HollowFang. com, the Internet newsletter for vampire aficionados. A funeral home in Orlando made deliveries, code for temporary sleep accommodations to traveling vampires. I requested a Majestic Imperial casket with the Sedona leather lining and hammered brass fittings. I *was* on vacation. Why not splurge? Besides, I got a "family" discount.

The delivery crew brought the casket up to my room, explaining to the hotel staff that it was a magic prop. I hoped to chat with the crew and touch base with the local *nidus*. But both humans seemed clueless about the true nature of their employer.

I pushed the bed aside and had the crew lay the casket in the middle of the floor. The casket was a vintage model, complete with a foldout crystal ashtray. Fortunately, instead of old stogies, the leather lining smelled of Vancouver Island sinsemilla. I dozed off dreaming of fanging topless Canadian women in dreadlocks. The DO NOT DISTURB sign on the room door kept the maid away and I slept—forgive me—like the dead for the next thirty-seven hours.

I started the first day awake with a mug of organic, fair-trade Bolivian coffee, a raspberry scone, and a 450-milliliter bag of whole human blood that I'd brought along in a cooler. Arterial type A-negative—the good stuff.

Since I had no idea where to start looking for this Goodman character, I continued on my original reason for coming to Florida, to find Carmen and quiz her about *The Undead Kama Sutra.* I drove south, as if the Florida peninsula was a drainpipe leading me to Key West.

Early evening, after the sun had set, I was on U.S. 1, midway between Islamorada and Duck Key. The fragrant sea air rolled in through my cracked window during the long drive across the intercoastal bridge connecting the Keys. The bridge was a ribbon of concrete that hopscotched from the Florida peninsula across a chain of islands that stretched into the turquoise sea. That the bridge continued to exist at all was a testament to Nature's forbearance rather than man's ingenuity. The ruins of the old bridge lay in pieces between the islands, where a hurricane had torn the structure apart. Small key deer picked at grass around the remaining abutments.

Traffic stopped suddenly as if the road ahead was paved
with glue. In a rush of noise, a couple of women on custom
choppers thundered past on my left as they white-lined between the lanes. One a brunette, the other a redhead. Tiny
bikini tops barely covered their muscular, tanned torsos.
Braids swirled behind their heads. Wraparound sunglasses
shielded their eyes. Lean shanks of leg showed between the
hems of their denim shorts and the tops of their cowboy
boots, which were propped on the highway bars alongside
the engines. Light flashed off the bangles on their wrists and
the chrome of their bikes.

I dropped my sunglasses to peek over the lenses at these
high-octane mamas.

Orange auras.

Vampires.

I immediately recognized one aura. Carmen. She wasn't
kidding about working on her tan. She sported the best
makeup job I'd ever seen on the undead.

I'd've followed Carmen and her redheaded friend. But I
was stuck behind a Dodge Caravan with a litter of snotty
kids wiping their boogers on the rear window.

Carmen rode a green bike with a flame paint job. She
cocked her thumb at me and shouted something to her fellow biker on a blue metal-flake chopper. They exchanged
nods and sped away.

I knew Carmen had seen me. Why didn't she stop? I
texted her:

WHAT GIVES? ON THE WAY FELIXG

It was late evening when I finally rolled into Key West.
No reply from Carmen. Along Truman Avenue, I searched
the rows of motorcycles parked in front of the strip joints
and dives. I found the two choppers outside a tavern called
Murphy's Scupper.

Inside, Murphy's was a zoo of sunburned bodies and
laughing drunks. I bought a beer, tucked myself into a corner, and scoped the auras by taking furtive glances over the

tops of my sunglasses. Where had Carmen and her friend gone?

Two tables away, a huge, bearded gorilla of a human saw me looking at him, his buddy, and their two drunken female companions, both of whom looked like they'd used volleyballs as breast implants.

He scowled and shoved his beer into the hands of the blonde next to him. His ball cap read: WOMEN NEED ME. FISH FEAR ME.

What class. Now I knew what attracted his mate.

He stood, pushed his way through the crowd, and came straight at me. His hairy face screwed into a snarl. Beefy, tattooed arms stretched the sleeves of his Hawaiian shirt, which was tight around his beer gut. Hammer toes clutched at flip-flops.

He pointed a fat index finger at me. "You. Yeah, you, faggot. Whatta you looking at?"

People parted around him and hushed. Dozens of eyes turned from him to me.

If it were just us two in an alley, I'd zap him with hypnosis and that would be the end of my trouble. I couldn't risk that in a crowd. We were going to tangle mano a mano. I hoped for his sake that he's had plenty of sex with balloon-breasts over there, because I was about to end his vacation with a vampire-swift kick to the nuts. Say good-bye to your jewels.

He grabbed a chair and threw it aside, to intimidate me, like the ape that he was.

The redheaded vampire biker chick suddenly darted from the crowd and stood before me. She dropped her top and shimmied her shoulders. The crowd whooped and banged the tables.

Mr. Fish Fear Me stopped and his eyebrows knitted in confusion. He grinned. "Outta my way little girl. I'll get back to you after tending to business. Me and my buddy could do with a new threesome."

The redheaded vampire grasped his arm and held him in place. "Stay with me lover boy."

His blond companion charged forward, shouting, "Don't mess with my man, you smelly-ass whore." She grabbed the redhead by the hair and started kicking.

The crowd chanted, "Fight. Fight."

Redhead looped her free arm around blondie's neck and put her in a headlock. Fish Fear Me tried to shake loose but the redhead kept him from moving. His grin turned back to a scowl, then to worry, as he couldn't wrench himself from her hand.

Carmen pushed through the crowd to my right. She took my arm in hers and led me along the wall to the side door.

"This way, Felix. Welcome to Key West."

CHAPTER
5

CARMEN PULLED me into the alley. A vampire scent trailed her, an aroma of damp moss and dried roses.

She stopped and faced me. Triangles of a neon-green bikini top barely covered her breasts. Gold-and-coral earrings dangled alongside her neck. She raised her sunglasses and revealed the reflective red disks of her *tapetum lucidum*. Her lips parted and showed the tips of her fangs. "Felix, it's a good thing we came to your rescue."

Like I needed rescuing from that fatso inside. I smiled back. "What are you doing here?"

She spread her arms. "Isn't it obvious?"

I took in all that taut, sienna-colored skin. Her tan looked perfect, too perfect even for an expert undead application of makeup. I sniffed and detected no trace of cosmetics. This tan was real? Impossible.

"I give. What's your secret?"

Carmen poked me in the stomach. "Geez, Felix, aren't you first going to ask me how I've been? Whadda ya think?" She put an arm out for me to inspect.

I dragged my finger across her wrist, still amazed at how authentic her tan looked. "This can't be real."

"As real as these." Carmen shimmied and her breasts wobbled.

Anyone else, and I would've been all over them. But Carmen's sexual manner was as subtle as a bear trap and she had the reputation of wringing even male vampires dry.

But a vampire with a tan? Pigs flying. Cats doing geometry. Dogs playing poker. All those would've amazed me less. "And you're not even wearing sunblock?"

"Nothing between me and the sun but this beautiful bronzed skin," Carmen said. "And what brings you to Key West?"

"I heard you're working on *The Undead Kama Sutra.*"

The ends of her smile pointed to the dimples in her cheeks. "You naughty boy."

A bar stool crashed through the window of the saloon and landed on the street.

My hands curled into claws and my talons grew. "We better go inside and help your friend."

Carmen laughed. "Jolie can handle a battalion of marines. Public brawling is her hobby."

Shouts and the smashing of wooden furniture boomed out the broken window.

"Sounds like Jolie's having lots of fun." I started for the door, hoping that she'd left some of Mr. Fish Fear Me for me to thump around the floor.

Carmen grasped my wrist and led me out of the alley toward the two choppers. "Don't spoil it for her."

The thin, almost-nothing strap of Carmen's bikini top bisected a sleek, muscular back. Her braid pointed to a trim waist. Denim shorts rode low on her hips. Her toned legs glistened like copper in the electric light of the saloon marquee.

Carmen looked over her shoulder. "You checkin' me out?"

Maybe I should risk getting wrung dry. I put on my best smirk.

She winked. "Thanks. Otherwise there's no point in dressing like this."

"Where we headed?"

Carmen unclipped the keys hooked to a belt loop on her shorts. "You asked about *The Undead Kama Sutra* and how I got my tan. It's time to show you." She grasped the handlebars of the green chopper, arced her leg over the frame, and settled onto the seat.

I asked, "Did you get my messages?"

"I did."

"Why didn't you reply?"

Carmen inserted the ignition key. "You asked what gives? I wanted you to come and find out. Show me how bad you want to know." She cocked her thumb to the pinion seat of the motorcycle. "Climb on. We're going to the dock."

"I can drive. You ride on the back."

Carmen shook her head. "Like hell. It's my bike. You can either walk or ride bitch."

"I'll follow in my car."

Carmen started the engine. She shouted above the roar from the exhaust pipes. "Quit being such a macho *caga palo*. Take the stick out of your ass. Forget your goddamn car. It's not going anywhere. Just get on."

You couldn't argue with Carmen. I swung a leg over the rear seat. Carmen reached with her left hand and groped for my arm. She pulled it across her waist. My right arm reached around so that I clasped both arms against her very trim and firm middle. For a vampire, she was surprisingly warm, or was that my imagination?

I had barely planted my feet on the rear pegs when the chopper jumped from the curb. The front wheel tucked to the left; Carmen barely straightened it before we flipped to the side. We swerved past a yellow Porsche Carrera, missing the rear fender by millimeters.

We skimmed close to a row of parked cars. I had to jerk my shoulders aside to avoid getting slapped by the mirrors.

"There's no rule that says you can't drive down the middle of the road," I shouted.

"You want to obey the rules," she shouted back, "then stay away from me. Shut up and enjoy the scenery."

Carmen took Duval Street and merged into traffic. We approached the harbor and parked alongside a steel-pipe barricade.

I got off the bike first, thankful that we'd made it without being flung against the asphalt. Carmen took a tightly wrapped paper bag out of one of the leather panniers. The quart-sized bag bore a crude inked stamp: YERBAS DE BO-TÁNICA OSHÚN. MIAMI, FLORIDA.

Herbs of Oshún Apothecary. My mother and aunts used to shop in Mexican *botánicas* for folk remedies, some of which worked and others were merely superstitions—and a waste of money. "Does what's in that bag have anything to do with your tan?" Maybe some of the superstitious recipes did work.

Carmen squeezed the bag and crinkled the paper wrapping. "I didn't buy this to make bread."

Typical Carmen answer. "Who's Oshún?"

"She's an orisha, a Santeria goddess."

"Santeria? So this is about voodoo? You're going to stick pins in a doll of me?"

"I don't need pins or Santeria. I can kick your ass on my own."

I stepped out of her reach, just in case she wanted to prove something. "How did you get involved with Santeria?"

"I'm Cuban." Carmen crouched to fit a lock on her front brake disk. "It's part of my heritage. The African slaves brought their beliefs to the Caribbean. You don't know much about Santeria, do you?"

"I know some. There's that song *Babalu,* by Ricky Ricardo. That's about Santeria, right?"

"He was Desi Arnaz when he recorded it," Carmen said. "And yes, the song is about Santeria."

"So who is Oshún?"

"The goddess of beauty and sensuality. We call upon her magic."

"For what?"

"To make us better lovers, of course."

"How come Desi Arnaz didn't write a song about her?"

"I don't know, Felix. If Desi was alive you could ask him."

Dozens of sailboats and yachts were moored to the pier and their lights twinkled festively over the water. Carmen walked down the ramp to a thirty-foot Bayliner cruiser and hailed someone on board.

I removed my sunglasses.

A man appeared from the cabin. A red aura surrounded him. Human.

Carmen stepped off the dock and into the cockpit of the boat. She and the man clasped hands, and he kissed her on the cheek. Her orange aura glistened with affection. Vampires only show that kind of attraction to "chalices," humans who willingly offer themselves and their blood to their vampire masters.

Carmen waved me aboard and I joined her in the cockpit. She introduced me to Thorne, a ropy-muscled man in his mid-twenties. The word "strapping" came to mind; someone who could satisfy her sexual appetite. Was he her research partner for *The Undead Kama Sutra*? A bandanna covered his neck, advertising his status as a chalice to those in the undead family. He didn't say much and smiled politely.

Carmen carried the *botánica* bag and stooped to enter the boat's cabin. She came out empty-handed and ordered that we shove off.

Moving athletically on his sturdy, hairy legs, Thorne cast loose from the moorings. Her hungry gaze followed him.

Thorne took the helm. He flipped switches across the instrument panel. The navigation lights flicked on. The engine coughed to life. Above the cabin, the radar antenna on the mast began to spin. He adjusted the volume of the radio so the squawks of harbor traffic faded into the background. The Bayliner cruised slowly away from the dock.

A woman's shriek—a cross between a drunken sorority girl and a hyena on fire—echoed from the pier. An orange glow streaked toward us. Jolie.

She bounded from the edge of the pier. Our boat was a good hundred feet away. Jolie sailed through the air and pumped her arms to keep the momentum. She used vampire levitation to land softly beside Carmen and me.

Jolie raised both her arms in a triumphant salute. "Ta-da."

"Yeah, great," Carmen chided. "Where's your motorcycle?"

Jolie's aura dimmed. "Shit. I knew I forgot something."

I introduced myself, then asked, "How was the fight?"

"Totally awesome. One of those assholes got the drop on me and nailed me good." She pointed to the shiner on her right eye. "I'll bet it's a beaut."

"Looks . . . wonderful," I said. "Hurt?"

"Stupid question." Jolie touched the swollen tissue around her eye. "'Course it hurts. Too bad it'll heal by the time we get home."

"Which is where?" I turned to Carmen.

She loosened her braid. She closed her eyes in a blissful trance as she raked her fingers to untangle the tresses. Leaning against the railing of the gunwale, Carmen silhouetted herself against the lights of Key West. Her hair shimmered like a lacy halo. "Houghton Island. It's in the Snipe Keys northeast of here."

Once in open water, Thorne opened the throttle and the Bayliner rocked on its wake. Jolie yanked off her boots and socks and scrambled barefoot to the prow, where she sat on the foredeck and sang—more or less—tunes from the eighties. Thorne played with the GPS on the instrument panel and adjusted our course. In the far darkness, red, green, and white lights marked the other boats floating by.

I took a seat on the fantail. "Aren't the Snipe Keys government islands?" I asked.

Carmen's aura sparkled with assurance. "That's what makes our resort so exclusive."

"A resort? How did you manage that?"

Carmen gave a dimpled smile. "We have chalices in high places."

"We?"

"There's a bunch of investors, a few select vampires and chalices. It was my idea . . . and Antoine's. You'll meet him."

"A few select vampires and chalices? High rollers, I'll bet. Fun and games on a private island. Must be paradise."

Carmen's aura prickled with worry. "It was. That's why I'm glad you came here."

"Sounds like someone's found a turd floating in the punch bowl, and I'm supposed to fish it out." Trouble followed me everywhere.

"Lovely visual, Felix. Yeah, I could use your help."

"Doesn't sound like research for *The Undead Kama Sutra.*"

"It's not." Carmen paused for a beat and then explained in a monotone: "A chalice has been missing for two days."

A missing chalice? I already had plenty to keep me busy, thanks to Gilbert Odin and the Araneum. But Carmen, as an experienced vampire, wouldn't have asked for help unless she needed it.

"You got a name?"

"Marissa Albert. She arrived at the Key West airport and disappeared. Too bad you didn't have a chance to meet her, you might have had a lot in common."

"How so?"

"She's a private investigator."

"Was Marissa here on a case?"

Carmen looked flustered. "She didn't mention it. She called last week and asked for a reservation to the resort. It was kinda sudden, but not too unusual."

"And you know her from where?"

"We met when I was traveling through Minneapolis." Carmen smiled at the memory. "She's a wonderful chalice. It'll be a shame if anything happened to her."

"Why would you suspect that? Maybe she ran into a friend and changed plans."

Carmen lost the smile. "She wasn't the type to not let me know. I wouldn't describe Marissa as flighty."

A missing chalice and an alien threat? Was there a connection? I wanted to share what the Araneum had offered but they had ordered that I keep the information secret.

A series of black humps appeared on the horizon. Thorne pointed the Bayliner toward the largest one.

"Houghton Island," he said.

As we approached, the island and its crown of trees looked like spiked teeth jutting from the water. The word "paradise" hardly came to mind—it looked like my ass was about to get bitten.

CHAPTER
6

THORNE SLOWED the Bayliner as we neared the island. A cluster of lights sparkled within the embrace of a lush bay. As we approached, the cluster became a row of burning torches arranged parallel to the shore, north to south. Farther up the beach, strings of electric bulbs in various colors lit the cabins of a small village. The glow of the torches and electric lights reflected off the beach sand and a small pier.

Reggae music beat the night air from a simple pavilion on the far side of the cabins. Under the thatched roof of the pavilion, vampires and humans danced together, their orange and red auras mixing like swirls of candy.

Carmen pulled off her cowboy boots and socks. Since we'd be walking on sand, I went barefoot as well.

Thorne docked the Bayliner against the pier. Carmen went below into the cabin and brought out the *botánica* package, which she handed to Thorne with instructions for him to bring it along. She and Jolie leaped from the boat and lashed the bowline to a wharf piling. I hopped onto the pier and started after them up the beach.

A tall black man, stout as a tree trunk, wearing a tank top and baggy shorts, came from the cabins to meet us. His orange aura announced he was a vampire. And one that liked to eat, judging from his belly. A crop of nappy hair ringed his bald scalp, and a goatee and mustache circled his mouth. The reflection of the beach torches danced on his shiny forehead. He smelled like he'd been grilling fish.

Carmen introduced me as a longtime friend from Colorado.

The vampire's name was Antoine, her business partner. Antoine gave a broad and welcoming smile. He hooked one arm around my shoulders and squeezed hard enough to make me gasp, "Pleasure's mine."

Most black vampires looked anemic. Not Antoine. His complexion was as dark and shiny as waxed ebony. Evidently, he shared Carmen's skin treatment.

Antoine let go and we continued up the beach. Jolie jumped onto Antoine's back and sat on his shoulders like she was riding in a rodeo.

Carmen strode alongside Antoine. "Any word on the missing chalice?"

Antoine sighed. "Nothing new on Key West. Any word from Miami?"

"No." Tendrils of anxiety snaked along the periphery of Carmen's aura. She closed her eyes and brushed a hand through her hair.

Jolie reached from her perch on Antoine's shoulders and tapped her foot against Carmen's back. "Chill. You've done all you can for now." Jolie unsnapped her bikini top and twirled it like a pennant. "Time to party."

Her pointy breasts dared me to leap up and nuzzle them. But from what I'd seen of Jolie, she was as apt to kick my balls as to fondle them. So I stayed on the ground and kept my mouth shut.

The four of us passed through the village. None of the lightbulbs matched. The cords had lumps of electrical tape where frays had been mended. The cabins were simple huts with painted shutters and doors. Colorful streamers— actually cut up sections of awning—dangled from the eaves. Everything looked cobbled together from a salvage yard. I had expected a luxurious Florida resort and it was instead a Third World shantytown fixed up for a party.

"Who built this place?" I asked.

"I did," answered Antoine. "You won't believe I got most of this picking through debris from the last hurricane. Saved a ton of money."

"No kidding?" I asked. "The guests ever complain?"

"I give them a retro experience. The Keys as they were back in the day of rum runners and nickel sandwiches."

A helicopter rested on a concrete pad between the cabins and the wood line. A threadbare tarp covered the bubble canopy and another tarp (in a different color, of course) covered the engine beneath the rotor mast. Black stains darkened the concrete under the engine. The copter was a vintage Bell 47 Whirlybird. Ropes secured the tips of the drooping rotor blades to eyebolts in the pad.

"You have a helicopter? Why didn't you fly instead of taking a boat?" I asked.

Carmen cocked her thumb at Antoine. "Ask him."

"The copter's mine." Antoine's voice sagged with remorse. "Won the damn thing in a poker game and it's been nothing but trouble."

"You fly?"

"I gave Howard Hughes his first lesson," Antoine replied. "I haven't renewed my license since but I still get around."

The Bell's right skid was missing and a stack of cinder blocks and a car jack kept the fuselage propped upright. Beach and kitchen towels hung from the lattice structure of the tail boom. "This thing's an antique," I said. "It'd be worth fixing up."

Antoine shrugged. The gesture said, *Mañana*.

Two snowmobiles sat on a rusted trailer behind the helicopter. Weeds grew through the trailer and around the flat tires.

"What are you doing with those?"

"Different poker game," answered Antoine.

We passed through a plume of charcoal smoke carrying the aroma of grilling fish. The smoke rolled out the chimney and the windows of a wooden shack.

"That's my gourmet kitchen," Antoine said.

"Looks like it's on fire," Jolie noted.

Antoine paused. His aura flared with concern. He yelled to the shack: "Hey, you guys burning my kitchen?"

From inside the kitchen, there came a clanging of metal and an "Oh shit."

A flame shot out the kitchen chimney. Antoine pulled Jolie off his shoulders. Together they sprinted for the shack.

Carmen shook her head in dismay. She grasped my hand, we turned our backs to the shack, and continued for the pavilion.

A combo band of undead and living played guitars, a baritone saxophone, a marimba, and a variety of drums at the south end of the pavilion. No one wore anything more than a brief swimsuit and dreadlocks. Some wore less.

Groups of chalices stood on the wooden floor of the pavilion, arms waving to the music. I counted seven orange auras besides us. I didn't recognize any of these vampires. Counting Antoine, Carmen, Jolie, and myself, that made about three chalices per set of fangs.

Along the floor's edge, vampires sat on the benches of picnic tables, chalices on their laps, the couples necking like teenagers. A wall of palm fronds decorated with flowers, ribbons, and bunches of rooster tail feathers stood on the far end of the pavilion.

Carmen took me to the center table. A female chalice, topless and fit as a Pilates instructor, removed the lid from a metal stockpot on the table. The smell of a rich bouillabaisse wafted out. Bread rolls filled a basket next to a stack of bowls and utensils.

Carmen patted my shoulder, indicating that I sit. "Antoine's lack of aesthetic style doesn't extend to his cooking. Enjoy." She rubbed my scalp and tousled my hair. "Chow down, Felix, you're going to need it. Meanwhile I have resort business to take care of."

I grabbed Carmen's wrist. "What do you mean, 'You're going to need it'? For what?"

She grinned and shook loose. "Every evening we have a party and tonight you're the guest of honor." She turned to leave.

The chalice ladled the fish stew into a bowl. The aroma of the bouillabaisse was a teaser compared to the wonderful scent of a thick blood stock, type O-positive, that she added from an insulated metal carafe. Another chalice—a bustier version of the previous one—poured mojitos from an enameled pitcher into short glass tumblers. This was the first decent meal I'd had all day, and after a second helping, I sopped at the last of the gelatinous redness with hunks of bread and washed it down with sips of the sweetened rum drink.

Two chalices cleared the table. Thorne, Carmen's male chalice, went around with a big pitcher and refilled glasses. This batch of mojitos had a better kick. Maybe it was the blending of different spices, a more potent rum, or something from the *botánica*.

The sax, marimba, and guitar players paused and let the bongos and conga drums carry the rhythm.

Antoine reappeared from the left side of the pavilion. Vertical red, black, and white stripes covered his torso. A wreath of leaves crowned his balding noggin. His broad lips gripped an unlit cigar. Glitter sparkled in his hair, mustache, and goatee. A necklace of cowrie shells glistened against the dark skin of his neck. He strutted in a cadence that matched the drumbeat, his thick legs parting his only attire, a blue sarong.

The drumming softened to a rumble.

A female chalice followed Antoine. Stripes of paint also covered her body.

They stopped before the wall of palm fronds. She stepped around Antoine to place votive candles along the floor.

Antoine pulled a butane barbecue lighter from his waistband and crouched to light the candles. After he lit the last one, he stood, put the lighter to the end of the cigar, sucked hard, and exhaled a dense puff of smoke. The smoke rolled through the air and spread a pungent tobacco smell.

The drummers slapped their congas and started a loud Afro-Caribbean beat. The guitars, marimba, and saxophone joined in with a fast merengue.

Antoine's aura crackled around him. He no longer looked doughy and friendly but demanding and stern. "It's time to make music," he boomed louder than the conga drums, "and dance to beckon the goddess of beauty and sensuality, our exalted Oshún."

The beat reverberated inside me. I swirled my mojito and wondered about the dark sediment circling the bottom of the tumbler. Maybe what Carmen had bought in the *botánica* was in the drink. Something psychoactive. I hoped so.

Jolie made her entrance from the left. She wore an iridescent loincloth the size of a napkin. Her red hair was fashioned into an octopus of braids. Jolie led six painted chalices, alternating male and female, who entered in a swaying gait. The rattles on their ankles and wrists shook with the rhythm. They carried censers that trailed plumes of smoldering tobacco, sage, marijuana, and sandalwood.

Antoine stamped his feet and chanted, "Oshún."

The other vampires and chalices in the pavilion sprang to the floor and picked up the chant. Their orange and red auras pulsed in time to the music. They shimmied and writhed as if they were Pentecostal snake handlers. Breasts and buttocks quivered like so much flesh Jell-O.

This was one party I couldn't sit out. I downed the last of the mojito, jumped from the bench, and joined the dancing. Chalices pawed at my shirt and tossed it aside.

I swung my arms and kicked with spastic abandon, doing the Chicano version of a frog-in-the-blender dance. I wasn't sure of the point to all this but it was a great party.

The wall of palm fronds began to shake. The music picked up speed. The chanting went faster and faster.

"Oshún. Oshún."

With my eyes closed, I shouted, "Oshún," over and over, enjoying myself until I realized that the music had stopped and I was the only one still chanting.

I opened my eyes.

The other dancers stood frozen in place. Their auras shimmered like a collection of neon lamps.

The wall of palm fronds before us had split apart. Carmen (who else?) glared at me from between the fronds. Her gaze burned through the eye slits of an elaborate feathered headdress.

A dozen cowrie-shell and glass-bead necklaces looped across her naked torso. Gold bells on her bracelets and anklets tinkled softly. A brightly colored loincloth dangled between her thighs.

In one upturned hand she carried a glass jar the size of a coffee cup. She swung her arm in a small circle, the torch lights refracting through the glass jar into rainbow bursts of jewellike colors.

The music started again, jumping back to the same loud tempo as a moment ago. Carmen dipped left and right in exaggerated postures, with the jar as the focal point of her movements. Her breasts trembled beneath the layers of cowrie shells and glass beads.

Vampires somersaulted in gravity-defying leaps. Chalices

wailed as if speaking in tongues, threw themselves to the floor, and bounded back up.

The music became louder, the dancing more frantic, and the atmosphere more charged with hedonistic frenzy. Jolie and a couple of chalices stood hunched over, hands on their knees, and twirled their hair while ululating like Arab witches. The fragrance of pheromones was as thick as the smoke.

I didn't know how well this shindig kept to Santeria traditions but I was having a hell of a time. And I still had my pants on.

We stamped our feet, faster and faster, and just as the beat couldn't get any more rapid—I was ready this time—we all stomped once. The music stopped. The silence seemed as deafening as had the music. Heaving, glistening bodies surrounded me, the body paint mottled by sweat.

I found myself standing directly before Carmen.

She faced me, the glass jar raised in offering. "Felix Gomez, Her Majesty Oshún channels me to summon you."

Carmen pushed the jar in front of my face. "Behold the secret to our protection from the sun. Oshún has given us this wonder, the Florida chartreuse-pine spider."

My head cleared slightly. This is what all the music and theater was about? I took the jar and held it up to the light of the tiki torches. Inside the jar scurried a small, bright green spider the size of my thumbnail. "Powerful medicine?" I fought to keep the sarcasm out of my question.

"Very powerful," Carmen answered reverently.

"Quite a show. The last time I bought aspirin at Walgreens, they did nothing like this." I tapped the jar. The spider reared back. "Where did you find this critter?"

"In the trash outside the kitchen," Jolie answered.

Carmen cleared her throat. "Oshún's blessings are everywhere."

"Is it poisonous?" I asked.

"Of course." Carmen removed her headdress and handed

it to a chalice. "But to us vampires, the venom in its tiny fangs is magic. One bite from this spider and our flesh is made new. We get color." Carmen lifted one side of her loin-cloth and flashed a sliver of pale flesh. "See, tan lines."

It was an exciting glimpse of white skin against a brown leg. I looked with admiration at the spider. "One bite? That's all?"

The little spider seemed to study me in return. Its tiny eyes sparkled like grains of sand.

A bite of its minuscule fangs and I could again enjoy the caress of the sun upon my naked skin. No more slathering on the sunblock? I could walk among the humans without a mask of Dermablend?

"What have I got to lose?"

Carmen gave a twinkling smile. "Good. Give me the spi-der and hold out your arm."

I returned the jar and extended my left arm.

Carmen removed the lid and upturned the jar on my fore-arm. The spider dropped onto my skin and stretched its tiny legs. I got a creepy tickle. I kept my arm steady to refrain from giving an embarrassing shiver.

Antoine moved behind me, wrapped his strong arms around my torso, and pinned my right arm to my side. Car-men and Jolie grabbed my other arm by the wrist and pulled hard.

"What the hell?" I tried to jerk free but the other vam-pires held tight.

I stared in panic at the spider. "I thought this wasn't going to hurt."

Carmen laughed. "What gave you that impression? Actu-ally, it's going to hurt like a motherfucker."

CHAPTER 7

CONSCIOUSNESS SLOWLY returned. I felt weak and spent, like a castaway sailor surviving a storm. I opened my eyes and found myself on a bed in one of the cabins. Our concert to Oshún echoed softly in my head and faded to silence. Judging by the angle of the sunlight streaming through the window, I figured it to be early afternoon.

A chalice crowded the bed. She slept on her side, her smooth back toward me. She was naked, as was I. A bedsheet covered our legs.

Red and blue blotches from bite marks dotted her back and along her neck under the edge of her short brown hair. The bruises looked as if someone had gone at her with a ball-peen hammer. As painful as the bruises looked, in reality the chalices wore them proudly, like hickeys.

Carmen, modestly clad in a T-shirt and black shorts, her hair tied into a frizzy ponytail, came through the front door.

"Felix, you're awake. Welcome back to the land of the undead."

I sat up and clutched my very sore abdomen. "What did you guys do while I was sick?" The words rasped from my throat. "Use my belly for kickboxing practice?"

Carmen tapped her foot against a metal wastebasket by the bedpost. Maroon muck clung to the plastic-bag liner. "It's from all your heaving."

"How long have I been out?"

"Two nights."

"No wonder I feel like I've crawled back from the world's worst bender," I muttered.

"It wasn't a pretty sight."

I pointed to the chalice. "And her?"

"The adaptation process makes you crazy with hunger. Chalices fight for the honor of providing sustenance."

"What a sport." I kissed the chalice's shoulder.

She snored. The bedsheet slipped from her hip and exposed the back of her thighs. Bruises and puncture marks trailed between her legs. More hickeys.

I noticed rows of scratches along the sides of my back and peeled the long, narrow scabs. I also had deep bite marks on my shoulders. Apparently, the adaptation process involved a lot of jungle sex as well as fanging.

"Quite the smorgasbord we both had. Too bad I can't remember a damn thing."

Carmen motioned that I get up. I swung my legs off the bed and stood. I felt woozy. She gave my nude body the once-over.

I said, "Sorry, but at the moment I can only get my flag to fly at half-mast." Normally anemic and translucent, my skin was an opaque hue of mestizo beige. The spider bite on my forearm was a fading blemish. "How did you find out about the pine spider?"

"From Antoine," Carmen replied. "It's a Seminole vampire legend. At least, they claim it was a legend."

I poked at the bite, a pale spot the size of a dime, and expected the flesh to give easily, but it remained firm. "I feel like a defrosted turkey."

"Then it's time to bake." Carmen took my hand and led me to the bright rectangle of light framed by the front door.

Carefully, on stiff legs, I shuffled beside her. The anticipation of feeling the sun's warmth made my breath shorten. My *kundalini noir* coiled, nervous and uncertain.

"Any surprises, Carmen? The last time I tried one of your tricks I got sick as . . ."

"A motherfucker," she said. "Not this time."

I pulled my hand from her grip. "Don't lie."

"I didn't lie. It's not my fault you didn't ask the right questions." Carmen continued outside through the doorway. The sunlight washed over her.

I paused in the threshold of the shadow and slowly extended my hand toward the sun. Conditioned by years as a vampire, I tensed to recoil at the lash of searing pain. Instead I got a warm, gentle caress. I put both hands out and enjoyed the sensation. I tried to scoop the sunlight. I cupped the palms of my warmed hands against my face. No more Dermablend. No more makeup. No more stares at my vampire complexion.

Freedom.

I wanted more sunlight and leaned away from the shadow. The warm beam pressed against my skin. I blinked uncomfortably. Carmen handed me a pair of sunglasses and I put them on.

My skin soaked up the heat. "Do we sunburn?"

"No one has yet," Carmen replied. "Seems our rejuvenation powers counteract it."

"Is this permanent?"

"Unfortunately, no," Carmen replied. "Might last a few months or a few weeks. Depends on the vampire."

"And then what?"

"You get another bite from our little friend, the spider."

I turned to let the sun kiss more of my body. At the present, putting up with the agony of another bite seemed worth it. "Does the Araneum know about this?"

"There are a lot of things the Araneum doesn't know," Carmen said. "I'll tell them when I'm ready."

"You're the head of the Denver *nidus*. You have responsibilities."

"I head the *nidus*. I'm not a hall monitor."

I twirled my arms and laughed like a giddy child. "If the Araneum learns about this and that you've kept it from them, they'll have a fit." I, in turn, had secrets from the Araneum that I couldn't reveal to Carmen. But at this moment I didn't care. I only wanted to revel in my nakedness and share the exhilaration. I ran between the cabins. "Look at me."

No one appeared. I barged into a cabin. Nothing. I ran into another cabin. Again nothing. The resort was deserted.

Disappointed, I trotted back to Carmen. Streaking time was over. I found a pair of beach trunks slung over a clothesline and slipped them on. I asked her, "Where is everyone?"

"Antoine's leading an Iyengar Yoga class on the other side of the island. Jolie's teaching a kung-fu samba workshop." Carmen flicked her hand to the dense brush. "The rest are here and there."

She waved that I follow her to another cabin. She opened a nylon briefcase on a table and pulled out a thick sheaf of paper bound with a rubber band. She handed the papers to me. "You asked about *The Undead Kama Sutra*? Here it is."

CHAPTER
8

I HEFTED THE manuscript. Finally, *The Undead Kama
Sutra*? "Is it true what I've read about this?"

"What's true?"

"The psychic-healing part."

Carmen opened her mouth in an exaggerated "ah," and
nodded. She put on a sly smile. "I'm convinced that it is but
I'm not sure how it works. I'm still doing field studies. The
original work is centuries old. The last complete manuscript,
in the Western world anyway, was destroyed when the li-
brary in Alexandria, Egypt, was burned. There's rumor of a
partial manuscript in the Vatican's collection of forbidden
texts."

I removed the rubber band from the manuscript. I flipped
through pages of 12-pt. Courier marked with sticky notes,
pencil scribblings, and yellow highlighter. Obviously, a work
in progress. I stopped on page 26. A paragraph described a
drawing of a vampire and chalice tangled together in a pose
named "Monkey Laughs at Moon."

I didn't know if I'd laugh having sex this way, but I would at least give a big smile.

I flipped to another page and a pose of a vampire standing with two chalices intertwined tightly against her torso. The title: "Jade Tree Ecstasy."

I turned to another pose. This one startled me. "Feeding the Melon."

Carmen read over my shoulder. "Whadda ya think?"

I rotated the page left and right. "Looks uncomfortable."

"It's an advanced pose, for sure. You got to work into it."

"Who did your drawings?"

"I did." Carmen displayed her hands. "These digits can do more than spank naughty bottoms."

"Why are you writing this?"

Carmen took the manuscript from me. "I'm convinced there is a supernatural component to lovemaking. Good sex can cure a lot of ills."

I nodded. "Of course. I've used that line lots of times."

"I'm serious. Sex in the correct sequence of these poses," Carmen tapped the manuscript, "can realign your chakras."

"Do you know what that means? You've found a way for us vampires to play in the sun," I held out my tanned arms, "and now with this *Kama Sutra*, it'll be like we're almost alive again."

"We're not in the Garden of Eden yet," she replied.

"Where did your manuscript come from?"

"I pieced together fragments of ancient writings. Tibetan. Sanskrit. What's left of the Aztec codices. Sumerian monographs. I had problems with that particular dialect."

"How old *are* you?"

Carmen's aura flashed a touch of indignation. "Since when is it okay to ask a lady her age?"

"My bad," I said. "Are you sure you're not using this as an excuse for marathon sex?"

"I don't need an excuse for marathon sex. But this is beyond that. Correcting the energy flow through your chakras will reverse psychic damage and heal your mental and emotional wounds." Carmen set the manuscript on top of the briefcase. "That's the theory. I haven't yet found out if and how it works."

She turned around and leaned against the table. Her eyes gleamed seductively. "We could practice a few of the poses. As research." She loosened her ponytail. With a shake of her head, wild, curly locks of black hair splashed over her shoulders. She heaved and the T-shirt pulled taut across her nipples. "Anything special you'd like to try?"

I matched her seductive gaze. "Oh yeah," I drawled.

She gave an expectant nod.

I said, "Coffee, if you got any."

"Coffee?" Carmen's grin faded. The glare from her eyes could've melted iron. She swiped at me with her open hand.

I caught her wrist.

Her lips pursed, then curved into a puzzled smile. "Goddamn you, Felix." She tore free.

"We're immortal. What's the rush?" Females, human or vampire, didn't come any lustier than Carmen. Truth was, I hadn't had sex with a vampire yet, and I wanted my first to be someone who wouldn't make me limp for the rest of the week.

"One day I'm not ever going to offer again," she said. "Then you'll have no choice but to kill yourself out of regret."

"Carmen, are you begging?"

"Ha, don't flatter yourself."

"Must be nice being the center of the universe."

"I love it just fine." Carmen went to the next room. Bags and cartons of foodstuffs sat on a shelf beside a water cooler. She brewed coffee over a small propane stove.

I thumbed through the manuscript and counted over two hundred ways of getting it on. What a scholarly triumph. "Who came up with the names for these poses? 'Tiger and the Wheelbarrow.' 'Painting the Lily.' 'Feast of Mangoes.'"

Carmen yelled her answer so I'd hear her from the next room. "Those are my translations. Colorful, huh?"

She came back with a couple of plastic to-go cups. "It's a

fair-trade Cuban blend. Sierra Maestra with goat's blood."

The coffee smelled great. I put the manuscript down.

"Hope you learned something." She gave me one of the cups. "I would call you stud but we wouldn't know that, would we?"

"I appreciate the compliment. What are you going to do with this manuscript?"

"Get it published, what else? The general public will get off on the New Age woo-woo angle and we vampires will have yet something else that we passed under the noses of the blunt tooths. In the meantime, I've got more research to do." She grinned. "The fun stuff."

We walked to the pier, sat on the edge, and dangled our bare feet over the water. The resort's Bayliner was docked next to us.

"You guys only have one boat?" I asked. "Seems you'd have more."

"Antoine's got one."

"Where is it?"

Carmen pointed to the water fifty feet from the pier. A white oblong object rested on the bottom of the lagoon.

I asked, "More winnings from one of his poker games?"

"Of course."

We sipped the blood-coffee blend and meditated on the beauty around us. Fish flashed like knife blades through the water. Crabs crept up the wharf pilings and, when they caught us looking at them, skittered back down to the rocky bottom.

The sun felt great against my skin. In the few minutes I'd been outdoors, my complexion had darkened but I needed to cook awhile more before I matched Carmen's toasted patina.

The rhythmic grunt of an engine announced the approach of a motorboat. A white boat appeared around the northern spit of land at our right, about a twenty-footer, with a fabric canopy over the cockpit.

"Expecting company?" I asked.

"No," she replied. "It's probably a fishing boat and the captain forgot how to read a chart. Happens now and then. Especially when we have naked chalices sunning themselves on the beach."

The boat turned and chugged toward us. Sunlight glittered off the gold metallic letters on the hull, which read: SHERIFF. Under that, in dark green letters, it said, MONROE COUNTY.

A man in uniform—white short-sleeved shirt, yellow chevrons on his sleeve, dark green trousers, gun belt, sunglasses—occupied the helm. I guessed him to be well over six foot. Some of that height came from a pompadour so pointy and stiff it belonged on the nose of a rhinoceros.

Carmen and I got to our feet, our *tapetum lucidum* hidden by our sunglasses.

I don't like cops. Any cops. Federal marshals, city police, and especially a deputy sheriff, like this guy. A visit by a cop was always a cure for a good mood.

The boat glided to within inches of the dock and stopped. The tall deputy with the pompadour hailed us.

"Know where I could find Antoine Speight?"

"He's not here," Carmen answered. "What's this about?"

The deputy moved to the front of the boat and tossed the bowline. It landed between Carmen and me.

"A little help," the deputy said.

Carmen didn't move. "You didn't answer me. What's this about?"

The deputy grimaced in annoyance. He hopped onto the pier and bent over to hitch the rope to the closest piling. He stood and his pompadour towered above us. When he looked at Carmen, his expression became all big-bad-wolf-and-I'm-happy-to-see-you. "Deputy Sheriff Toller Johnson."

He removed his sunglasses and forced them through the crust of gel holding his steeple of hair in place. His gray eyes went from Carmen to me and then back to Carmen. He addressed her breasts. "You work here?"

"I have a face, if you don't mind, Deputy."

Johnson's gaze rose to her face, and that hungry smile of his widened. I wanted to sew it shut with wire.

He pulled a memo pad from his hip pocket. "And you are?"

"Carmen Arellano. I'm business partners with Antoine, so yes, I work here."

Johnson pointed the memo pad at me. "And you?"

"I'm a guest."

"Your name?"

Johnson needed that memo pad shoved up his rectum. I answered curtly. "Felix Gomez."

Johnson's stare didn't move from Carmen. "Are you missing someone from your resort?"

Carmen didn't say anything. I'm sure she and I shared the same thought. Why was the deputy asking?

True, one of the women guests was missing. That the Monroe County Sheriff's Office was on to it meant bad news.

The deputy made a point of resting his elbow on the pistol holstered to his waist. The gesture signified that he had the authority to carry a gun and pry answers out of us. "Well, is anyone missing? Female?"

"A woman. Yes."

"And her name?"

Carmen looked irritated at having to answer to this over-coiffed blunt tooth. "Marissa Albert."

"How well do you know her?"

"As well as anyone else here."

"Really?" Johnson gave a smug nod. "Then I need you to come with me."

"Where to?"

Johnson flipped the memo pad closed and tucked it into his pocket. "To the morgue on Big Pine Key, *Miz* Arellano." He worked the sunglasses back out of the pompadour and set them over the square bridge of his nose. "We have the body of a dead woman that needs identifying."

CHAPTER
9

CARMEN'S BRISK, angry steps churned the sand as we returned to her cabin.

"Fuck," she kept repeating.

"You mean about the missing chalice or the deputy?" Deputy Johnson had told Carmen that she had to ride to Big Pine Key in his boat. We were on the way to her cabin to change clothes before we left.

"Both," answered Carmen. "I was hoping to find her alive. She was a doll. Christ, now we got the goddamn authorities involved. What the hell happened to Marissa anyway?"

"Maybe it's not her in the morgue."

"Keep believing that, Felix. She's been missing for three days and poof, this peckerwood comes around asking me to identify a body."

We entered the cabin. Carmen plucked a sundress from a peg on the wall. "Naw." She put the dress back on the peg and bent over to shift through a basket of laundry. She pulled out a tiny red tank top, whipped off her T-shirt, and stretched the tank over her head and torso. The tank looked as thin as a coat of paint. "How's this?"

"I thought you didn't want Johnson to stare."

"The more he stares, the more that lech stays distracted."

We put on our contacts. No telling how long we'd have to be among humans and we'd better take care to remain disguised. I got a T-shirt and boating mocs.

Carmen gathered her hair into a ponytail and pulled it through a scrunchie to hold it in place. She pushed her feet into a pair of flip-flops.

We rounded up her chalice Thorne. Poor guy had an ice pack on his crotch. Strapping or not, sex with Carmen had put his connecting unit through the wringer. The three of us returned to the dock. Johnson sat on a wharf piling. When he saw Carmen, he immediately stood at attention. His mouth gaped and his eyebrows arced over the top of his sunglasses. I expected his eyeballs would come flying through the lenses.

Carmen climbed aboard Johnson's boat and Thorne and I got in the Bayliner. The two boats motored out of the bay and turned northeast from Snipe Keys. The sun hovered above us.

I went to the front of the Bayliner and stretched out on the deck. As a vampire, I never thought that I'd get a chance to work on my tan.

I watched Carmen and Johnson in his boat. They talked and he wrote on his memo pad, but I couldn't hear what they said. I slipped off my contacts and read their auras. Carmen's orange glow bristled with annoyance. Johnson's red aura bubbled with lust, even though the conversation should have been about a dead body.

While I baked like a ham, I thought about what was happening around me. I came to Florida in search of the author of *The Undead Kama Sutra*. Then Odin's mortally wounded alien impersonator hired me to find his killer and, in his dying breath, offered the name Goodman. And he added that little gem of needing to save the Earth women. Then the Araneum warned me about aliens and made a puzzling reference to a crashed charter airplane.

Next I found Carmen, leader of the Denver *nidus,* who turned out to be recreating this *Kama Sutra.* She's also found the secret that keeps vampires from withering in the sun and she's co-owner of a resort for vampires and their groupies. One of her chalices was missing. And now, Deputy Johnson asked us to identify a body.

I'm after the one who murdered Odin and within days a second corpse turns up. Suspicious? Definitely.

Because of my experience with psychic powers and the supernatural, I am aware of a grand cosmic design that binds our actions with what we call coincidences. In this case, what connected the many, many dots?

We continued east, parallel to the Keys. Dozens of boats cruised around us and we rocked over their wakes. Small airplanes droned overhead.

Our two boats approached a concrete pier, beyond which stood a jumble of nondescript, rectangular buildings on Big Pine Key. An American flag snapped from a pole erected on a lawn between the pier and the buildings. The Bayliner's engine slowed to a putter.

We berthed alongside an assortment of boats representing the agencies working the Keys: Monroe County Sheriff's Office, DEA, Department of Fisheries, and the Coast Guard.

We docked next to Johnson's boat and, after I tossed the bowline to an attendant, Carmen and I disembarked and left the Bayliner in the care of her chalice.

Johnson saw that I followed him and he halted. "It won't take two of you to make an ID."

"I want Felix to keep me company," Carmen said. "Or do the corpses complain about too many visitors?"

Johnson relented with a brisk wave of his hand. He led us

around the largest building, past a parking lot, and through the entrance of the Medical Examiner's Office.

Government buildings always gave me the willies. Everything seemed stamped with "official business" as the worker cogs turned on their petty duties and counted the days to retirement. It was like a treadmill in a mausoleum.

Johnson had us wait at a counter while he went ahead. The clerk behind the counter was a sad-faced, middle-aged woman. She did a double take at Carmen.

The clerk's pale scalp showed from under wispy strands dyed henna-red, with silver roots. Ignoring us, she perked up and clicked a remote toward a television sitting beside a water cooler.

She increased the volume for a commercial of a product called NuGrumatex. Photos showed a man with a monk's crown surrounding a bald pate smooth as a balloon. More photos and a video clip had the same man running and playing tennis—activities that demonstrated how his youthful vigor had been restored by the growth of new, thick hair. The next photos showed a woman suffering with bald patches where her head had been gnawed at by alopecia areata. She looked as miserable as a cold, wet dog, and wore a schoolmarmish blouse cinched tight against her throat. In her "after" photos, she had the luxurious curls of a forties cheesecake pinup with bare shoulders, inviting cleavage, and come-do-me-now smile.

The clerk nodded self-consciously and touched her thinning hair. The commercial segued into the usual rapid-fire disclaimers, which I tuned out, except for increased salivation and heightened libido. How wonderful. Thanks to modern pharmaceuticals, America could now be a nation of hairy, drooling, horny nimrods.

As the ad faded, it mentioned the Swiss conglomerate Rizè-Blu Pharmaceutique, Making Your Life Better Than Ever™. I'd seen a rash of Rizè-Blu's ads lately, as if their marketing department had gotten the hives.

Deputy Johnson returned. Maybe that pompadour of his was courtesy of NuGrumatex. But the only thing that made him drool now was Carmen.

Johnson had the desk clerk sign us in and issue visitors' badges. He led us past one door, a turn, then to a steel door, where we stopped beside a cart piled with paper face masks and disposable booties.

"Put these on," he said. "For your protection."

Carmen turned her back to Johnson and rolled her eyes.

Once we all put on masks and booties, Johnson swiped his ID badge through a reader on the wall. The lock on the steel door retracted with a snap.

We entered a morgue. The chilled air smelled of antibacterial cleaner and decaying human flesh. The door made another snap when it closed behind us.

At our end, with its collection of bottles and jars and the white decor, the room looked like a science lab.

Johnson introduced us to the medical examiner, a woman in her thirties, dressed in green scrubs, matching head cover, and a paper face mask. Because of the silver piercings in her ears and her trendy glasses, I would have expected to find her serving lattes instead of sawing through cadavers.

The morgue extended into an open examination area with a steel table in the center of a linoleum floor. A white sheet covered a corpse on a table. The examiner went to a computer monitor and tapped on the screen to bring up her files.

Johnson walked to the table and grasped a corner of the sheet. "We found Jane Doe this morning. Hopefully you can give us her real name."

Carmen looked at the corpse. "Why are you asking me?"

"Just take a look," he answered.

Carmen and I stood alongside the table directly opposite of Johnson.

He pulled back the sheet and uncovered Jane Doe's head. The eyes were clouded marbles recessed into the dark, wrinkled pits of the eye sockets. A delicate nose pointed from a face molded of spotty, darkened flesh pressed against the skull. Black hair jutted from her scalp in matted tangles. As an amateur specialist in corpses, I guessed the woman had been dead three days. Too bad; alive she must have been a looker.

Something had left ragged edges at the lobes of Jane Doe's ears and the loose skin of her throat.

I looked at Johnson.

"Crabs," he said. "They had a munchfest."

Carmen's foot nudged against mine and pressed. The movement was deliberate yet secretive. What was she trying to signal?

Johnson leaned against a file cabinet and drummed his fingers. "Well?"

Carmen pulled her foot from mine. She returned Johnson's gaze and shrugged. "Who is this?"

Johnson stopped drumming his fingers. His eyebrows slanted downward and wrinkled the skin over the bridge of his nose. "Your missing guest was Marissa Albert. This isn't her?"

"Nope."

Johnson pulled the sheet back but kept his attention on Carmen. "Are you sure?"

The knobs of Jane Doe's shoulders were splayed back as rigor mortis had arched her spine upward. Her breasts lay flat against the rib cage like a pair of rotting apples. There were more spots of hamburger lacerations where the crabs had fed.

"Holy shit," Carmen pointed, "what happened there?"

In the center of the woman's sternum was a deep, thumb-sized hole lined with charred flesh.

My fingers tingled as my vampire sense went on full alert. The wound was identical to Gilbert Odin's. Jane Doe had been killed with an alien blaster.

CHAPTER
10

THE COLD trail of Odin's killer had grown red-hot. The killer was here three days ago. Before that he had been in Sarasota. Where he was today was anybody's guess.

My vampire sixth sense sounded a warning, and my fingers trembled against the edge of the table. A warning of what?

Johnson noticed my twitching fingers. "You're going to toss your cookies?" I heard the sneer in his voice.

The medical examiner held up a paper barf bag. "Not on my floor, please."

I took the bag to appease her. "Thanks."

Carmen appeared puzzled at my reaction. A vampire getting queasy around a corpse? Her expression seemed to ask, What is it?

Johnson turned to Carmen. "Doesn't seem to be affecting you."

She shrugged. "I lived in Detroit. It'll take more than this to shake me up."

Johnson's breath puffed against the inside of his paper mask. "You sure you don't recognize her?"

"I've already told you that I didn't."

Johnson looked at me. "What about you?"

"She's still Jane Doe."

Carmen leaned over the corpse and studied the chest wound. "What killed her?"

"Don't know yet," the examiner said. "We wanted to ID the body before we started an autopsy."

Carmen's finger hovered over the wound. "I'll bet it was this."

The examiner narrowed her eyes. *Smart-ass.*

Johnson was clearly furious that Carmen couldn't identify the body. Why? My instinct was to remove my contacts to zap him and the examiner, and interrogate them both. Why was Johnson so upset? Wasn't this just another Jane Doe? Why ask us?

Before I did anything drastic, I surveyed the morgue. Two security cameras watched; one covered the front door, the other the examination table.

We were being taped. Causing trouble might be too complicated to undo.

Johnson covered Jane Doe with the sheet. He acted like his disappointment was our fault.

Outside the morgue we took off the booties and masks and dumped them in a trash bin. Johnson took us back to the entrance desk, where we turned in our badges.

He offered Carmen a business card. "In case you need to chat."

"About what?"

He gave her a final once-over. His frown morphed into a grin, quick as a chameleon changing colors. "Whatever."

Carmen refused the card. "I know where to find you."

Johnson tightened his lips in annoyance and acted like he wanted to shove the card against her face.

She gave him an innocent look. "Anything else, Deputy?"

His lips curled upward and he dropped his gaze to her chest. His eyes flicked left to right. He shook his head and cocked a thumb to the door. *Dismissed.*

Carmen and I went out and headed to the dock.

"I'm surprised he remembered Marissa's name," Carmen said. "On the way over here Johnson did nothing but stare at my boobs. I feel I need to wash them. The next time I meet up with that bastard, I'll drain every drop of his blood. Al dente."

That meant fanging someone without secreting enzymes to deaden the victim's pain. The agony was like having acid pumped through every blood vessel until the organs boiled. It was a ghastly death, usually reserved for the most vile of human enemies.

"He was setting me up." Carmen stared ahead as we walked.

"How so?"

"Because Jane Doe was Marissa Albert."

"She was? Why did you lie?" I asked.

"To give me time to figure out what Johnson is up to. They find Marissa's body this morning and then he comes to *my* resort looking for someone to ID the body. There are hundreds of hotels, spas, hideaways all over the Keys. He knew who she was from the beginning. Otherwise, why did he come to my resort?"

"How do you figure into this?"

"My guess is that once I identify the body, then the investigation turns to the resort and me. What did I know about her? Why had she come here? It's a matter of misdirection by Johnson."

"Because he knew who killed her?" I asked. "If that's the case, why recover the body?"

"Maybe the body wasn't meant to be found." Carmen quickened her pace. When we got to the dock, she gave Thorne the signal to start the engine. Carmen grasped my arm and turned me so our backs were to Thorne. As a chalice, Thorne could be trusted with any vampire secret, but we still took precautions.

She squinted at me. "That's not all that bothers me. What shook you up in the morgue? Very unvampire-like behavior."

Here goes. The Araneum told me to keep my investigation of the extraterrestrials confidential. Now I had to violate that trust to keep Carmen's. Tell Carmen the truth and she'll have a conniption fit over my not sharing what I've known. My dilemma fastened around me like a pair of pliers.

Carmen gestured impatiently. "Well?"

I felt the pliers squeeze. "Marissa was killed with an alien blaster."

Carmen's brow lowered. "How do you know?"

"I've seen those wounds before."

"Where?" Her eyes narrowed and crinkled the center of her brow.

I confessed how I'd found the alien Gilbert Odin, the space blaster, and the delivery of his rotting corpse to the UFO. The more details I gave her, the more her eyes narrowed, until they looked like slits. Her nostrils flared and one corner of her mouth twitched. I thought she was going to lunge at me and bite.

Her eyes opened a bit and glistened like hot rivets. "When the hell were you going to tell me?"

"I'm telling you now."

"Anything else?"

There was no point in holding the rest back. I told Carmen about the message from the Araneum.

Her expression turned from anger to worry. The glint in her eyes dimmed. "You were only doing what you were told. I would've done the same."

"Before Gilbert Odin died, he told me, 'Save the Earth women.'"

"And who's supposed to save the Earth women?" Carmen's voice sharpened with sarcasm. "You?"

"Very funny. But the point is that since we know Marissa was killed with an alien weapon, maybe she's the first of these women that needed saving."

Carmen cast a look past me and across the horizon, as if searching for the meaning of what I'd just shared. "Or the first that we know about."

I added what I knew about the charter plane that had gone down.

Carmen remained quiet and her eyes focused back on me. "And the connection?"

The best I could do was shrug and say, "Don't know."

We started for the boat. Carmen's arm moved in a blur and by the time I figured out what she was doing, she had already slugged my left shoulder.

I rubbed the spot where her punch had landed. "What did I do?"

"Besides bringing me all this goddamn trouble, I'm so goddamn jealous."

"Of what?"

"Of what?" Her voice rose. She stopped, then moved close to whisper, "Isn't it obvious? You've seen UFOs twice. Once at Rocky Flats and then here. I'd give my left testicle to see a UFO."

"Carmen, you don't have testicles." Though I wasn't really sure about that.

"And I haven't seen a UFO either. What's your point? I'm queen of the space cadets—and *nada*. You, on the other hand, practically get inside one. Probably a Class Three Sigma the way you described it. Tell me again about the blaster."

Carmen watched my hands as I described the shape.

"Did you shoot it?"

"No. The UFO took it from me."

"Using a tractor beam, right?"

"I guess."

She hit me again. "You guess? You know jack shit about

UFOs and it's you the aliens come to see. Where's the justice?"

"Don't ask me."

"Maybe things aren't so bleak," Carmen said. "I'll bet Deputy Johnson knows more than he lets on."

"I can start with him," I replied. "I'm going to stay behind and have a chat."

"Keep him busy. I'll come back tonight with Jolie and take Marissa's corpse. I want her to stay missing for a while."

"Careful, there was plenty of security back there. Lots of cameras."

"Felix, the night I can't sneak into a morgue and steal a corpse is the night I'll start wearing a chastity belt."

"What about the computer records?"

Carmen showed her fangs. She extended the talons from her index fingers and brought them together. A spark jumped from each tip. Zap. "Jane Doe? What Jane Doe?"

"How did you do that?"

"The answer will cost you, Felix. The poses on pages 29, 46, and 92 of my *Kama Sutra* manuscript."

"I'm not that limber, Carmen."

"Then sign up for Antoine's yoga class."

I undid the bowline and tossed it on the boat. Carmen hopped into the fantail. Thorne gunned the engine and the Bayliner rocked backward from the dock.

Carmen faced me and flashed a vampire's smile of pointed teeth. She looked ready to meet Johnson again. Al dente.

CHAPTER
11

THE BAYLINER cruised out of the harbor. Carmen
waved good-bye. She joined Thorne at the helm and
cupped his butt. No doubt she'd be getting a nooner on the
high seas before they arrived at Houghton Island.

I returned to the medical examiner's office. My plan was
simple. Catch Johnson privately, zonk him with hypnosis, and
cull the secrets from his brain. But I didn't know when Johnson would leave and I couldn't stand around without attracting attention. I circled the building to check for the exits.
There was one on the southern side and another in the back. If
he used that one, he'd have to come around the building to
leave the premises and I'd see him.

I stood in the grassy square outside the entrance. Three
palm trees grew in the middle of the square. From the treetops I could view the medical examiner's office and catch
Johnson on his way out. I checked if anyone was watching

me—I saw no one—then put my fingers against the rough bark of the tallest tree and walked them upward, pulling my body along. I hid in the center of the dense fronds. If anyone asked, I was checking for tree mites.

I remained in the shadows under the fronds and kept watch. A seagull rode the afternoon breeze and hovered close to me, its beady eyes inquisitive.

Was this gull a friend of the crow and here to spy? I gave the gull the finger. It shifted its head to see if I offered some food, saw that I didn't, then peeled away for the shore.

At a quarter to five, the day shift swarmed out and headed to the parking lot. No Johnson. He couldn't have gone out another way without me seeing him.

The swing shift trickled in. The sky darkened and the lamps in the parking lot flicked on.

A little after ten, Johnson appeared. He had changed into a light-colored Hawaiian shirt and dark blue beach shorts. He carried a gym bag. His pompadour looked unusually shiny, as if he had shellacked it. He walked briskly across the square on the far side, about two hundred feet away.

I started to climb from the palm when a man and a woman wearing white lab coats came out of the office. They strolled beneath me to share smokes from a pack of Winstons. With these two below, I couldn't get down. Though my frustration grew with every moment, I couldn't do anything except fold my legs and remain tucked against the fronds.

Johnson made a beeline through the parking lot to a red Mustang convertible with the top up. He fumbled with a set of keys, opened the car door, and tossed his bag into the backseat.

Damn, he was so close. I kneaded my fingers in irritation. Below me, the two smokers chatted like parakeets. If this had been a coconut tree, I would've beaned them.

Johnson climbed into his Mustang and cranked the engine. The convertible top retracted. Mötley Crüe belted from the speakers. He used the light from a lamppost to check himself in the rearview mirror and patted his pompadour into place. My throat tightened as I saw him preen. All I could do was watch him escape.

The smokers ground their cigarette butts into the mulch and walked back to the office building. About time. I floated down from my perch and started after Johnson.

The Mustang rumbled out of the lot toward the highway. He headed to Key West. I cut across the strips of sand and broken shells along the road, hoping to head him off.

Johnson didn't waste time putting the pedal to his V-8 engine. The Mustang whipped into traffic.

I vaulted over a guardrail and sprinted on the highway shoulder. A delivery truck whooshed by. I jumped and clung to the rear doors, my fingers and feet holding firm with supernatural sticky force. I moved around the truck to the right side of the cab and stepped on the running board.

The driver, a chubby white guy with a mustache, sunglasses, and a ball cap, leaned against his door. He brought a plastic cup to his mouth. He munched ice and tapped his fingers against the steering wheel in time to country music on the radio. I could've done jumping jacks and the driver wouldn't have noticed me.

Six cars ahead, the Mustang continued in the left lane. I tracked Johnson's aura, having memorized its outline and wave patterns so I wouldn't lose him in the night traffic.

I opened the passenger door and got in. "Hey buddy, can I have a lift?"

The driver jerked upright. The truck swerved to the left. The cup rolled from his lap and ice cubes splattered on the floor.

With vampire swiftness, I lifted my sunglasses and plucked his from his brow. "Surprise." His eyes opened wide, the pupils dilating. His mouth gaped.

Hypnosis should hold him for a minute perhaps. The truck slowed and swayed across the lane. Cars behind us honked. I grabbed the steering wheel and straightened the path of the truck.

I dragged the driver over the bench seat and took his place behind the wheel. I sped up to match the traffic flow.

The driver remained slumped where I'd shoved him against the passenger door. His hands twitched and he blinked. Normally I'd use fangs to keep him unconscious but I couldn't bite and drive.

So I slugged him across the jaw. "Sorry pal, but I'm on a mission to save the Earth women."

His eyes rolled back into their sockets and I expected to see them display TILT!, like a pinball machine.

I coaxed the truck across the lanes until I was behind Johnson. He kept reading his mirrors, though he seemed clueless that I tailed him in this big white truck, as conspicuous as a beluga whale on roller skates.

Once at Key West, he continued south on Truman Avenue and parked beside a strip joint called Bottoms Up. I pulled over.

Johnson hustled out of his Mustang. Bumps like welts formed along his aura, signaling anxiety. He turned against the car like he was going to pee. Johnson lifted his shirt and checked an automatic he had tucked inside the waist of his shorts. His aura calmed.

Off-duty cops carried guns. Did Johnson check his pistol because he thought he might need it? Against whom? Was he undercover?

Johnson made a brief call on his cell phone. He climbed the short steps to the porch. A doorman greeted him. When the door opened, a roar spilled out, sounding like that rude, fun place between a drunken riot and bedlam. Johnson disappeared inside.

The street was too busy for me to abandon the truck there. I turned the corner and parked in a loading zone. I left the driver snoring behind the steering wheel, his chin hooked over the rim. He'd been such a good sport about this—the hijacking and the punch to the face—that I tucked a hundred-dollar bill under his cap.

I turned the corner when Johnson appeared in a side exit

of the Bottoms Up. His aura roiled with excitement. Why the side exit and not the front? He held a cell phone against his cheek and talked with great animation.

I halted and retreated behind the cover of a myrtle bush. He was two hundred feet away and too far for me to pick up what he was saying.

Johnson hesitated outside the threshold of the door. He looked down the street as if checking to see whether someone followed him.

Johnson put his phone away and proceeded at a brisk pace, going west on Windsor Lanc. I gave him a minute's head start. With my contacts out, I would have no problem tailing him.

He cut left and right through the neighborhood, stopping occasionally to pretend he was making a phone call, as he scanned back over where he'd been. I was able to hang back a block and track him by glimpsing his aura. When he halted, I stayed behind the cover of garden shrubs lining the sidewalk. Because of the shimmer of his aura, I could tell he was only being careful, though I wondered why he seemed to be taking these precautions against being followed. Why had he left his Mustang at the Bottoms Up and where was he going?

Had he spotted a tail, meaning me, his aura would've flared in alarm. Instead it remained at an even, nervous burn.

Johnson continued in a westerly direction. When he reached Caroline Street, he stopped and glanced around.

He walked the last block to the marina and got on the dock. He unfastened the lines of a twenty-foot cruiser and got aboard. I kept in the shadows and darted across the marina. A bank of lampposts lit the dock and I couldn't get closer without being spotted.

Johnson nudged the throttle and drifted from the dock. He turned the running lights on.

The harbor was full of boats and I needed something before Johnson motored out of view. Closest to me was a rust bucket of a powerboat. It was an older hull, the cracked vinyl seats mended with duct tape and the windshield missing one panel. Empty cans and the ragged pieces of a Styrofoam cooler littered the floor.

I checked the tank—it was full—and lowered the outboard Evinrude into the water. The lock on the throttle lever was no problem to break. I reached under the instrument panel, hot-wired the ignition, and fired up the engine.

Johnson cruised past the buoys and out of the harbor. I kept my distance, at least a quarter mile back. He sailed around Wisteria Island and then southwest into the open sea. His running lights blinked off. Against the darkness, his aura was as obvious as a red signal flare. A half-hour later, he turned east, toward a cluster of small islands.

He slowed and beached his boat on the sandy shore of the center island, about three hundred meters wide, with a dense cover of vegetation. I idled my engine and drifted. The surf splashing on the beach masked the noise of the Evinrude.

Two men crept out of the brush, assault rifles at the ready. Johnson greeted them. All their auras burned with worry and excitement. I tried to listen, but against the churning surf, their voices were but murmurs. The three of them melted into the darkened interior of the island.

Now I had these armed men to consider. I motored forward quietly and anchored in a dark little inlet swaddled in mangroves. I stepped off the boat and into the peaty muck. A cloud of bugs settled around me. Swathes of mosquitoes landed on my arm, tickled my skin, and took off. Why didn't they bite? Professional courtesy, I guess.

I lashed the bowline to a mangrove knee, climbed out of the inlet and onto sandy ground. The mosquitoes must've passed the word, because as I moved about, the bugs kept clear.

Johnson and the two other men moved noisily through the brush, fronds, and branches. I followed in the shadows.

They stopped in a clearing. One of the other men spoke into a handheld radio. *"Bueno. Estamos listos."* He spoke with a Cuban accent. *"La noche es bien lindo."*

Of course the night was beautiful, that's why they carried guns and sneaked around. This was code for what?

Was Johnson here undercover? I couldn't believe it. The man was sleaze; I could almost smell it on him.

I stepped forward. A palm frond rustled against my leg. One of the men panned his gun in my direction. They hushed and studied the gloom.

I froze until they seemed satisfied no one else was out there. I needed a form better suited to sneaking through the darkness. Like a wolf.

I backtracked and found a clear spot of sand surrounded by saw grass. I took off my clothes, stowed them under a stunted pine, and lay in the sand.

Summoning the transformation, I tensed my fingers, then my limbs. A searing pain racked my body. My bones twisted and re-formed. My spine elongated into a tail. Skin burned as fur pushed through. My jaws stretched and my teeth grew long.

For several moments I lay still, letting the agony subside as I gathered strength and oriented myself in this new flesh.

The air was rich with fresh smells. My hearing caught the tiniest of sounds. I rolled onto my belly and pushed up on my paws. I padded through the darkness. My feet avoided anything that could betray my presence. Leaves and branches brushed silently against my fur.

I circled downwind of the men. They reeked of insect repellent and greasy meat. The odor from their oily guns cautioned me to keep my distance.

The tallest of the strangers gave Johnson a satchel; he opened it and counted piles of the green paper humans hold more dear than life. Johnson looped the bag's strap over his head. The three got up and headed to the south side of the island, where they stood on the beach. One of the men flashed a hand lamp toward the water. A tiny light answered.

A dark shape pushed a curl of water. The shape turned into a boat crowded with human auras. The men aboard called out to Johnson.

The boat crossed the surf and bellied into the sand. Men jumped off and formed a line from the boat to the trees. Others lifted bundles that were handed down the line, to be piled among the trees.

I sniffed and caught the sharp smell of cocaine.

Slinking around them, I kept watch on my prey: Johnson. These men had many weapons, which meant I had to corner Johnson alone and unsuspecting.

A thumping echoed faintly in the sky, a noise still too small for humans to hear. I perked my ears. Motor sounds approached from the water. More humans were coming, though Johnson and his companions hadn't yet noticed.

Weapons. Cocaine. The paper they valued so dearly. There was going to be trouble.

But how to get Johnson? If trouble started, he would be in the middle of it. I might never get at him.

The thumping grew loud. The men on the beach dropped their bundles and shouted in panic. Their auras raged like fire.

A beam shot upon them from overhead, a circle of bright light that held steady on the boat. The whirring wings of the flying machine reflected the light. The loud thumping made my guts tremble. More beams flashed over the water and the men scurried across the beach.

The light stung my eyes. I retreated into the shadow of the palmettos.

A lone figure, tall, his aura bright with desperation, sprinted up the beach. Johnson.

A beam of light snagged him.

Johnson raised his arm, pointed his gun into the beam, and fired.

CHAPTER
12

WEAPONS CHATTERED and their deadly stingers hissed through the air. In the glare of the spotlights from the water, men on the beach staggered and fell. Their boat exploded and threw a ball of fire into the night sky.

The heat splashed against my snout and I melted into the shadows.

Johnson ran across the sand toward me. Tufts of sand erupted around his feet.

No, Johnson was mine. My front paws clawed at the ground in anticipation.

When he was close to the brush, he screamed and fell to his knees, wounded by a bullet. Another beam ensnared him, the two shafts of light holding him like pincers.

I yelped in distress at losing my prey. Bounding from the shadows and onto the edge of the beach, I lunged for Johnson and leaped into the brilliance surrounding him.

Our eyes met and his opened wide with terror. I wanted him to whimper and wet his pants in fright. I locked my jaws on the garment around his neck and dragged him into the brush, my vampire-wolf strength easily handling his weight. His human odor swirled through my nose, bringing the smell of warm blood, insect repellent, gasoline, and terror. Johnson grasped my foreleg and I shook him until he let go.

Wild and noisy shooting surrounded us. One of the lights sweeping over us went dark. The second light swung across the beach to follow the men dashing from the burning boat and toward the brush.

Hurriedly, I pulled Johnson deeper into the undergrowth. Branches and stiff reeds scraped against us. Letting go, I stepped away, not sure of what to do next. I needed him to answer my questions, and, as a wolf, I couldn't hold a conversation in English. I doubted he would wait patiently while I transmutated back into a vampire.

Johnson brought his legs under him and kneeled. He clutched his side and grimaced with pain. In a pathetic human gesture, he clung to the bag of money strapped around his neck. He gazed at me and back to the beach, looking amazed that I had saved him. His aura blazed with frightened confusion and then with angry determination.

He brought his hand weapon up and fired at me. I sprang to one side. He lurched to his feet. I readied to pounce on him.

The flying machine roared over us. The thumping of its wings pounded my ears. A bright light stabbed through the trees and dazzled me. I leaped into the shadows. When I turned around, Johnson was gone.

The flying machine circled above, the wind from its whirling wings beating the treetops and scattering palm fronds. Its light hunted for prey. A swarm of bullets snapped at the brush.

I darted through a dark grove of tangled vines. I sniffed

deeply, turning my snout from side to side. To my left, I found the meaty scent of Johnson's blood.

Mindful of the flying machine, I kept low and padded out from the vines and through a thick patch of tall grass.

Up ahead. The red haze of a human aura. Johnson.

I sprang into a gallop. Johnson's scent grew stronger.

As I bounded over a fallen log, I saw Johnson running to where he had left his boat. He clawed at branches whipping against his face. I circled to ambush him.

Johnson reached a clearing and slowed to a limp. He looked over one shoulder back in the direction of the shooting. The flying machine hovered over the fighting. Its beam of light sliced through the night.

I crept into a black hollow between two palmettos and waited.

Johnson emerged from the clearing and came straight at me. He limped, favoring his right leg. He held the money bag tight against his chest while a stain grew on the side of his torso. Moonlight glinted off his weapon.

I flexed my legs and bared my fangs. The muscles on the back of my neck tightened and the fur bristled.

Johnson stopped. He looked about, as if realizing that he was being watched.

Silently, I stepped forward, closing in for the attack.

Johnson's shiny eyes searched the gloom. The two black orbs of his pupils locked upon me. He raised his weapon in my direction.

"What are you?" he whispered to himself. Adrenaline and desperation tainted his scent.

Being a wolf, I couldn't answer.

Johnson winced, his expression distorted with confusion. He adjusted his grip on the bag.

I put one paw forward.

Johnson motioned with his weapon and I stayed still.

I stared at his neck.

Johnson's aura shimmered with deliberation, as if he was

wondering what to do about me. His aura flared, signaling an attack.

I jumped away. His bullets pumped at the brush and the blasts slapped my ears. I bounded around him, weaving back and forth to confuse him.

His weapon went silent. I lunged and jammed my paws against his chest. His arms beat my flanks. My teeth snapped at his throat, tearing flesh and tasting delicious blood.

Johnson fell. I tumbled over him. I set my jaws for the final bite. Something hard thumped against my skull and I staggered away, momentarily dazed.

Johnson crouched, keeping the weapon high over his shoulder to use as a club. Blood seeped from his neck.

I circled, looking for the chance to strike again. Like any wounded animal, Johnson was desperate and still dangerous, but so was I.

The flying machine returned, a noisy blur of wings and flashing lights. Its noise beat my ears and shook my insides. The beam of light speared Johnson. He bared his clenched teeth and looked like a cornered rat.

Holes appeared on his chest. Blood sprayed into the light. Johnson fell backward, his legs twisted beneath him. His aura burned with terror and pain, glistened vainly for an instant, then vanished.

My best lead in this case was dead.

CHAPTER
13

A SHAFT OF light hunted for me. I slunk back and hid until the flying machine left.

I sniffed Johnson's body, now a lifeless, bloodied heap.

The humans in the flying machine had cheated me. I snarled at them, frustrated. Angry.

In the distance, lights swung through the brush, silhouetting a line of men and their weapons against the glow of the burning boat. The fighting on the beach had stopped, the last echo of gunshots disappearing into the night. Above, the flying machine circled with the *chop, chop* of its wings drumming against my ears.

I didn't have much time to search Johnson, and I couldn't do so as a wolf.

I lay in a smooth patch of sand. Closing my eyes, I summoned the transformation back into a vampire. My legs stretched from their sockets, elongating and twisting as pain surged through my bones. Skin burned where fur retracted into flesh. The worst of the agony was when my snout blunted and my skull and jaws re-formed.

I opened my eyes. The pain ebbed and my muscles relaxed. As I gazed about, the world seemed emptier, the sounds duller, the smells fainter.

Naked, I rolled to my hands and knees.

The line of men moved closer. Radio calls and static crackled through the night. The helicopter hovered above, shepherding the group with its searchlight.

I crawled to Johnson's body. I pulled the satchel with the money from his shoulder, opened the bag, and thumbed the pads of hundred-dollar bills, estimating a hundred and fifty thousand dollars. No sense in wasting the cash. I looped the satchel's strap over my head. Searching his pockets, I found a magazine of ammunition, cigarettes, a lighter, keys, a coke spoon, coins, and his wallet.

A loudspeaker boomed over the island. "This is the United States Drug Enforcement Administration and the Monroe County Sheriff's Office."

The Sheriff's Office? Johnson, the stupid criminal bastard, had betrayed his own. This death might have been a favor.

The loudspeaker continued: "You are surrounded and outgunned. Put down your weapons and come out with your hands behind your head." The message was repeated in Spanish.

Red auras floated through the brush like a string of glowing balloons. The auras belonged to police agents advancing closer, now about two hundred meters away. No time to go through the wallet. I stuffed it inside the satchel.

The agents called to one another. There was no doubt this was a drug war; they were as well-armed as infantrymen and very trigger-happy. Laser pointers from their guns traced before them, like glowing red feelers probing the shadows of the brush.

Except for the bag of money slung over my shoulder, I stood naked with my dork hanging in the sea breeze. I crouched to hide behind a bush. To escape the island, I had to get to my boat, which was moored in a swampy inlet behind me, about a hundred meters away. The agents were fifty meters away and moving closer. I could slip into the brush and make it to the boat except . . . my wallet and ID remained in the pile of clothes I had stashed when I had transmutated into a wolf. *Damn.*

The clothes were to my left, somewhere within a grove of palmettos and saw grass. The agents hadn't reached the spot yet. I counted fifteen red auras, clumped into groups of three. One group turned in my direction.

"The grass here is trampled," an agent said. The optic tubes of his night-vision goggles gave him a lobster-face. "And I see shoe prints."

Despite his night-vision goggles, I had the advantage with my vampire eyes. But they had the advantage of numbers and guns.

"The copter nailed one of the assholes around here," a companion added.

The first agent stopped. "Hold on. There's another set of prints. Someone barefoot."

I glanced at my naked feet. Those were my prints.

These agents were no more than twenty meters away. A laser pointer swung toward me. The red line quivered across the branches and leaves above my head. Careful. Steel-jacketed lead slugs could hack my flesh as effectively as silver bullets.

If they were looking for a barefoot suspect, I'd give them one. I lay on my back next to Johnson and shut my eyes.

Brush scraped against fabric. I smelled perspiration from the agent, and hot oil and burned ammunition from his recently fired gun.

A strong light played over my face, making the insides of my eyelids glow. "Here's the second guy."

Boots scuffed the earth by my head. "Son of a bitch is naked."

"You noticed?" Another man's voice. "You feds got a real grasp of the obvious." A gloved hand touched my shoulder. "Don't see a mark on him."

The first man said, "Don't recognize him from our list of suspects. Maybe he's got ID in that bag or shoved up his ass."

His breath and the odor of a menthol cigarette puffed against my face.

I opened my eyes.

He crouched beside me. His nose was inches from mine. I hit him full-force with vampire hypnosis.

His aura flared like a match. His pupils dilated and his expression went slack. He fell on his ass. The submachine gun slipped from his grasp and clattered to the ground.

The other two agents stepped back. I rotated on my heels, zinging upward in the classic vampire fashion.

"What the f—" one gasped and then froze when I zapped him.

His companion jerked an M-16 to his shoulder. I locked onto his gaze and instantly hypnotized him as well.

Their jaws drooped and they stood slump-shouldered. Hypnosis would hold them long enough for me to escape.

Another group of agents moved toward where my clothes were stashed. I had to act fast.

The palm trees grew close together, the fronds overlapping. I sprinted for the nearest tree and hustled up the trunk, where I leaped to the next tree. From that tree I bounded to the next.

"What was that?" An agent turned on the flashlight attached to his submachine gun and panned the cluster of fronds where I had been. I kept still.

"The wind. I don't know."

"Wind, hell, let's see what jumps out." The agent shouldered his submachine gun and opened fire. The bullets chopped the tree and tattered palm fronds whipped through the air. He quit shooting and examined the gnarled tree with the light from his gun. He turned off the light and lowered his weapon.

An agent at the far end of the line halted at the spot where my clothes were. He yelled, "I found something."

Better hurry. I leaped from tree to tree, nimble as a monkey, silent as a bat.

Three agents clustered around my clothes. I jumped and landed beside them.

Startled, they turned toward me. First snatching my clothes, I shook my nakedness and taunted, "Wooga, wooga, wooga." No need to hypnotize them; I wanted them to panic.

Pie-eyed with surprise, they opened fire and shouted into their radios. By then I was back up the tree, my clothes tucked under one arm and the satchel of money swinging from my shoulder.

I bounded to the next group and repeated my "wooga" introduction. They started shooting. Bullets clipped the brush in every direction. The other groups opened fire and, within a minute, they were gunning for one another and yelling:

"Watch out. We got one wacked on meth."

"Shoot the bastard. Drop him."

The helicopter returned. Its searchlight probed the ground and held for a moment on the outline of an agent huddled among the palmettos and bushes.

"Police. Police," he shouted, panicked like he was about to shit his pants. "Don't shoot."

I ran through the brush toward where my boat was moored in the bog. I stepped through the muck and tossed the satchel and my clothes into the boat. I cast loose and climbed aboard. The helicopter and the confused shooting masked my starting of the Evinrude. I kept the throttle cracked enough to quietly back out from under the overhanging vines and cypress moss and into the surf. I pointed the bow to the dark sea and, with the muffled outboard churning the water, slipped away.

I wasn't worried about what the agents would report. That a naked Tarzan whacked on meth jumped from tree to tree?

My path to the island had been to follow Johnson, and now I had to guess a reverse course. An hour northwest at moderate speed, then turn northeast until I returned to the Keys. The compass ball mounted to the windshield didn't move. I tapped the plastic housing, to free the compass. The cheap housing broke apart and the compass ball fell to the deck.

What now? I found the Big Dipper and fixed the North Star to keep myself oriented. Sooner or later I should run into one of the islands in the Keys.

What did I have to show for tonight's work? My best lead was dead, a crooked deputy shot and killed by his fellow cops.

I pulled Johnson's wallet from the satchel. Maybe I'd find something. I went through his wallet. Monroe County Sheriff Office ID. Credit cards. Gift cards and coupons. After I read each one and decided that it added nothing to my investigation, I tossed it overboard.

Just as I was about to fling one business card away, I stopped and read it again. The card belonged to a hotel resort in Hilton Head, South Carolina. Along the bottom was the name of the resident golf pro. I remembered Odin's enigmatic clue: Goodman.

Now I knew where I could find a Goodman. The golf pro. His name was Dan Goodman.

CHAPTER
14

F INALLY, THE trail was once again hot, hotter than
   before. I had a strong lead to the name Odin had given
me—Goodman—and where I could find him.

But a golf pro? What would a golf pro have to do with the
murder of an alien and the chalice, Marissa?

I slipped the business card into the satchel and laid the
satchel on the deck by my feet.

Before me, the horizon lightened from indigo to cerulean.
The eastern stars faded. Sunrise approached.

Despite my spider-bite vaccination against the sun, I had
my doubts. My mouth went dry. I was scared. For centuries,
it had been the first rays of the new day's sun that inciner-
ated vampires. It was like facing a tiger I knew could never
be completely tamed.

Even worse, I should've spotted land by now and I was
getting hungry and lightheaded. Rummaging through the
boat I found nothing but empty bags of Doritos. There were

obviously no cups of blood lying about. The fuel gauge indicated that the tank was full to the brim—a lie, considering
I'd been motoring for a good part of the night. At any moment I expected the Evinrude to cough and quit. Well, I did
have all those hundred-dollar bills, which meant I had plenty
of paper handy in case I had to blow my nose.

I could've planned this sojourn better. For starters, stealing a better ride instead of this piece of rusted junk.

My consolation was that I knew how to find Goodman—
Dan Goodman—who might be the man the alien Gilbert
Odin had fingered as his murderer. Goodman killed Odin
for what reason? It had to be more than Odin being an alien.
And, if so, would I have to include Goodman as part of my
investigation ordered by the Araneum?

White light scrolled up from the horizon. Dawn was about
to break.

Not wanting to take more chances, especially when it
came to my privates, I shook the sand out of my cargo shorts
and put them on. I crouched behind the instrument panel.

The rays of the sun unfolded in a rush of brilliance. Not
burned to a crisp yet. Still, I waited until shadows slanted
across the deck, telling me that the sun had risen safely
above the horizon.

I stood. The yellow ball of the sun hovered majestically
before me. Its heat warmed my skin, a gentle, loving caress.

Had we broken the sun's tyranny? My fear at the cruel
bite of solar rays ebbed as I noticed how much I'd tanned.
The sun was no longer a ravenous beast to be cowered
from—I'd seen those morning beams devour vampires—
but more like a friendly dog that wanted to cuddle.

If the sun could be defied, then what else about our vampire nature could be altered? Enjoying the sunlight without
protective cosmetics was a human privilege. Was this a step
to becoming more human, and, if so, could we find a way to
forever quench our barbarous thirst for blood or reverse our
accursed undead immortality?

Become human again? I nurtured the idea like a tender sprout. What would those fruits be—real love? No longer living as fraud beneath a disguise of makeup? Shedding the fear that I might be outed as a vampire and destroyed?

Suppose I did become human again? Would the Araneum let me live with the secrets of the supernatural realm? Or would I be killed—this time for sure, no undead funny business—to protect those secrets?

I had barely figured out how to exist as a vampire, and these new questions made my head hurt.

Squinting toward the east, I spied slivers of land in the haze of the distant water. I tapped the throttle lever anxiously, hoping that enough gas remained in the tank.

The slivers of land grew into a series of humps that I recognized as the Snipe Keys. If vampires counted only on skill for survival, we'd be extinct by now. I was grateful for all the breaks that Lady Luck pushed my way.

At last I saw Houghton Island and I chugged victoriously into the lagoon and headed for the pier.

Carmen and several chalices—she was topless, they were nude—tended the mooring lines of her boat. Carmen saw me and walked to the end of the pier, where she waited, smiling.

I nudged the speedboat against the pilings.

Carmen set her hands on her hips. Man, what a great pair of boobs. It was a good thing I wore shorts or she would've seen me weathervane toward her. I stayed behind the instrument console and let the moment pass.

Carmen stood on tiptoes to get a better look inside the boat. "You're wearing shorts? I was hoping you were naked. This *is* southern Florida; all you really need is a tan and a smile."

I spread my arms to show off my bare torso. "Here's my tan. And here's my smile."

"Well, you do look good. The parts I can see." Carmen moved to the edge of the dock and planted a foot on the gunwale of my boat. She kept her expression calm but her aura grew writhing tendrils of apprehension. "Anything about the murders?" Her voice was low. "Marissa the chalice? The alien?"

I picked up the satchel and flashed the business card with Goodman's name. "Pay dirt. I find this guy and chances are good that I solve the murders, save the Earth women, and learn what the aliens are up to."

CHAPTER
15

I DABBED MY lips with a cloth napkin. After a good meal, I felt much better.

A chalice lay across the picnic table. She was naked except for a striped bedsheet covering her body from the waist to her ankles. Bruised puncture marks dotted her neck. An expression of ecstasy faded from the chalice's face; many chalices swooned and achieved orgasm when vampires dined on their blood. The chalice relaxed and sighed, content and sleepy.

Carmen and I sat on benches on opposite sides of the table. We had taken turns enjoying the chalice's rich blood.

A thatched awning provided shade from the noon sun. We were alone in the pavilion of Carmen's resort. The other vampires and chalices were either asleep in their cabins or playing cannibals and missionaries somewhere else on the island.

Carmen pulled the bedsheet to the chalice's neck. "Don't want the poor girl to catch cold." Despite the hedonistic ambience of the resort and her predilection for walking around topless, Carmen wore a T-shirt and had pulled on beach trunks over her bikini bottoms.

She had wanted me to wear Speedos—an orange banana hammock—but I had put on camouflaged cutoffs and a tank top. I grabbed a plastic bottle from the table and squirted aloe vera lotion into the palm of my hand. After rubbing the lotion on my body, I stretched my legs from the shade and into the warm sunlight. "How did your corpse heist go?"

Carmen smirked. "Stealing ice from an Eskimo would've been more of a challenge."

"Where's the body?"

"Antoine, Jolie, and I gave Marissa a proper burial at sea. Bothers me that I have to cover up her death when I had nothing to do with it."

The sea breeze mussed my hair. A rock placed on a sheaf of papers kept them from blowing off the table. I had told Carmen how I followed Johnson, what happened to him on the island, and how I discovered Dan Goodman's business card. Earlier today we had gotten on the Internet, using the resort's satellite link, and printed Goodman's photos and a bio. Considering how much trouble it had been to find him, it was now laughably ironic how simple it was to get all this information.

I took the papers and perused them. "Talk about skating through life. Goodman got his officer's commission from West Point and spent his career golfing for the army."

"That's possible?" Carmen raised an eyebrow.

"Apparently so. After retiring as a colonel, he hired on as the head golf pro with the Sapphire Grand Atlantic Resort at Hilton Head Island. It's so high-end it's where the owners of four-star hotels go for pampering."

"The lap of luxury," Carmen noted.

"Lap hell, it's the moist crotch."

In the photo accompanying his bio, Goodman looked the prosperous, middle-aged country squire with one foot perched on the front bumper of a golf cart, his hands clasping the grip of a nine iron. He wore shorts that showed off well-muscled legs. Unlike with most retired men, there was no hint of a roll around his waist. The logo of the hotel decorated the left breast of his polo shirt. One tip of his collar was flipped up as if to express his carefree attitude.

Goodman projected the confident air of a man with few regrets. Friendly eyes squinted into a bright, inviting sun. An admirably healthy shock of blond hair—cut moderately short on the sides—framed his angular, handsome face.

I handed Carmen the picture of Goodman.

She asked, "This is the man who murdered my chalice and killed your alien friend?" Her voice was skeptical. She returned the photo.

"The trail leads to him," I said. "Gilbert Odin tells me to find Goodman. Johnson turns up with a dead woman, your guest, with a blaster wound identical to the one that knocked off Odin."

The chalice on the table started to snore.

Carmen stroked her hair and shushed her as one would a baby. "Why Marissa?"

"You said she was a private investigator," I replied. "Are you sure she wasn't here on a case?"

"I don't know." Carmen's aura tightened and dimmed with doubt.

"So why kill her?" I asked. "With an alien weapon?"

Carmen crossed her hands on the table and kept quiet. One finger tapped the opposite wrist and stopped. "What if no one was supposed to find her body? Then it didn't matter how she was murdered."

"Good point but it doesn't answer the question," I said. "Why kill her?"

Goodman's face stared back at me from the photo. I couldn't believe that this man who had slummed his way through an army career as a duffer was my prey.

Carmen must have sensed my dilemma. "Johnson was human, right?"

"Definitely."

Carmen kept quiet and let her silence raise the next question.

"You're suggesting that Goodman might not be?" I asked.

"Gilbert Odin did a good job masquerading as human when you first met him," Carmen said. "Fooled even you."

I folded the papers and slipped them into a pocket. "Or this golf pro could be a decoy to hide the identity of the one I'm looking for." I remembered the terrible wounds that killed Odin and Marissa. They must have suffered. And the warning: save the Earth women. From what? Was the murderer human—an earthling traitor—or an alien?

Carmen slipped off her bench and stood in the sand. "There's only one way to find out, Felix. Let's go rattle some cages. When do we leave?"

"There's no 'we,' Carmen."

"Like hell. Marissa was mine." Carmen wasn't a big vampire. Standing barefoot, she almost reached my nose. But though I outweighed her by at least fifty pounds, there were lions I'd rather tangle with.

Her lips twitched and the tips of her fangs started to protrude. "You're saying I can't handle this investigation?"

"Carmen, don't put words in my mouth."

Her forehead remained furrowed while her mouth curved into a malicious grin. "It's not words I'd like to put in your mouth."

"Settle down, Carmen. The answer is no."

"To what? The investigation or putting things in your mouth?"

"Both. We can't rattle cages, not yet anyway. We start clomping around and we'll give ourselves away. This investigation is going to require more subtlety than zapping Goodman and munching on his neck."

Carmen's fingernails extended into talons. Her aura

brightened like a flame. "I'd gladly do that interrogation."

I couldn't back down, not if I wanted to stay in control of the investigation. "The murders were to protect some big plan and Goodman is the key. Until I find out what that plan is, I go alone."

"On one condition," Carmen demanded.

"I'm not negotiating."

"Well, I am. I let you go alone, for now, and in return, you owe me two hours of *Kama Sutra* sex."

"No, Carmen."

She grinned and tapped her foot. "Five hours."

"Nothing doing."

"Eight hours. You better load up on oysters."

I raised my hands in surrender. "Okay, five hours." If I had to, I'd borrow Thorne's ice pack.

Carmen's victory pulled her grin into a pearly smile. "I'll put you on my calendar."

CHAPTER
16

HOW TO go after Goodman? I could either circle like a shark, moving closer until I knew enough about him to strike. Or I could go straight after him, like a cruise missile.

Why waste time then? Why not go after him directly?

Because, as a vampire, despite my superpowers, I only had to make one mistake. What if Goodman was bait? Who or what protected him? If humans caught me and discovered I was a vampire, the best I could expect was a quick execution by the Araneum. To protect the secrets of the undead, they'd strike to destroy any evidence of a supernatural creature. Felix Gomez would be a pile of ash scattered to the winds.

I'd investigate Goodman by hiding in plain sight. First, I had Deputy Johnson's money, a hundred and fifty grand in hundred-dollar bills, that wasn't doing me much good as cold cash. I went to Key West, got my car, and cruised up the Intercoastal Highway to Miami to visit a dozen check-cashing stores and buy money orders. As long as each cash transaction was under ten thousand dollars, I should stay off the government's radar. I mailed the money orders with deposit slips from my checkbook to my credit union in Denver. Despite an afternoon of stopping in one seedy strip mall after another, I still had a third of the money left. Laundering drug money was tedious work. I converted a bunch of the hundreds into twenties, which were easier to spend.

I made reservations at the Sapphire Grand Atlantic Resort, where Goodman worked. Fortunately, I had stashed most of Johnson's money into my bank account. A few days in even the cheapest suite—the hotel had nothing for the budget-minded—would've maxed out my credit card. I transferred funds to cover the difference.

I drove straight from Florida through Georgia to South Carolina and arrived at Hilton Head in mid-afternoon. The drive on Highway 278 snaked around the island developments: shopping centers, restaurants, houses, golf courses, and lots of condos. I navigated a traffic circle and pulled up to a guardhouse done in pink stucco.

The guard wore the uniform of a private security firm and he carried a pistol. I told him I had reservations at the hotel. He gave me a onetime in-and-out pass that I had to exchange for a guest pass from the hotel.

The two-lane street curved under a tunnel of live oaks draped with Spanish moss. A bike path ran parallel to the street. I drove past more condos, some tennis courts, and plenty of fairways. Hilton Head seemed like one giant golf course where people happened to live. I had to stop twice to let golf carts cross the street. Groundskeepers in teal overalls tended the flower beds and shrubs along the shoulders.

The street looped past a second guardhouse, this one vacant, and turned into a roundabout in front of the hotel entrance. Dozens of tall palms lined the street and sidewalks.

Considering its exclusive clientele, the Sapphire Grand Atlantic Resort looked understated. I expected a gargantuan edifice of Las Vegas proportions that screamed: Look at me.

The main hotel building was only four stories tall, the rows of dark windows flanking a simple portico. Yet the architecture remained thoughtfully constructed. Its pink marble façade curved toward me, as if leaning forward for an expensive hug.

A sign pointed to guest parking on the north side of the building. I entered a parking garage, left my Cadillac on the second level, and dragged my roll-along bags inside.

Once in the hotel, the pretense of austerity stopped. The enormous atrium could've been used as a hangar for the space shuttle. The sun's rays filtered through skylights high above. Terraced gardens with café tables faced the central corridor with its artificial lagoon and schools of koi. Ubiquitous black spheres housing security cameras peeked from the foliage and the corners. Nautical trim and prints of sailing ships decorated the walls and furniture.

The corridor led into the lobby. Gigantic chandeliers of amber glass hung from the vaulted ceiling. The carpet was plush enough to hoe and sow corn.

I checked in and went looking for Goodman. I followed a map of the resort, which took me through the lobby mezzanine, across a glassed-in corridor that bridged over the outside sidewalks, and to the adjacent clubhouse.

The corridor emptied into a foyer. Arrows on the wall read: PRO SHOP, LEFT. GOLF COURSE ADMINISTRATION AND TRAINING, RIGHT.

I went right, down a hall to an arched threshold with double doors and beveled glass inserts. Both doors were open, revealing a round vestibule lined with office doors. In the middle of the room squatted a wide, circular desk of teak trimmed with brushed aluminum.

Behind the desk sat a slender black woman, who looked

to be in her early thirties. The brushed aluminum nameplate on the desk said that she was Mrs. Mikala Jamison. Sitting perfectly upright, dressed in a tailored business suit that matched the room décor, Jamison looked like she'd been ordered out of an office-supply catalog. She stared at a thin monitor screen. A headset boom jutted around her left cheek. Her manicured fingernails clicked across the keyboard. She had a gold wedding set so heavy and ornate that it would have been the envy of any Babylonian queen.

Large paintings of fairways at famous golf courses hung along the walls around us. Corporate plaques and trophies filled the spaces between the paintings and office doors.

The only golf pro I had ever known before, my uncle Pancho, would have found such sumptuous digs beyond comprehension. His office was a plastic crate behind the pro shop at the Fresno public links, where he used to sit, smoke, and hold court.

I announced myself to Mrs. Jamison and added, "I'd like to see Dan Goodman."

She nodded and raised a hand, gesturing that I wait. Her fingers tapped on the keyboard while she muttered in business-speak, as if talking to herself. She clicked some buttons and turned toward me. "And your business, sir?"

I raised my sunglasses.

Her eyes popped open, the whites broad, concentric circles around the caramel rings surrounding the dilated pupils. Her aura lit with a luminescent burst of crimson.

I closed and locked the doors.

I stepped next to Jamison and swiveled her chair toward me. Cupping her chin, I stared deep into her eyes to strengthen my hold. Her chin was sharp and delicate. Her skin had the texture of a fresh rose petal.

I gave her another stare. "Is Goodman here?"

Jamison didn't answer. She held her breath. I stroked her cheek with my thumb.

She slowly exhaled. "The colonel is not in."

Colonel? Interesting. Goodman was vain enough to use his rank despite being retired.

"Where is he?"

Another pause and a breath. I took Jamison's hand and massaged the web of flesh between her thumb and index finger, to deepen the hypnosis.

I repeated my question.

She answered in a whisper: "Chicago."

"When is he expected back?"

Jamison's jaw muscles tightened. Hypnotic interrogation wasn't a simple process. Press a reluctant victim too hard and her subconscious could tighten into a protective ball, like an armadillo's hide. Better to gently coax the answers from her.

I let go of her hand and touched her neck. My fingertips traced across the tender spots of her throat. Her aura simmered into a low burn of contentment.

She said, "I don't know."

I looked about the vestibule. "Where's his office?"

"Over there." Jamison lifted a finger in the direction of the widest door on the opposite side of the entrance.

Figuring the door might be locked, I asked Jamison for a key. She groped in a desk drawer and brought out a key on a ring with the logo of the resort.

I took the key and was about to tell Jamison to close her eyes when I thought to ask: "Is his room under surveillance?" I hadn't seen a security camera in here.

Jamison shook her head. Good.

I told her to fold her arms on her desk, close her eyes, and lay her head down. I kissed the back of her taut, delicious neck. "Be a nice girl and take a nap."

I entered Goodman's office, a cavernous, opulent space. I expected to find a throne. Tall windows along the far wall overlooked palmettos, myrtle, and a green fairway. His desk was to the right and matched the materials and design of the other furnishings in the hotel.

The nameplate on his desk read: COL. DAN GOODMAN, RET. U.S. ARMY. Laminated diplomas and certificates hung behind his desk. To the left was Goodman's "me" wall: photos of himself with other people. The photos were of Goodman in various stages of his life, always a group shot with other golfers. In some of the photos he wore a polo shirt or windbreaker with U.S. ARMY written across the front. He shared the lens with dozens of celebrities: entertainment, business, sports, political. It was as if he had served his military career on the pages of *People* magazine. In one older color print, a boyish Dan Goodman—in the dress uniform of a West Point cadet—received a trophy from Arnold Palmer.

At the far end of the photos was a framed certificate of his commission as an officer into the regular army. Next to that was a shadow box displaying awards and decorations. Along the top were rank insignia arranged left to right, from second lieutenant to colonel. Under those were his decorations, two of which surprised me: Bronze Star and Purple Heart.

How did a career duffer end up with a medal for bravery and another for wounds as the result of enemy action? Who had he played against? Did the Taliban field a golf team?

His cabinets were unlocked. I thumbed through the files and found tournament invitations, resort brochures, invoices for lessons and equipment, nothing out of the ordinary for a golf pro. Instead of a computer, he had a docking station for a laptop, which was missing. I searched his desk drawers and looked for a note, a business card, a scrap of paper, anything that could point the way forward.

Nothing.

I set the door lock from the inside and left the office.

Jamison snored like a hibernating bear. Her arms dangled to the floor. Both of her feet had twisted out of her pumps and wrinkled the panty hose around her ankles.

I stroked the top of her head and commanded her to wake up.

Jamison's eyes fluttered open. She smacked her lips and straightened in her chair. Her eyes turned toward mine and I gave her a hard stare, to refresh my hypnotic hold.

"When did Goodman leave for Chicago?"

"Yesterday."

"What's he doing there?"

Her eyes blinked lazily. "Consulting."

"For whom?"

"RKW."

I knew enough about current events to recognize the initials. RKW stood for Rockville Kamza Worthington, the military and security subsidiary of Cress Tech International. Cress Tech built oil wells, highways, shipyards, bridges, airports, pretty much any project measured in the billions of government dollars. The running joke on late-night TV was that the White House was the marketing branch of Cress Tech.

"What was Goodman consulting for?"

"Government work."

"What kind of government work?"

"I don't know."

I had to trust Jamison. Victims couldn't lie under hypnosis. "Where's he staying?"

Another "I don't know."

"You have an itinerary?"

Jamison turned her eyes to her computer monitor. She tapped robotically on the keyboard.

Goodman's calendar came on the screen. This week he was in Chicago. Last week . . .

I brought my face closer to the monitor to make sure I read the calendar correctly.

Last week Goodman was in Key West, Florida. And last week Marissa Albert arrived in Key West and disappeared.

I knew what to do next. I was going to Chicago.

CHAPTER
17

I MADE AIRLINE reservations for Chicago, but as I hate
layovers, the earliest direct flight wouldn't leave until the
next morning. Still, it beat driving. I decided to use the time
to check out the hotel and resort grounds.

I put my contacts back on and visited the pro shop. It re-
sembled the showroom of a BMW dealership, only swank-
ier. After scanning my room key, the clerk signed over a set
of Ben Hogan clubs and a red E-Z-GO golf cart.

While still parked outside the pro shop, I fiddled with the
cart's stereo receiver and scanned channels on the satellite
radio. Considering how well-marked the course was, I found
the dash-mounted GPS an excess even for this place. Then
again, maybe the GPS was a necessity for inebriated and
disoriented guests to navigate their way around. Maybe the
GPS was also a way to track the whereabouts of every cart.

With rockabilly tunes twanging from the stereo speakers,
I drove past the first tee and began my reconnaissance.

The front nine holes were north and west of the hotel. Stands of pine and oak, and sloughs with alligators basking on the muddy banks, separated the guest grounds while disguising the less picturesque support buildings. I paused where a narrow road passed behind a green wooden fence. The gate opened to a parking lot. On the left stood a large maintenance shed. Two men in the resort uniform—teal polo shirt over khaki cargo shorts—pushed a riding mower into one of the bays. On the right, a couple of panel trucks— May River Commercial Laundry—backed up to the service entrance on the side of the hotel. Men guided the trucks and shouted commands in Spanish.

The gate closed by remote control, creaking on steel wheels, moving like a curtain drawn shut to hide family secrets.

I kept on the cart path to an open area beside the closest fairway. A Bell Long Ranger executive helicopter in bright colors sat on a concrete pad. In the calm air, the orange windsock hung limp as an empty condom.

Condos bounded the north side of the resort grounds. I turned around and drove the cart to the nine holes south of the hotel. I passed tennis courts, two swimming pools, and a pond watered by a fountain. I continued over a wooden bridge toward the back nine. The course faced east toward Calibogue Sound and Daufuskie Island. A growth of dense juniper—ten, twelve feet high—continued as a straight row from the back of the main building of the hotel to a distance of about two hundred meters.

I wasn't sure what I was looking for. This place seemed too perfectly neat, except for the big wrinkle that Goodman worked here.

A narrow asphalt road followed close to the back of the hotel. I couldn't tell where the road came from but it headed into a break in the junipers to my far left, the entrance to the enclosed area. To the right, pampas grass and sea oats atop sand dunes marked the boundary with the beach.

I stopped, got out of the cart, and walked until I found a path across the dunes. The beach was a wide, flat stretch of sand. At low tide, the Atlantic surf splashed a hundred meters away. Pelicans dove into the ocean and dolphins broke the surface in graceful arcs. A breeze cooled the air enough that the few people strolling the beach wore long pants and windbreakers. From back here, the resort blended into the clumps of palms and pink buildings stretching along the beach.

The loud thumping of rotor blades announced a Blackhawk helicopter banking over the water. It entered a descent for an area between the beach and the back of the hotel. Unlike the Long Ranger in its colorful livery, this helicopter was painted in a drab, military finish. The Blackhawk tilted its nose up to decelerate and disappeared over the tops of the junipers. If there was a helicopter pad on the other side of the hotel, why did the Blackhawk land here?

I returned to my golf cart, walking unhurriedly, like just another casual tourist. The arrival of the military Blackhawk stoked my suspicions about Goodman and the hotel. When I got to the cart, the helicopter rose straight up from behind the junipers. The dense stands of trees muffled the roar of the turbines and rotor blades. The Blackhawk rotated to the south and accelerated, leaving tree branches and palm fronds quivering in its wake.

The junipers obscured my line of sight and prevented me from seeing anything but the flat roofline of a three-story building, its stucco painted to match the hotel. I'd already seen the maintenance shed. With its forest of antennas, what was this building?

Thorny rosebushes grew parallel to the path. I found a gap and rumbled through.

Immediately, my GPS display flashed: OFF COURSE. TURN AROUND.

Loud beeps shouted from the stereo speakers. I turned the volume down on the speakers but the beeping continued. I mashed the GPS off button but the GPS kept resetting itself. I reached under the dash, found a bundle of wires, and yanked. The beeping stopped and the display went black.

I steered the cart closer to the junipers so I could study the rear of this building. The few windows on the wall were squinting, horizontal slits. The roof was a jungle of spindly radio whips, clusters of dishes pointed up, and ladderlike masts festooned with pods. Definitely high-grade communications equipment, not the sort of getup you'd need just for HBO. Why all these antennas?

A small green John Deere Gator truck appeared around the far end of the junipers and turned toward me. I took my contacts out, stored them in their plastic case, and put my sunglasses back on.

The Gator was a utility vehicle, not much wider than my cart and with an aluminum bed on the back. It halted by my cart.

The tiny cab of the Gator had no doors. Radio traffic cackled from a speaker. A man in the resort uniform swung his lanky, hairy legs out and stood to face me. The resort logo decorated the shirt and his ball cap. Unlike other employees, he had a special ID tag swinging from a cloth lanyard looped around his neck. The ID tag bore iridescent hologram markings, the resort logo, and his photo and last name: Lewis.

Coming close, Lewis rested an arm against the roof of my cart. He moved with the confident swagger of an ex-cop.

"Good afternoon, sir." He forced the polite tone. Blue eyes contrasted with his bronzed complexion. "Is there a problem?"

Lewis expected a dumb-ass executive, so I gave him one.

"Problem? Damn right there's a problem. It's my friggin' game. Sliced my hook."

He grinned. "Sliced your hook?"

"Yeah," I replied innocently. "Must be something wrong with my clubs." I leaned over the steering wheel. "My ball went flying this way."

Lewis glanced from the distant fairway to the grass around my cart as if doubting that I could have hit the ball this far. "Don't see it." He tilted his head and examined my dash panel. "Why isn't your GPS on?"

"Is that what this is? Goddamn thing started beeping like crazy." I pounded the dash panel. One of the buttons popped loose and fell to the floor. "I think it's broken."

Lewis reached and pulled my hand away from the dash. "I'll take care of it, sir." He looked over his shoulder back to the ruts I had crushed through the roses.

"Did I do that? Didn't see them. Sorry."

Lewis set his cap on the back of his head. His jaw muscles tightened.

"What about my ball?" I lowered my voice and pretended that I was sharing a secret. "Listen, I got money riding on this game and right now I ain't doing too good."

"Take a mulligan," Lewis said with growing irritation. He rapped his knuckles on the roof. "First, you need to get back from the fence."

"What fence?"

"I meant the junipers, sir."

But he had said "fence." "Maybe my ball went on the other side." I extended a leg to dismount.

Lewis planted a big hiking boot in my way. The corners of his mouth bent into a frown. "Sir, please return to the path. I'll look for your ball."

"If you cost me this game, so help me."

"You got a problem, talk to my supervisor." He leaned close and sneered. "You rich, dopey assholes think the rules don't apply. Well, you can stick it up . . ."

I lifted my sunglasses.

The pupils in his eyes dilated into circles the size of dimes. His face went slack and his jaw drooped. Saliva pooled over his lower lip.

I grabbed his collar and walked him back into the cab of his truck. Pushing him into the passenger seat, I turned his head and fanged him, drinking only enough to keep him docile and quiet. I savored his blood as if it were a chocolate truffle melting in my mouth.

I took his cap and left him doubled-over. I scooted behind the steering wheel and turned the truck toward the far end of the junipers. Driving close, I saw that they had overgrown a tall chain-link fence.

I reached the end of the junipers and paused. The tree line turned north. A cinder-block tower with dark windows overlooked the entrance.

"Unit 83," a voice beckoned over the radio speaker. "Are you 10-6?"

Looking back to the hotel from this perspective, I appreciated the architectural sleight of hand used by the designers of the resort. The wings of the hotel curved away. The windows were carefully angled so that guests had splendid views of the grounds yet no one could see into the area defined by the perimeter of junipers.

The voice started again. "Unit 83, you still 10-6 with the wanderer nosing around the annex?"

Another voice hailed, this one stern. "Eight-three, you copy?"

I noticed the number 83 written on the radio console. They were asking for Lewis and the "wanderer" must be me. The annex was this secret building with all the antennas and security detail.

"Eight-three?" the first voice asked again.

If I replied, they would recognize that I was not Lewis. Under hypnosis, humans weren't good at conversation, so I couldn't expect him to answer convincingly.

"Eight-three, you there?"

I picked up the microphone and keyed the transmit button twice, radio shorthand for "I acknowledge."

The stern voice returned. "Eight-three, this is tower one, when you're called, respond immediately."

Asshole. Again I clicked twice.

What was on the other side of the fence? I couldn't risk getting closer to the entrance without being further challenged by the tower. If the measures here were sophisticated enough for the GPS transmitters to narc on the golf carts, then the fence was certainly wired to catch trespassers.

I returned to my cart and left Lewis conked out in the cab of his truck. I covered his face with the cap to make it look like he was dozing off.

I drove back to the pro shop, wondering: why so much secrecy?

The fenced area was well protected against human intruders. But what about a vampire? Let me find Goodman first. Then I'd come back and I'd find out.

CHAPTER
18

A SOMBER CROWD accompanied me in the Savannah Airport. People stared apprehensively at the various monitors scattered throughout the concourse.

A commuter plane had crashed en route from Kansas City to Chicago. The news programs showed the crash site from a distance, a smoky black smudge rising behind a stand of trees. There were shots of ambulances and police cruisers parked along a road, and of the response team from the National Transportation Safety Board disembarking from a helicopter.

The news announcer described the doomed aircraft, a Raytheon Beech King 1900D twin turboprop, as its photo flashed to one side of the screen. The airliner belonged to a small regional service, Prairie Air. All on board the small commuter, the crew of three and sixteen passengers, were accounted for. No survivors.

Even I got a case of the nerves. Nothing like a plane crash to temper the romance of flying.

I remembered the Araneum's message with the article about the charter plane that had gone down. That airplane had been a smaller Cessna Caravan, a completely different type from the Beech King 1900D. Were these two crashes related? Were aliens involved? How so? For what purposes?

If the aliens suspected that I was on their trail, how vulnerable was my airliner? The UFO in the gulf had stalled my Wave Runner and paralyzed me. Had they done the same thing to the Beech King and crew?

Our flight to Chicago was especially quiet, which made the groans and squeals coming from the belly of the Boeing 767 that much louder and more worrisome. The attendants did a brisk business keeping the adults, including me, medicated with alcohol.

While I killed off a trio of Smirnoff miniatures, I thought about how I would find Goodman. Okay, so he was in Chicago. What was I to do? Put his face on a milk carton? Go out to Wrigley Field and announce, "Has anyone seen Dan Goodman?"

I paid the extra five bucks to watch the TV display attached to the back of the seat in front of me. While I wanted to distract myself from thinking about a plane crash, I kept flipping back to news about the wreck anyway, partly out of morbid fascination and partly out of superstition that watching the news would protect me from a similar fate.

Every fifteen minutes, CNN kept showing the same clip, a fast-paced montage that implied detailed reporting. (The commercials were from Rizè-Blu.) First CNN showed the smoke above the crash site, then stock footage of passengers boarding a Beech King 1900D turboprop, emergency technicians donning hazmat suits, and finally police escorting grim-faced investigators past a barrier of orange cones and yellow tape.

About the sixth time the clip repeated, I had memorized the choreography and could pick out more of the details.

One. Like the way the smoke above the crash curled into the shape of a chicken head.

Two. In the stock footage, there were sixteen passengers on the Beech King (in appropriately politically correct demographics), eight men, eight women (wearing enormous shoulder pads), six of the group black, three Asian.

Three. The emergency techs slipping into the blue hazmat suits were two men (the dumpy guy in the foreground had a walrus mustache) and a muscular blonde who looked like she ran marathons while French-curling an anvil.

Four. A state trooper parted the way for two men to pass through the barrier and a gauntlet of onlookers. The clip showed the men from the back. Both wore dark windbreakers. The second man glanced to the right for an instant before the clip ended.

It was him.

The tousled mat of blond hair, a flat brow, the chiseled nose, a well-defined jaw with a fleshy pan on his dimpled chin, the tanned complexion.

Dan Goodman.

The image of his face sobered me right up. I waited anxiously for the clip to be shown again.

The sequence returned. Smoke. Airplane. Hazmat suits. Trooper. Second man turns his head.

Goodman.

As a vampire, I have a *kundalini noir*. And as a private detective, I also have an internal stink-o-meter. Right now that stink-o-meter jumped to the red zone.

Gilbert Odin had been killed by an alien blaster.

He gave me the name of his killer: Goodman.

One of Carmen's chalices showed up dead from a blaster wound.

The man who had found the dead chalice was a dirty cop, now also dead, named Deputy Toller Johnson.

On Johnson's body I found a business card for a golf pro named Dan Goodman.

This Dan Goodman, a retired U.S. Army colonel, moon-lighted for a secretive defense contractor.

Now Goodman was involved in the crash investigation of a commuter airliner.

A big fat *why* hovered in my brain.

And even more sinister, Goodman had left for Chicago yesterday. The plane crash happened this morning.

Coincidence? Not according to my stink-o-meter.

Did that mean Goodman either knew of or was responsible for the plane crash? How?

And how did that tie into the other mission Gilbert Odin handed me, to save the Earth women? What about the Araneum's alien connection?

My first task was to track Goodman. He sat in the middle of the bull's eye. I'd start right where the TV showed him to be. The crash site south of Oswego, Illinois.

CHAPTER
19

THE INTERNET gave me the map grid location of the
crash site. I rented a Lexus SUV because of the onboard
GPS, and followed the directions southwest on I-55, then
north on Highway 30 to Oswego, where I took a county
road.

I looked for a column of smoke in the afternoon sky. On
TV, dense smoke had risen from behind a tree line, as ominous as a death shroud. Shouldn't be hard to find.

But the sky was clear now. Helicopters marked the spot as
they orbited like flies over a picnic. A sheriff's white patrol
car with lights flashing was parked beside a portable barricade straddling the road. The barricade read: LOCAL TRAF-
FIC ONLY.

I rolled my window down and slowed for the deputy wearing a safety vest. I told him, "I live at the new development."
There were always new developments, anywhere you went.

He glanced into my car and waved me through.

A quarter mile from the crash site, an impromptu bivouac of news vans crowded the shoulder of the road. Masts with antennas telescoped from the van roofs. On the opposite shoulder, state troopers, federal marshals, and more deputies milled alongside a yellow barrier tape. The tape stretched for hundreds of feet on either side of a second road leading into the woods.

Journalists with microphones and video cameras waited in clusters. A black Suburban appeared in the second road. The lawmen parted for the SUV to pass and the newspeople crowded around it. The SUV turned left and headed west. The journalists relaxed with their equipment and slunk back in boredom.

I'd return later tonight. The police weren't expecting anyone more bothersome than a persistent reporter, so I should have no problem sneaking through as a vampire.

I figured most of the local hotel and motel rooms would be taken by the news media or crash investigators. Besides, for hospitality I wanted the personal touch.

I drove north into Oswego. A brunette in black spandex jogged around the park of a residential neighborhood. She filled out her top nicely and, for proportion's sake, had a fair amount of junk in the trunk. She stepped away from the park and went up an adjacent street. I removed my sunglasses and contacts. Her aura was calm. Nothing bothered her except for the sexual frustration that appeared in her aura like small fractures in glass.

I replaced my contacts and slowed alongside her. I could use vampire hypnosis and get my way regardless. But I never liked that—I preferred to cast the bait and see if the woman responded. I used to rely on vampire hypnosis later in the liaison, mainly to keep secret the pale, translucent skin that I didn't cover with makeup. But I had a tan now. Would I need hypnosis at all?

I halted against the curb and gave her a "rescue me"

smile. "I'm kinda lost. Can you help with directions back to the highway?"

The woman stepped off the sidewalk and braced her forearms against the window opening on the front passenger side of the Lexus. Her perspiration had activated her perfume and the scent was a tempting appetizer. "Nice car," she said.

The hook was set. I didn't think it would be so easy.

Her left hand dangled into view. She wore an engagement ring. Considering her lingering sexual frustration, future hubby wasn't taking care of business.

She tucked a stray lock of hair behind her ear. "Where you from?"

"Colorado."

She twirled a lock of her hair around a finger. "What are you doing here?"

"Business." I told her I was a talent scout for a marketing company. "I'm looking for a great pair of hands. We need them for jewelry and soap commercials."

She spread her fingers. "I have nice hands."

"You do," I answered.

"How do you audition hands?"

Depends on your needs. "It's an involved process."

"I'll bet it is." She drummed her fingernails against the door. "How about a lift to my house so I can clean up? Then maybe we can talk about auditioning my hands."

My door locks popped open. She got in and scooted across the leather upholstery. Her scent became even more tempting. We exchanged names; hers was Belinda.

If you're a vampire, getting into a woman's pants is easy. There's the hunt and the conquest but without an emotional connection, after a while it's like eating in a restaurant by yourself. It might have been the fanciest meal in town but the experience wouldn't beat sharing a plate in a greasy spoon with a friend.

I've learned that I can't have a normal relationship with a

woman. I've tried and the result was like flying in the *Hindenburg*. I had concealed my undead nature but the deceit built up like hydrogen gas before exploding and tearing us apart.

What I most had to hide with hypnosis was my translucent vampire skin. Now with a tan, I was free of that masquerade.

The mystery now was how well I could get to know Belinda and how well would she get to know me.

An hour later we were in her town house, frolicking naked in the big tub like a couple of otters. I couldn't believe my freedom. No more tricking a woman to hide my vampire persona. I had dropped my skivvies and there I was. Everything a nice shade of pecan brown. We compared tans.

I held her hand and rubbed my thumb over her engagement ring. "What about your fiancé?"

"He's postponed the wedding twice. He's lucky I haven't pawned the ring for a big-screen TV."

Belinda took the ring off and set it on the rim of the tub. "My hand doesn't need the ring for the audition, does it, Mr. Talent Scout?"

The way she said that meant I was busted about being a talent scout, but the way she pressed her bare breasts against my chest meant it didn't matter. We adjourned from the tub to Belinda's bedroom. She pulled an open carton of Trojans from under the bed.

I thought about trying some of the *Kama Sutra* poses, but my hostess wanted only the quick basics, and gentleman that I pretended to be, I couldn't refuse her.

The sound of a toilet flushing awoke me. Had I fallen asleep? The night's activities had done wonders for my mood, leaving me so relaxed that my body settled against the mattress like a bag of jelly.

The digits of the clock radio read two A.M. A border of light outlined the bathroom door. The rumpled sheet on Belinda's side of the bed conformed to her shape. Her pillow carried a pleasant damp scent. Ice melted in an empty pitcher of margaritas on the night table.

I smacked my lips and tasted B-negative. Of course I had fanged Belinda. After all, she was *my* dinner.

As a vampire, I fang for nourishment, to deepen my hypnotic hold, as the first step in converting a victim into a vampire, or to kill.

We vampires secrete enzymes through our fangs. One enzyme induces deep amnesia, another accelerates healing to hide our puncture wounds, yet another gives an almost hallucinogenic pleasure; without it, the victim feels like fire is surging through their veins.

Belinda might have two faint yellow bruises where I'd fanged her. The enzymes in my saliva expunged the memory of my bloodsucking.

The bathroom light went dark, the door opened, and Belinda came out. She knotted the belt of a terry-cloth robe that couldn't hide the voluptuousness of her full breasts and wide hips.

I smiled and fluffed her pillow. I was ready for more fun. The sex had been uncomplicated and easy. No interruption on my part to hypnotize her and erase the memory of my vampire nature. I didn't even have to remove my contacts. Having a natural "human" tan was liberating.

Belinda ignored the invitation and sat her rump on the edge of the mattress. She poured the melted ice and what was left of the margaritas from the pitcher into one of the glasses. She opened the top drawer of the nightstand and took out a bottle of pills. Aspirin? After popping a couple of pills, she chased them with a drink from the margarita glass.

If she had a headache, I could recommend a better cure.

Belinda turned and looked at me like she didn't recognize who I was. Had I given her too much of the amnesia-causing enzymes? Better ease up on the vampire mojo this second time around.

"What was your name?" She took another swallow.

I couldn't believe I'd been so careless with my fanging that she'd forgotten my name.

Belinda didn't wait for me to answer. "You better go. I have to get my sleep. It'll be easier for me in the morning if you're gone."

She was kicking me out? Just like that? My emotional compass spun in circles. What had I done wrong?

"No hard feelings," she added. "I had a good time."

A good time? She'd had enough, and out the door for me? She didn't even remember my name. "What am I? An anonymous piece of ass?"

Belinda put the glass back on the nightstand. "What are you complaining about? You had fun."

"Yeah but . . ." My brain went numb with confusion. This had nothing to do with my fanging her. I wanted Belinda to treat me as she would any other man, and she did. Take a number, wait your turn, now get the hell out.

No hard feelings? I was a vampire, the supreme sexual predator, and I felt . . . used, as disposable as last night's condom.

I stewed in humiliation. Now what to do? The spider-bite treatment hid my vampire persona, which it did too well. Show her my fangs and talons? Belinda, you had sex with a vampire.

Big deal, apparently, because that didn't change the fact that she was giving me the boot. This wasn't about my being a vampire, it was about my pride. A very human pride that I thought I no longer felt.

If I showed her my true self, the bloodsucking monster of the night, what then? I couldn't let her live with that knowledge, so I would have to either erase her memory—and we're back to her judging me as worthy of only one bout on the mattress—or I'd have to kill her—which I wouldn't do.

Naked and embarrassed, I slipped from under the covers and gathered my clothes. Belinda sat cross-legged on the bed, watched me get dressed, and yawned.

I saw why her fiancé was ambivalent about tying the knot with this fickle bitch. Getting out now was a good idea. I checked my pockets to make sure I hadn't forgotten anything.

"The front door will lock behind you," Belinda said in a tone that meant "scram."

CHAPTER
20

I DROVE OFF, reliving the evening, thinking how my clever macho talk, my smooth moves in the sack were all a setup for her punch line: Beat it.

My vampire savoir faire had little to do with getting laid. Hell, if Belinda had been horny enough, I could've been a buck-toothed hick driving a Yugo and she would've jumped my bones.

I couldn't stop the chatter in my head, the constant search for a stinging comeback I should've made to placate my ego. But I had to get on with my investigation. I stopped in a convenience store, bought a tall cup of coffee, and added a good amount of blood from a plastic bottle that I had brought in checked baggage. Fortunately, the blood was A-negative, which tended to have a soothing effect on me, like valerian root.

My mood tempered, I drove through the darkness and returned to the crash site. The cluster of vehicles had thinned to four state police cars.

THE UNDEAD KAMA SUTRA   115

As soon as I parked, a trooper came out from the shadows and asked if he could help; in other words, what was I doing here?

When he got close, I zapped him. I fanged the trooper only enough to keep him under—barely tasting his blood—and locked him in the backseat of his cruiser.

I scanned the area and saw the red auras of woodland critters but no humans.

Two trailer-mounted generators hummed alongside the road. I followed a line of cables from the generators toward a glow in the woods beyond. Rows of plastic bins held jagged pieces of metal, most the size of my arm or smaller. I peered into the woods with my night vision and didn't see anything of concern to me.

A circle of construction lights on towers illuminated an oblong black area gouged into the ground. The area was a couple of hundred feet long and about a hundred feet wide. Scorched brush surrounded the perimeter. Small flags dotted the site. Wreckage, either a tail fin or a wingtip, flattened a shrub to my right.

I stood in a patch of burned weeds and studied the impact hole. There was no crater; rather it was a jagged trough scooped into the earth.

I walked around the perimeter. The plane must have hit the ground at a steep angle, ricocheted, and exploded. Good luck trying to collect the remains of these dead.

So where were the remains? And that wreckage in the bins, where was that going?

What did this have in common with the Cessna Caravan the Araneum had mentioned? Other than both planes had smacked the earth, killing all souls on board, I didn't see a connection.

I returned to the road and found another trooper patrolling the area. I zapped her and asked where the remains were stored.

She said they were in a hangar at a small private airport

nearby. I made her give me directions. Then I shoved her in the backseat of the cruiser with the other trooper I'd fanged. I unbuttoned their shirts and loosened her bra. Would they admit to finding themselves in a situation that risked the wrath of human resources? I took the male trooper's ID badge.

The airport was seven miles away. I got there at a quarter after four in the morning and parked in a deserted lot. I clipped the trooper's badge to my shirt and got out of my car.

The early morning hour—oh-dark-thirty, we used to call it in the army—plus the smell of prairie grass and aviation fuel reminded me of assembling for helicopter assaults in the infantry.

A corporate jet climbed noisily from the main runway. Strobe lights flashed on its belly and tail. The jet looked too fancy for a pop-stand airfield like this. Was Goodman on the jet and had I just missed him?

The operations building was locked. This was a rinky-dink enterprise: a few prefab hangars, a concrete runway, and a dozen small private airplanes and ag sprayers tethered to the parking apron.

I walked around the south side of the operations building. Construction lights illuminated an area in front of the largest hangar at the far end. I approached down the taxiway and circled around a fueling point.

A couple of big RVs, several black SUVs, and three panel trucks sat in a row beside the hangar. Traffic cones and police tape marked a perimeter around the area. Two red auras identified a couple of men, both bored, standing guard next to an unmarked Crown Victoria at the entrance into the perimeter.

I could break into the hangar from the back or the roof. But getting past these two guards shouldn't be much trouble, so why bother?

The men gossiped and sipped coffee from paper cups.

I scoped the area. Nothing but the lights, the vehicles, and the two wide doors of the hangar shut together. Light from inside leaked through the edges of the doors. Nothing waited in the darkness beyond.

I angled my path so that I stepped into the long shadow cast by the two guards and the lights behind them.

The men noticed me and placed their cups on the roof of the Crown Vic. A sign leaning against a traffic cone said:

RESTRICTED AREA
NATIONAL TRANSPORTATION SAFETY BOARD
U.S.D.O.T.

Badges glinted on the men's belts. The rectangular silhouettes of pistol butts showed against their hips. The embroidery on their dark polo shirts read FEDERAL MARSHAL.

I kept my face in shadow. "Illinois State Police. I'm a liaison from the governor's office."

"Kinda early in the day, isn't it?" the taller of the marshals asked.

"The governor calls and I jump. I don't ask him the time."

The marshal chuckled. "I hear that." He pointed to the tape marking the boundary. "But I can't help you, pal. This place belongs to the NTSB right now. If you need access, come back when the staff is here."

I kept walking toward them. "What time will that be?"

The marshal shrugged. "Six maybe. Seven for sure."

His partner beckoned me. "Let me see your ID. Nothing personal. We have to log in all visitors, whether they get in or not."

"No problem." I stopped four feet in front of them and let the light wash across my face.

Both marshals fixed their eyes on me. One muttered, "Sweet Jesus." The other whispered, "Holy shit."

Their auras flared like two hot coals in a Weber grill. Their eyes opened wide as half-dollars.

I let their auras settle before asking, "Does either of you know Dan Goodman?"

Big guy answered no. His partner couldn't get a word out and I didn't have time to prod his subconscious. I needed to look inside the hangar.

Fanging the marshals was the preferred technique to keep them under, but I tried something else. I banged their heads together like coconuts and let them drop.

I proceeded toward the hangar and examined the parked vehicles in case I overlooked someone. Around the corner to the south, there was a smaller door with a brightly lit window. I didn't see any security cameras. I kept my distance from the window and looked inside. A female marshal sat at a desk ten feet from the door. She leafed through a copy of *Flying* magazine. A coffeemaker with a half-empty carafe rested on the desk.

I waited a couple of moments to see if someone else appeared. No one did. I stood to one side of the window and placed my hand against the door. The metal vibrated with the hum of electric motors—something like ventilation fans or compressors. Satisfied that she was alone, I opened the door and walked in.

The marshal brought her gaze from the magazine and up to me. She began to stand. "You need . . ."

She froze midway up. Her pupils dilated and her aura brightened into a crimson sizzle.

I shut and locked the door. I brushed my hand across the row of light switches. The hangar fell dark as a tomb. Perfect.

I stepped around the desk and cupped the marshal's neck. She had a firm, athletic build. I brought my fangs close to her throat. Her shampoo had a tea tree scent, while her deodorant smelled of something exotic and tropical. I was sure the marshal bought these products at a health food store, so I bet she paid attention to what she ate.

My fangs broke her skin. The warm blood pumped into my mouth. I took a swallow and savored the taste. Nothing artificial in her blood. A strictly organic diet for sure.

I worked my saliva to the wound. As the enzymes seeped into her flesh, the marshal gave a low moan and relaxed. I held her arm and eased her back into the chair. My fanging should keep her under for at least an hour.

I flipped through the papers and binders on the desk. Most were procedures or lists of people. I sorted through a stack of loose faxes, invoices, and receipts. One form was a flight manifest for a Gulfstream corporate jet. Among the six passengers was a D. Goodman.

The trail was hot again.

The Gulfstream had left just as I arrived—so he was aboard.

The destination of the Gulfstream? Kansas City, the origin of the doomed airliner.

An investigation team would look into evidence at the point of departure. But why was Goodman involved in the first place?

I asked the marshal if she knew Goodman and she answered no. I closed her eyes and left her content and unconscious.

Airplane wreckage lay scattered across the hangar floor. A metal easel held a schematic of the Beech turboprop that mapped how the pieces belonged together.

The noises of a fan and compressor came from a semi-trailer parked inside the hangar against the northern wall. The back of the trailer faced the hangar doors. A ramp led to the trailer doors, which were secured with a padlock.

Boxes of latex gloves, booties, and paper masks rested on a bench beside the bottom of the ramp. Two gurneys had been pushed against the bench. A sign taped to the left trailer door said:

AUTHORIZED PERSONNEL ONLY.
CRASH INVESTIGATION EVIDENCE.

Another placard had the symbol for biological waste and was labeled BIOHAZARD.

I picked through an open toolbox and found a heavy pry bar that I used to force open the trailer door. I slipped the broken padlock into my pocket to hide the obvious evidence of my entry.

When I opened the door, a wave of refrigerated air carried the odor of decaying human flesh. On the inside of the door someone had taped color head shots labeled with names, a birth date, and some kind of reference number. There were nineteen smiling faces, which I presumed were the crash victims, now charred and torn to pieces and no longer smiling.

Body bags sat on the shelves along the inside of the trailer. Some bags held lumpy forms scarcely the size of a child. Others were almost flat. Smashing into the ground at several hundred miles an hour didn't leave much to recover.

Humans have this perception of the inviolate forms of their physical bodies, until they encounter the laws of physics. Then their precious bags of flesh, tissue, and bone become messy, fragile projectiles that go splat.

I counted seventeen body bags. Masking tape on two empty shelves had been marked with the names Vanessa Tico and Janice Wyndersook. Where were their remains? According to the most recent news, all the bodies were accounted for. Were these two released to their family for burial? Considering the crash happened this morning, I doubted it.

I examined the pictures of the missing women. Vanessa Tico's portrait looked like a glamour shot. She was an African-American with a middle-dark complexion, straight hair that seemed sprayed armor-stiff, and wide, bright eyes that begged you to share a laugh. Janice Wyndersook faced the camera in a fuzzy blowup of a snapshot. Her small eyes squinted at the viewer through narrow glasses. Tufts of blond hair jutted from her scalp in the current trendy style. Her rosy complexion made each round cheek look as inviting as a freshly picked apple. Vanessa was twenty-seven, Janice twenty-eight.

They weren't much younger than Marissa Albert, the murdered chalice in Key West. I touched the pictures on the door. A hunch—I was a private detective, what else did I have—told me that Vanessa and Janice were still alive.

Then why the charade of their deaths in this crash?

I bet Goodman would know.

CHAPTER
21

I BACKED OUT of the trailer and closed the door. I turned the hangar lights back on, dropped the padlock into an outside drain, and hustled to my car. The marshals by the Crown Victoria remained unconscious.

Each new thing that I learned so far—the murders, the aliens, my orders from the Araneum, the crashed airplanes— was like another big rock in my mental knapsack. More weight to carry to what destination?

I got back to Midway Airport, bought a round-trip ticket for Kansas City, and sat with a cup of coffee in the passenger terminal where the morning sun could hit me. I watched the red orb rise over the ragged horizon beyond the airport perimeter.

As a vampire, I'd seen the sunrise through the thick, dark lenses of welder's goggles, while wearing heavy clothing to protect my skin. Now I was so used to my human skin that I didn't feel the slightest tremor of fear when the sun advanced past the edge of the earth. The sun grew bright enough to sting my eyes through the contacts and I looked away, a reminder that I only looked human. I felt the gentle warmth against my cheek and the back of my hands.

Because of all the stupid pain-in-the-ass security rules, I had to sneak blood with me. I hid three ounces of B-positive (a whole three ounces!) in a travel-size bottle of shampoo the TSA screeners had waved through.

I emptied the bottle into my coffee. The small amount of blood was enough to quench my vampire thirst until my next big fix. The rest of my supply had to travel in checked baggage.

Again, as before, the question was where to find Goodman. The man flitted before me, elusive as a mirage.

Once in the Kansas City airport, I scouted the counter for Prairie Air. I followed a maintenance worker to the men's room, zapped him, pushed him into a stall, and took his badge.

I swiped the badge to unlock a door to the secure part of the terminal. The employee lounge for Prairie Air wasn't anything fancy: two long tables in the middle, stackable plastic chairs scattered across the linoleum floor, a microwave, refrigerator, and coffeemakers. Copies of the *Kansas City Star* and the *Chicago Tribune* lay on the tables. Headlines on the newspapers announced yesterday's crash. A wipe board on the far wall had been scrawled with red and blue markers:

NO MEDIA CONTACT, PERIOD!
SEE YOUR MANAGER FOR NTSB GO TEAM INTERVIEW
NOTE CHANGES IN WORK SCHEDULE!

There was a list of names with one crossed out. Karen Beck. Who was she?

Women and men in Prairie Air uniforms—shirts or

blouses that were dusty brown at the shoulders and faded to a bleached straw color around the waists, plus meadow-green trousers or skirts—hustled through the doors leading to the check-in counters. Everyone looked busy and it would've been difficult to snag anyone without attracting attention. Maybe I could find someone outside on a smoke break or getting off work.

I went out the employee exit and stepped into the bright sunlight. I slipped the badge into my pocket. The smell of cigarette smoke lingered in the air, menthols and unfiltered, but the smokers had since left. A concrete walkway led to an employee parking lot on the other side of a chain-link fence.

The door opened behind me and slammed against the stop. A short blonde with a pixie cut, in her early thirties, slender, wearing the Prairie Air uniform, carried a card-board box jammed with framed photos, stuffed animals, ceramic cups, her brown work shoes, and a wadded pair of panty hose. She was bare-legged. Cheap flip-flops slapped the bottoms of her feet. A paper visitor's tag pinned to her collar had her name written with a felt-tip pen. Karen Beck.

She plowed past me. The box raked my arm and she didn't even glance back to apologize.

I raised my sunglasses. Her aura looked like the surface of a red sea in turmoil. Tendrils of anger writhed from the periphery of the penumbra.

I lowered my sunglasses. "Ms. Beck."

She kept walking.

I followed and repeated her name.

She stopped and turned around. Her green eyes burned like twin flares. "What do you want?"

"A talk."

"I'm done with talking. If you need something to do, go fuck yourself."

Interesting Midwestern pleasantry. I smiled to deflect her anger. "Need help with the box?"

She gave me the once-over. "I can manage." Her voice softened. "Sorry. I had a really bad day. I just got fired."

Was that why her name was crossed out on the wipe board?

"Sorry to hear that."

"Not as sorry as I am, believe me. It was a shitty job but I needed the money." Karen shifted her grasp on the box.

"Why'd you get fired?"

"The real reason? I work for a bunch of assholes."

"Is there an official reason?"

"I wouldn't cooperate."

"With what?"

Karen opened her mouth and stopped. She closed her mouth and her forehead creased in puzzlement. "Where's your badge? Who are you?"

"My name is Felix Gomez."

Had Karen gotten canned for refusing to cooperate with a crash investigation? What did she know or do that made it worth losing this job? The hunch returned and I decided to chance it.

"I'm here because of Vanessa Tico and Janice Wyndersook."

The creases in Karen's forehead deepened into a V. "Are you with the media?"

I shook my head. "I'm an investigator. A friend of the family hired me."

Karen squinted suspiciously. "Which family?"

"Vanessa's," I lied.

"The crash happened just yesterday," Karen said. "Seems pretty damn quick to hire an investigator."

Time to redirect the conversation to the questions I wanted answered. "Were Vanessa and Janice on Flight 2112 to Chicago Midway?"

Karen looked past my shoulder to the entrance. "If I talk to you, are people going to get in trouble?"

"Some will."

"Good." She nodded toward the parking lot. "Let's continue this discussion someplace else."

CHAPTER
22

KAREN LOADED her fork with cashew chicken, pea pods, and steamed rice. We were in the Ling Ding Chinese Palace and Karen was finishing her fourth plate from the lunch buffet. The torn remnant of the paper visitor's tag dangled from a safety pin on her collar.

"Good thing it's a big buffet," I said.

Karen brought her hand to cover her mouth while she chewed. "Sorry, but I was starving." Rice dribbled onto her blouse.

Having lunch had been Karen's idea. If someone with information you needed wanted to talk, then put them in a comfortable environment and let them blab.

I moved food around on my plate and didn't do much except pick at it. The buffet looked good enough, but without blood even the most sumptuous of gourmet meals tasted like wet sawdust.

"What do you get from all this?" Karen asked.

"It's my job."

"How did Janice Wyndersook's parents get you on the case so fast?"

Had Karen forgotten that I said Vanessa's folks had hired me or was she testing me?

"I work for Vanessa's family."

"Oh, that's right." Karen nodded. She looked away for a moment.

"You don't act like you're heartbroken about being fired," I said.

"You can't believe what they expected me to live on," she replied. "I'm trying to get back on my feet financially, so I scrimp on everything. I've been living on cream of wheat and canned ravioli from the food bank."

"Back on your feet from what?" I brought a helping of Szechuan pork to my lips and set it back on my plate.

"What else? An asshole criminal of an ex."

"Criminal?"

"Really. A fucking crook. He cleaned out our joint bank account, maxed out our credit cards buying gold coins, and split town in *my* car with his cousin the stripper. First cousin, I need to add, the incestuous tramp." Karen shoved food into her mouth between sentences. "God, if love is blind then my eyes must have been plucked out of my head on this one."

"You needed the job at Prairie Air and yet you let yourself get fired."

"As much as I've been butt-fucked in life, you'd think I'd be the last person to stand on principle on anything. But this was wrong."

"In what way specifically?"

"The manifest on Flight 2112." Karen put her fork down and wiped her lips with a napkin. I didn't think she was done eating so much as taking a breather.

Karen set her elbows on either side of the plate and leaned toward me. "I got fired because I was asked to lie about the manifest. Vanessa Tico and Janice Wyndersook were booked for the flight but never boarded."

"You sure?"

Karen grabbed a fried wonton and munched it. "Absolutely. When their names didn't show up as having scanned their boarding passes I called the plane and spoke to the attendant. She gave me a head count. There were four empty seats out of twenty. Should have only been two. Wasn't hard to miss."

"Why did you go to the trouble of checking to see if Vanessa and Janice had boarded?"

"Because this was the first time I've ever had passengers miss a flight. Since they boarded on the ramp versus down a Jetway, there was the possibility they had gone out the door of another commuter airline. Not likely, considering security, but it has happened."

"What were you asked to lie about?" I asked.

"That Vanessa and Janice had boarded and that the manifest reflected that."

"Why and who asked you to lie?"

"The why I don't know. The who were my boss and his boss."

"Both employees of Prairie Air?"

Karen nodded. "Yeah."

"Do they routinely deal with the manifest?"

She shook her head. "No."

"Is changing a manifest something out of the ordinary?"

Karen rolled her eyes. "Hell yes."

"Why would your bosses ask you to change it?"

"That's the why question, right? Like I told you, I don't know. Maybe it was the feds?"

The question made me pause. "Feds?"

"One of those Go Teams arrived early this morning to investigate the crash. They did interviews and took records from the booking clerks and the maintenance crew."

"And they interviewed you?" I asked.

"Not directly. They were in the office when my bosses were asking me to change the manifest."

"But the manifest is on the computer, right? There would be a record that it had been altered."

"That's why they wanted me to go back and change it. To make it look like it had been my mistake by not putting those two passengers on the manifest. And they wanted me to sign an affidavit that I had made a mistake and not Prairie Air."

"And if you didn't cooperate?"

"I'd get fired for insubordination."

"And these feds? What were they doing during the interview?"

"Just watching. Once they made me wait in the hall while they discussed something with my bosses."

"How did you know they were feds?"

"Because my boss kept calling them 'the feds.' Two of them had NTSB badges and the other an ID with the initials RKW."

Rockville Kamza Worthington. The consultant firm Goodman worked for. He was within tackling distance. Why was Goodman interested in changing the manifest? The corpses of Vanessa and Janice weren't in the morgue trailer and, according to Karen, they had never boarded the doomed flight. So why the charade of claiming they had been killed in the crash?

My *kundalini noir* twitched with suspicion. What about the other crash, the Cessna Caravan? Were any of those victims missing?

I asked, "What did the man . . . it was a man who wore the RKW badge?"

"Yeah. About your height. More filled out. Short blond hair. Quiet. Late forties I'd guess. Looks like he works outside a lot. Wore one of those official blue windbreakers."

Goodman, for sure.

"You get his name?"

"No. As far as I was concerned, he was just another bureaucratic busybody."

"Your bosses threatened you with dismissal?"

"Not in those words. It was more like sign this or you're out on your ass."

"And your bosses were comfortable with this?"

"Charles, my immediate supervisor, wasn't. He's a nice enough guy otherwise but I could tell he didn't want to join me in the unemployment line. My other boss is a real career prick. He couldn't understand why I wouldn't admit to making a mistake. Of course, I didn't make a mistake. Even if I cooperated, I knew this wouldn't be the end of the story. Something else comes up, a criminal investigation for instance, and do you think they'd admit to pressuring me to sign that affidavit?"

Karen and I locked eyes for a moment. I sensed her gratitude; she'd found someone on her side. Maybe she would extend that gratitude to the bedroom.

"Who else could verify the manifest?"

"The flight attendant. After the crash, now it's just me."

I tried to remember which of those corpses in the trailer belonged to the flight attendant. Not that I could've gotten her to talk.

I scooped rice with my fork and pretended it tasted good. "What now?"

Karen sighed. She ran a hand over her scalp and fluffed her hair. "Find work. And pronto. My rent is due at the end of next week and I won't have enough to cover it."

Karen had been more than helpful. Thanks to her, the light on Goodman shined even brighter. This Dan Goodman was my man.

I fished a roll of hundreds from my pocket and kept the roll below the level of the table so Karen couldn't see what I was doing. I removed twenty bills, cupped them in my hand, and offered them to Karen.

She stared at the money. "What's that for?"

"To give you a little breathing room until you find more work."

"What's the catch?"

"There is none. My client gave me a good advance and so far, you've been my best lead."

Karen took the money and counted it. "You sure about this?"

"Of course."

She folded the bills and shoved them into her purse. "Don't expect no quid pro quo. Like putting out."

"Didn't cross my mind."

"Well, make sure that it doesn't."

The way she snapped at me meant I was wrong in thinking there was chemistry between us. How could I have misread her? Usually, when I'm with a woman alone like this, sex is not a matter of if but when. My vampire lure is always out there. Why wasn't she interested?

The waiter came by and took Karen's plate. She asked for hot tea. After the waiter left, she asked me, "What's next?"

"After lunch?" I was hoping for a chance to check out Karen's bra size, but considering her tone, I didn't want a repeat of the debacle I had with Belinda in Oswego. "I keep going with the investigation."

The waiter brought hot tea. Karen poured a cup and took a sip. "Got time for a break?"

"As in?"

"As in, I got the afternoon off. Duh." She sipped again. "You play pool? There's a sports bar about a half mile from here."

"I can hold my own." Okay, maybe I did have a second chance.

Karen laughed. "Hold your own. Good luck with that. I'm going to kick your ass."

Did chemistry flicker between us?

I paid the check for both of us. Karen and I had come to the restaurant in separate cars; I drove a Monte Carlo rental, she a little Metro. Karen had taken the last spot behind the restaurant while I parked down the street. I went back to my car and would follow her Metro to the sports bar.

If the afternoon unfolded as I imagined it would, and we ended up together, I wouldn't make the same mistake as I had with Belinda. Karen was getting a dose of vampire hypnosis.

A woman screamed.

The scream had come from Karen's direction.

My fingers and the skin on my arms tingled with dread. My *kundalini noir* writhed in alarm. So much for my sixth sense giving me a warning. The scream I heard meant the worst had already happened.

I sprinted down the sidewalk and through an alley back to the tiny lot behind the Ling Ding Chinese Palace.

A woman stared pale-faced at the ground beside Karen's Metro. Two busboys stood at the back door of the restaurant and also looked at the ground.

Karen lay on her back. Both legs were twisted under her hips. Her head faced the Metro and lifeless eyes gazed at the car door. Wet, shiny blood pooled around her head and matted the blond hair against the asphalt. Blood oozed from two small holes at the back of her skull.

Death had been lightning-quick. Karen had collapsed and rolled backward on her hip.

I panned the faces around me. "Anybody see anything?"

The two busboys shook their heads. The woman didn't react to my question.

Karen's key ring was by her right hand. Her purse remained tucked under her left arm. Nothing was taken.

I crouched and examined the bullet wounds in her skull. The holes were identical round punctures an inch apart. Too small to be 9 mm or .38. Most likely a .22.

I scanned the ground for the cartridge cases. Nothing but gravel, gum wrappers, and cigarette butts.

Why hadn't I heard the gunshots?

A silencer? Of course .22s were easier to silence than larger-caliber weapons. And a couple of .22 slugs into the skull was enough to flatline anyone.

The shots looked expertly delivered. Karen hadn't been simply murdered, she had been assassinated.

CHAPTER
23

ANOTHER GOOD lead and another one dead as well.
Only Karen didn't deserve it.

Why kill her? What few personal effects Karen had were still on her body. Robbery wasn't the motive.

Maybe the killer wasn't after what she carried but what she had in her head: information. And with her dead, that information was gone forever.

If this was an assassination, why kill her like this and leave evidence of a professional hit? Why not run her down, or break into her house and make it look like a burglary gone bad? Or did she have to be shut up immediately?

Now I knew what she had known. Did her killer realize that? And if so, was I next?

Karen had been dead less than a few minutes. The killer had to be close by.

My *kundalini noir* coiled like a snake in its den—wary, suspicious, prepared.

Pedestrians gathered to gawk at the body. Was one of them the murderer? I could take out my contacts and read their auras but that would give away my vampire nature. There were about a dozen people around me, too many to hypnotize.

A waiter appeared in the back door of the restaurant, the same Asian guy who had served us. A busboy mumbled to him and motioned toward the Metro. The waiter's expression went from concern to shock. He walked to the Metro and halted to stare at Karen's body. His face turned ashen-white. He looked at me and pointed a finger. "She was with you."

The crowd gave a collective accusing gasp.

The wail of an approaching police siren told me this attention was only going to make it worse for me.

I backed away toward the alley. I wanted to turn and run, but if I did that, then everyone would presume I was guilty of something.

"Where are you going?" The waiter scowled. He stepped around the Metro and followed me.

What was up his tight ass? He was no cop.

The waiter jabbed a finger toward Karen's body. "What happened to her?"

The siren echoed within the walls of the alley.

The waiter trotted after me. "The police will be here. They'll want to talk to you."

Maybe this guy was the assassin. He grabbed for my arm. I moved at vampire speed and was instantly out of his reach.

He stared dumbfounded. He yelled over his shoulder in Chinese and chased me, changing his shouting to English. "What happened to your lady friend? Why are you leaving?"

I turned away to remove my contacts. Where the alley emptied onto the street, I whirled about and faced the waiter.

The pupils of his dark brown eyes gaped like tiny mouths. His aura pulsed once. I zapped the waiter hard to keep him out for a full minute at least. I lifted him into a Dumpster and dropped him on a pile of yesterday's fried rice and peanut sauce.

I returned to my car and sped off. Even though I had an open ticket back to Chicago, I wondered if flying was the safest bet.

In the rearview mirror, I could see people run onto the sidewalk. A police car flew past me and skidded to a stop in front of them. People ran to the driver's door and gestured after me.

The police car raced from the curb and U-turned to pursue me. Going to the airport was out of the question.

I mashed the gas pedal and the Monte Carlo catapulted forward.

A second police car shot from the next intersection and swerved into me. His front left fender crunched against my right rear. My car spun ninety degrees and I faced the wrong direction down a one-way street.

I gave the Monte Carlo more gas and bolted down the one-way. The second cop car swung around the corner in pursuit. Cars and trucks juked around me, horns blaring like shouted curses.

A city bus lurched into the next intersection. I jerked the wheel and cut in front of it. The cop behind me tried the same maneuver only to have his cruiser T-bone the bus.

I zigzagged through the city and wound up on State Highway 210 going east. A helicopter shadowed me. Blue and red lights flashed in my mirrors. The noose tightened. No way could I escape by car. Maybe I should crash into a building and disappear on foot.

Up ahead, patrol cars blocked the highway. Cops scrambled out of their cars and readied weapons.

The pursuing cars slowed and let me approach the barricade by myself. I would be the only one in the field of fire.

Well, if they wanted me, I'd make them work for it.

I gunned the engine and steered to the right. The Monte Carlo flattened sign posts and rumbled over the shoulder and across the rough grass toward the Missouri River.

The engine revved into a scream. The Monte Carlo bounced over a small cliff. The front of the sedan angled toward the water. For an instant I was airborne. The brown water of the Missouri River filled my windshield. I braced for the impact.

My front bumper smashed into the water. The airbag detonated and slapped my face.

CHAPTER
24

WATER SPLASHED across the windshield and windows. The Monte Carlo bobbed in the turbulent river. Steam curled from under the hood. Lights sputtered on the dashboard.

A voice called to me from the stereo speakers. She had the perky earnestness of a Girl Scout rehearsing for a life-saver merit badge. "*On Star* here. Do you need help? Are you okay?"

"Help? Think you could make me invisible?"

"Pardon?"

Bullets peppered the roof. The cops weren't even going through the pretense of rescuing me.

"Sir, I show that you're in the Missouri River. Is that correct, sir?"

"I'm looking for my boat."

"Uh-uh," the voice said. "I'm going to summon the police."

A bullet punched through the side window. "Don't bother. They know exactly where I am."

"Sir. Sir. Could you verify that you're . . ." The voice cut out. The lights on the dash dimmed and went dark.

I tilted the steering wheel up, undid my safety belt, and smashed the driver's window with my elbow. Cold river water cascaded in and splashed the contacts out of my eyes. The Monte Carlo tipped to the left as brown water flooded the interior.

In seconds the coupe was rolling underwater and still sinking. I pushed the door open and swam clear. The current grabbed me like a giant hand and shoved me against rocks and mounds of silt.

The police expected the river to carry me downstream. I dug my feet into the muddy bottom, turned upstream, and plodded forward. The river current pummeled me and I groped along like a blind crayfish.

I came across a pile of rocks and climbed them. My head broke the turbulent surface. A bridge loomed over me, about three hundred meters from where I had ditched the car.

In the distance, police cars rolled close to the riverbank. A couple of helicopters hovered high above the water. Just as I thought, they expected me to float down with the current.

Would they issue an APB? Did they know who I was? If they had the license number to the Monte Carlo, then the rental agency would give them my name. I could see SEEKING FELIX GOMEZ, PERSON OF INTEREST flashing on those Amber Alert highway signs.

If I climbed out of the water now and ventured into public, my wet, soggy appearance would attract even more attention. I couldn't risk it. Better that I hide until dark.

I used cracks in a concrete river wall as handholds to move upstream. Water poured from a culvert above my head. The opening looked big enough to squeeze through. With luck, it would take me far enough from the river, where I could get out and escape.

I reached for the lip of the steel pipe and hoisted myself up. The inside of the culvert was layered with smelly muck. I crawled through the mess for a hundred meters and emerged in a sewer, where I could stand up. Rats clung to my shoulders. Narrow shafts of sunlight beamed through the holes in a manhole cover above. I shooed the rats and hiked through the sewer to get more distance from the river.

My overnight bag was still in the Monte Carlo. I had packed light, a few extra clothes and toiletries. My other luggage and the bulk of the cash remained in my Cadillac back at the airport in Savannah. When I pulled my cell phone out of my pocket and opened it, gritty water dribbled out. The screen remained dark.

My watch was gone, lost in the river along with my contacts. After what seemed like hours of spelunking through the sewer, I stopped in a chamber at the intersection of two tunnels. A steel ladder led to a manhole cover. Circles of light marked the holes around its inner circumference. Traffic rumbled on the street and the sunlight blinked as vehicles passed overhead. I'd wait here for darkness and pass the time in a cold, miserable, and disgusting funk.

I couldn't believe the ordeal I put myself through. Other vampires lived in penthouses and were attended by a coterie of rich, beautiful women. The low point of the day was when the martini glass ran dry.

So what the hell was I trying to prove? Why was it my lot in eternity to champion the wronged and find justice? I was no superhero; I didn't even own a pair of tights.

About the time in my youth when I gained my identity as a man, I'd always chosen the path that set me as a bulwark between the privileged and the underdog. I helped my mother and her sisters deal with unscrupulous salesmen and landlords. Later, when I joined the army, I might have talked about benefits, security, and opportunity, but deep in my heart, I saw myself as a patriot, the enemy of tyrants. Ironically, it was in service during a war we had no business starting that I murdered the innocent in the name of freedom, and it had taken my conversion to the undead to wipe the cosmic slate clean.

Maybe the slate wasn't clean enough and I needed to atone a little bit longer, perhaps for another century.

The rays shining through the manhole cover slanted as the time passed. The lights dimmed and disappeared as night settled. I climbed the ladder, put my hands against the bottom of the cover, and pushed.

I had to rotate the cover until it lifted and allowed me to look out over an intersection. People loitered on the sidewalks of a seedy part of town. Good. There were plenty of smelly, dirty citizens I could hide among.

I tilted the cover up and scrambled onto the street. The cover dropped into place behind me.

I walked across the street toward an alley. An illuminated billboard for Rizè-Blu beamed its cheery message of chemical self-improvement onto the homeless and drunks.

Damp, filthy clothes and black slime covered my body. Before I did anything or went anywhere, I needed to wash up and change clothes. I smelled, well, like I'd been swimming with rats and turds.

Dumpsters covered with graffiti and piles of trash were set against the walls of the alley.

The skin on the back of my hands tingled. Danger.

CHAPTER
25

T HE WARNING barely registered when something hard
whacked against my back. I staggered forward from the
blow. Out of the corner of my eye I saw a broomstick swinging to hit me again. I caught my balance, reached for the
broomstick, and wrenched it free.

An obese homeless man stumbled from a doorway. "Hey,
leave my stuff alone." He grabbed the handle of a shopping
cart to steady himself. A tarp covered a lumpy pile in the
cart.

In the moonlight, the homeless man's head looked as dark
and wrinkled as an overripe fig. His clouded eyes were a
pair of burnished nickels. The aura surrounding him pulsed
with defiance.

I gave him the scariest stare I could manage, to snag him
with hypnosis. Nothing. Great, I had let a blind man get the
drop on me.

The homeless man stared vacantly at me. A sweatshirt rode over the enormous swell of his belly, exposing a hairy navel big enough to screw in a hundred-watt bulb. He yanked the shirt to cover his gut.

I tossed the stick and sent it clattering down the center of the alley. The homeless man's aura blazed with alarm. He jerked his head toward the noise.

"I'm not after your stuff," I said.

His head jerked back to me.

I stepped toward him.

He raised his arms and stumbled backward against his shopping cart. "I can see good enough. Come close and I'll give you a whipping."

I addressed him in a soothing tone. "I'm not here to hurt you."

He circled his fists. "Folks say that before they hit me and take my things."

"I need your help," I said. "I need clothes and a place to wash up."

He put his arms down and leaned toward me. He sniffed, then grimaced. "Damn right you need to wash up. I thought the sewer had backed up again."

"I can pay." I peeled a damp bill from my roll of hundreds.

The homeless man did nothing.

"Here." I took his hand.

He tried to jerk it away but I held firm. I jammed the money into his palm.

He brought the bill an inch from his face. He wrinkled his nose and waved the bill as if to shake away the smell. He brought the bill close to his face again. His right eye bulged like the lens of a microscope as he examined the bill.

"You got a name?" I asked.

"You must not be from around here. If you were, you'd know who I was."

"You're right, I'm not from around here."

"Then where are you from? Stink-alvania?" He laughed. The shirt rode over his belly again and he pulled it down. "Name's Earl." He handed the money back to me. "This is a hundred-dollar bill. No way anyone around here is going to accept that from me. Got any twenties?" He stood with his hand out.

I smoothed a twenty and swapped it with the hundred.

Earl fingered the bill. "Just the one?" He brought the bill to his eye. "You owe me eighty."

"How do you figure?"

"You offered a hundred to begin with, didn't you? That's how I figure. You don't want my help, then stay dirty and stinking. Move along then, 'cause you're ruining my dinner."

A bag stenciled with the name DARRYL'S BAR-B-Q rested in the doorway behind him, along with an upright paper bag big enough for a bottle of wine or a fifth of liquor. I would've preferred the aroma of barbecue over my own disgusting smell. I'd pay a hundred bucks for a bath.

"Okay, help me and you get the extra eighty. Where could I wash up?" I asked.

"The rescue mission. But you got to put up with all that preaching and holy-roller shit."

"I can handle that." I looked up and then down the alley. "Which way is the mission?"

Earl pointed to his right. "That way."

"Well, let's go."

"Don't bother. It's done closed for the evening."

I wanted to shake a straight answer out of Earl. "Where then?"

"The gas station up the block." Earl turned around and groped for the bag of barbecue and the bottle. He slipped them under the tarp covering his shopping cart.

"Is the gas station open?" I asked.

"Nope." Earl pulled the cart away from the wall and guided it up the alley. He pushed the cart in a shambling gait. His heels flattened the backs of a pair of dirty white cross-trainers.

"Then where are you going?"

"The gas station. The folks who own it won't let you wash there when it's open." Earl said this like every idiot in Kansas City knew it as a fact.

I walked behind Earl.

He mumbled over his shoulder. "Don't get too close and for God's sake, stay downwind."

I put a couple of extra steps between us.

We turned on Holmes Street and continued to the next road. Traffic emptied from the interstate and whooshed past us into a spaghetti maze of on-ramps, off-ramps, and intersections.

Earl pushed his cart off the sidewalk. The wheels clattered onto the pavement. As if blind—gee, after all, he was—he trundled across the street. A Lincoln Continental with green lights in the wheel wells and a bass stereo loud enough to drown out an exploding volcano rounded the corner and, not bothering to slow down, zoomed around Earl.

He kept shuffling, rammed his cart against the opposite curb, and levered it onto the sidewalk.

At the end of the next block, Earl veered into the lot of a dark and deserted Gas-U-Mart. Electric wires jutted from the posts where the security lamps would have been. Scarred and chipped plywood sheets covered the vending machines. Behind the mart, a Dodge Caravan rested on flat tires beside a Dumpster and barrels filled with oily water.

Earl pushed his cart until it collided with the wall. It was an inside corner, where the building made an L by the rear entrance. A heavy chain and two hasps, all fastened with padlocks the size of fists, secured the door.

"Now what?" I asked.

Earl folded back the tarp on his cart. He wrestled with a stuffed nylon duffel bag and pulled it free. He hefted the bag and tossed it to land by my feet. "You can't believe the nice things folks throw out. Find you something that fits."

I bent over and unzipped the bag. Clothes and shoes popped out like meat from a split sausage casing. I sorted through the first garments: a turquoise prom dress, some kind of blue dress pants with silver stripes, a yellow blazer, and assorted sweats. I picked out a Lilith Fair T-shirt, black sweatpants with cargo pockets, and a pair of sneakers a size too big. Lucky for me, there was a pair of Foster Grant sunglasses in a pocket of the sweats.

"Got any underwear or socks?"

"That's one thing nobody tosses out. Least anything you'd want to wear." Earl cradled a box of broken electric appliances that he set on the ground. Someday he might need a waffle iron with a frayed power cord.

Earl pulled a length of garden hose from his cart. He waved to the ground around the door. "There's a spigot around there someplace."

I saw it. "There's no faucet handle."

Earl rummaged in his cart through yet another box. He fished out a pair of locking pliers.

Earl reached for the wall and stepped close until his shin knocked against the spigot. He grunted and sank to one knee. He screwed the brass coupling of the hose over the spigot.

Sludge caked my skin and hair. "What about soap? Shampoo?"

Earl cocked a thumb to the cart.

I found tubes and bottles of body wash, shampoo, and conditioner stacked next to spray cans of Raid and Velveeta cheese.

Earl locked the pliers over the stub of the valve stem. As he twisted the valve open, the spigot squeaked. Water rumbled through the hose, and its length snaked across the grass.

Earl grasped the end of the hose. He braced one hand against the wall and levered himself upright. "Should be a grate in the corner that you can stand on."

I unbuttoned my shirt. "Any chance someone can come by? I'd hate to be busted for public indecency."

Earl chuckled. "Cops come by all the time. But would I care? It won't be me buck-naked."

I carried the body wash, shampoo, and a bundle of clothes across the weeds and broken glass to the corner. I stepped on the grate and set the items on the ledge of a boarded-up window. As I stripped, I tossed my dirty clothes into a pile on the grass.

Earl squirted the hose. He missed.

"I'm over here, Earl."

"Sing something and I'll find you."

I hummed "Chances Are."

The cold spray jolted me. I lathered up and scrubbed at the funk with a rag. I wiped dry with a couple of T-shirts and slipped into the clean clothes. The sweatpants bunched around my ankles and I rolled them up to my shins. I collected things from my old clothes and pushed them into the pockets of the sweatpants.

Earl turned off the water and unscrewed the hose. He grunted the entire time. He dropped the pliers into their box and coiled the hose in his shopping cart.

Being clean refreshed me almost as much as fanging a virgin and drinking her unsullied blood—the Godiva chocolate of hemoglobin.

"Say, Earl."

He stopped for a moment.

"Thanks."

He packed his boxes. "I didn't do it for thanks. I did it for the hundred dollars."

"I haven't forgotten. How'd you wind up like this?"

"You asking how is it I'm a homeless bum?" Earl reached into the cart and grasped the bottle in the bag. "Bad luck and bad decisions." He uncapped the bottle and sipped from it. "Doesn't help that I stay a little off balance."

I pulled out my money. "I don't have any more twenties. How about a hundred?"

"That all you got, then I better get creative about breaking it." He held out the bottle. It smelled of Night Train wine.

"No thanks. Do you need anything else?"

"My life starting at age fourteen," Earl deadpanned. "Don't suppose you can do that?"

"Sorry."

"Didn't think so." He took another sip. "Since you're being so generous, then four hundred bucks outta do it. I've got a daughter in Cincinnati I'd like to visit."

I counted the bills. "Here's four. That's five hundred and twenty you've gotten from me." I touched Earl's hand and he turned it palm-up to clasp the money.

"Earl, you never asked me my name."

"Figured a guy who crawled out of the sewer and didn't ask for the police wasn't interested in spreading his identity around." Earl brought the money close to his eye and scrutinized every bill. "How about I call you Cash Machine?"

"Fair enough." I put the sunglasses on. "Time to go. Thanks again, Earl. Say hello to your daughter."

"My daughter?" Earl's eyebrows worked up and down. "Oh right. My daughter." He folded the bills into his front trouser pocket and groped for the handle of the shopping cart. "Yeah, we'll see you later, Cash Machine. Try staying out of the sewers. Might not find another Earl to help you."

I turned about and started north. A few blocks later I walked up to a mini-mart and approached a man gassing a Ford F-150 pickup. His back was to me as he watched the gas pump.

"Excuse me," I asked. "You wouldn't happen to be going east?"

He glanced over his shoulder and gave me a dismissive glare. "Can't help you, buddy."

I removed the sunglasses. "Guess again. You and I are going on a road trip."

CHAPTER
26

ONCE WE got to Savannah, Georgia, I left the F-150 and its driver in the parking lot of a crowded McDonald's and proceeded on foot to a bus stop. A mile down the road, I got off the bus and flagged a taxi that took me to the Savannah airport, where I'd left my Cadillac.

The taxi dropped me off near the west end of the airport parking lot. I scanned the cars and searched for the telltale glow of an aura belonging to someone on a stakeout.

The area looked safe. The few people I saw were encapsulated in auras swirling with petty worries. No one cared about me. But I had to assume that my cover was blown and that Goodman knew who I was and what I was up to.

I walked around my Cadillac. A film of dust covered the body and windows. I stood still for a moment and cleared my mind. I held my hands up, fingers raised, at mid-chest level. A faint breeze brushed against my skin, but nothing tingled. My sixth sense didn't detect any threat.

Didn't mean I wasn't in danger. In a previous case, I had an electronic bug planted on me that I had had no idea was there. My car could now have a listening device or a GPS transmitter stuck on it. I got on my hands and knees and inspected the undercarriage. I ran my hand inside the fender wells and the bumpers. Plenty of dead, crusty bugs, but no electronic ones.

As I stood and brushed myself off, I felt disappointed. All this time I'd been looking over my shoulder and priming my muscles for a desperate fight. I could've flown back here from Kansas City first-class and spared myself the long drive and a numb butt.

Maybe Goodman and his cronies had no clue about me. Maybe they were so fixed on their plan—whatever it was— that they didn't bother to notice I was sneaking up on them.

I was done with that. I knew where Goodman should be, and I would go straight to him. No more hide-and-seek. I started my Cadillac, tuned to a satellite radio channel, and cruised directly to the Sapphire Grand Atlantic Resort.

Goodman's image loomed foremost in my mind. I was sure he had killed Karen Beck and was responsible for me taking a swim in the Missouri River and hiking through the sewers of Kansas City. I rehearsed scenarios, how I would corner him and punish his body.

I passed the first guardhouse entrance. Down the road, orange cones funneled traffic to a security guard beside the second guardhouse. More guards and a phalanx of the Gator utility vehicles waited on the shoulder. Why all this security?

The guard waved me to a halt. He asked if I had a reservation, which I didn't. He said the hotel was booked up and closed to the public for the weekend. He wouldn't elaborate and asked that I clear the entrance.

A convoy of white Chevy Suburbans with tinted windows lined up behind me. I couldn't hypnotize the guard in front of so many witnesses, so I turned around and left.

I stopped up the road and examined the convoy with my naked vampire eyes. Everybody had a red aura with the typical range of emotions. Curiosity. Anticipation. Anxiety. Boredom. Nothing that threatened me.

Why was I turned away and the others let in? What was going on? Feeling not so much frustrated as puzzled, I checked into a multistoried motel off South Forest Beach Drive. I brought in my extra bags from the Cadillac and changed into fresh clothes and put in new contacts.

Despite the heightened security, I was getting back in the Grand Atlantic. However, I couldn't let myself get complacent about Goodman. Maybe I was tracking all the wrong clues. What if this involved something supernatural that I wasn't familiar with? What if my pursuers were in plain sight and I didn't know? Even though I saw no evidence of being followed or spied upon, I remained wary as a cat sneaking through a kennel.

After I inspected my motel room, I sat still in one of the chairs to let my sixth sense magnify the sounds in the motel. A distant toilet flushing. The gentle hum of the ventilation system. The conversations of guests walking down the hall. Nobody made noise like they wanted to kill me.

I got my spare laptop and searched online for a mention of Karen Beck. The *Kansas City Star* reported that she'd been the victim of an attempted robbery. Her assailant escaped when he ran off the highway to avoid a police roadblock and crashed into the Missouri River. His body hadn't yet been recovered. No kidding, because here I was. There was no description of the suspect—again, that would be me, though I hadn't harmed Karen.

Sooner or later I was going to meet Dan Goodman face-to-face. We'd settle the matter of whether he was behind the murders of Gilbert Odin, Marissa Albert, Karen Beck, and quite possibly all those aboard the crashed airliner. And, of course, what was his part in this scheme that threatened the Earth women?

CHAPTER
27

I TURNED OFF the laptop, clicked on the TV, and channel surfed. At this time in the afternoon, my choices were
soap operas and talk shows. Most of the commercials were
for prescription medications. Corporate America had figured out that turning the nation into a herd of hypochondri-
acs was great for the bottom line.

The present commercial showed a woman standing before a mirror. She looked dowdy and frustrated. An aura
magically surrounded her, like a shimmering cocoon. "Luvitmor," a woman's soft voice repeated in the voice-over,
"from Rizè-Blu."

The woman stepped clear of the aura (obviously, the creative talent behind this effect had no experience with real
auras). She was now beautiful, confident, and very busty.

"Reclaim the real you with Luvitmor, the only nonsurgi-
cal breast-enhancement pill guaranteed to increase your
bust size."

Then the disclaimers: occasional headaches, mood swings, muscle soreness, and heightened libido.

Hold on.

Heightened libido? Bigger boobs? Rizè-Blu was going to rake in millions. Make that billions.

Not surprisingly, the next commercial was for another Rizè-Blu product, Olympicin. "Free yourself from the tyranny of the razor." A woman marched out of a gloomy dungeon and onto the sunlit sidewalk of the big city. Her bare legs glistened like polished bronze from under the hem of her miniskirt.

I switched channels to a talk show bubbling with women's laughter. Four women, in their early thirties, I guessed, sat on a stage beside their male partners. Each woman was dressed like she was about to step out for the evening: slim gown, high heels, hair done up. And each had enormous breasts that threatened to avalanche over the tops of their gowns. The women described their use of the trifecta of Rizè-Blu's new cosmetic drugs. NuGrumatex to restore the lushness of their hair. Olympicin as the world's most effective depilatory. (Close-ups on their legs.) And with the help of a lingering camera shot on their ample cleavages, the women claimed that Luvitmor was the only proven way to enhance a bustline without surgery.

The petite blonde of the group explained that she had been an A-cup; an accompanying photo showed her in a loose and dismally flat halter top. With a shimmy of her shoulders, she demonstrated how proud she was to be the owner of a pair of new FFs.

She and the man beside her shook their clasped hands in the air like they had just finished a race together. "Sex is now more than amazing," she announced with unbridled perkiness. "It's spectacular."

Thanks for sharing. What's next? Details about the wet spot, aka the winner's circle?

Forget AIDS, cancer, and the other diseases that ravaged

the Third World. Rizè-Blu gave society lusher hair. Smoother skin. Bigger boobs. And, ladies, there's more: Rizè-Blu can guarantee a libido to match your new bra size.

The elevator on my floor pinged, making a sound as faint as that of a tiny bell. The doors clunked open.

I clicked the TV off. Footfalls clicked softly on the tile foyer and became muted as they trod onto the carpet. The brisk steps were those of a woman. The footfalls stopped at my door.

My sixth sense perked up.

Someone knocked.

My fingertips tingled. The hairs on my arms and the back of my neck stood on end.

Another knock.

Who was it? What did they want? Why didn't they announce themselves?

I got up from my chair and levitated so that my feet moved soundlessly over the carpet. I stood to the right side of the door. A common trick of assassins was to call upon the target and, when he answered, shoot through the door.

Well, I was not a victim. I took out my contacts. My talons and fangs grew to combat length. At the first shot, I'd spring to the ceiling and counterattack from above.

One more knock.

The faint rustle of clothing.

Silence.

I primed my muscles to jump to one side. "Who is it?"

"Felix, quit screwing around and open the goddamn door."

Carmen?

Was it a trick?

She pounded the door. "You owe me five hours of sex and if you don't open this fucking door right now, it'll be ten."

It was Carmen.

My fangs and talons retracted. I freed the deadbolt, swung the door open, and winced in surprise.

Carmen had a blond helmet of hair that spilled around her face and curled back up where it touched her shoulders. The artificial sheen made her skin seem dark as hot caramel. Her orange aura looked like a scoop taken from the sun.

A pair of large sunglasses with white rectangular frames was stuck into the wig. She wore a white sleeveless dress with wide yellow stripes. The skirt ballooned around her hips and the hemline orbited her knees. This was a very un-Carmen getup but there was no hiding that smile or those sparkling eyes.

"Well, aren't you going to let me in?" Her lacquered red lips twisted into a devilish grin. "Partner."

CHAPTER
28

I STEPPED ASIDE. "How'd you find me?"

"Your credit card." She strutted past me on high-heeled pumps that matched the yellow stripes of her dress. An enormous leather tote bag hung from her right shoulder. "Better be careful. If I could find you this easy, what about Goodman?"

"I'm aware of him."

Carmen dropped the bag on the floor by my bed and settled on the mattress. Her dress crinkled like crepe paper. She raised her heels out of her pumps and kicked the shoes into the air. One of the pumps landed between my feet, the other clattered against the wall.

"Don't mind me," I said. "Make yourself at home. Before we discuss the 'partner' thing, what's with the outfit? The last time a woman dressed like you, *Sputnik* was orbiting the Earth."

"Whatever happened to 'Carmen, you look great, as usual'?" Carmen took the sunglasses from her hair. "This, since you asked, is a getaway disguise." She tossed the sunglasses on the bedspread. "I was visiting a chalice in Washington, DC, and for the sake of brevity let's say that we were almost caught in the Smithsonian museum."

"Caught doing what?"

Carmen removed the plastic bangles from her wrist and let them rattle in a heap on the sunglasses. "Doing field research for my *Kama Sutra* book."

"And this outfit belongs to the Smithsonian?"

"Not anymore." Carmen propped back on her arms. "I would have preferred to exit au naturel but in this post-9/11 world, walking around naked in the nation's capital could be construed as an act of terrorism. Wouldn't be worth the hassle."

Carmen stretched her stockinged legs and circled her feet. "Which brings the story to you." She pointed her toes at me. The nails alternated yellow and white. "Partner."

"Let's get this straight. I have no partner."

Carmen yanked the wig from her head. She threw the wig at me. "Yes you do. Now shut up for a minute and listen to me."

I caught the wig. In my hand, it looked like the pelt of a golden retriever and smelled of Chanel and Aquanet.

Carmen's natural hair had been plastered into a glossy black skullcap. "I have news."

I set the wig on the dresser. "What kind of news?"

Carmen gave a teasing smirk. "The kind of news I'd only share with a partner."

"It better be good."

"First, say the P-word."

The request confused me. "You mean, 'please'?"

"No, I mean 'partner.'"

"Let's hear the info first."

"Nope." Carmen cupped a hand behind an ear. A diamond stud earring caught the light. "I'm ready."

No point in arguing with her; I'd be better off arm-wrestling a squid. "Okay. *Partner.*"

Carmen smiled victoriously. "I have the lowdown on Dan Goodman." She let the smile linger.

"You were going to keep this a secret?"

"Not from a partner. Are you ready? Our mysterious Dan Goodman was an assassin for the U.S. government."

I had a problem believing that anyone could rise to the rank of bird colonel because he was handy with a nine iron. But to hear that Goodman was Uncle Sam's hired killer defied comprehension. "Are we talking about the retired colonel Dan Goodman? The golf pro at the Sapphire Grand Atlantic?"

Carmen nodded. "None other. Here's his public résumé. West Point graduate. Spent his career in the army's Morale, Welfare, and Recreation Command."

Carmen tugged at one of her bangs and stared at it cross-eyed. "His golfing was simply cover. Most of his time he was getting 'sheep-dipped.' That meant being discharged from the army and doing something dirty for the CIA. Afterward, he'd go back into the army. Technically then, the army never had an assassin on their payroll and the CIA could say, 'Dan Goodman who?'"

Instead of clarifying matters, this information only stirred up the muck. "How did you find out about this?"

"One of my chalices works for the Directorate of Operations in the CIA. If anyone in the government would know about an army colonel doing funny business, it would be that chalice. He's one of those spooks with a silly top-secret clearance. As if he wouldn't tell me anything I wanted to know."

"And you went to see him about my investigation?"

"That and to have him and his wife contribute to my book. That's how we ended up naked in the museum."

"Spare me those details. Right now, tell me more about Goodman."

"Years ago my chalice gave the then-major Dan Goodman a target folder of one Olivia Martinez-Cisneros."

"Target folder?"

"It's a dossier the government keeps on people it wants to get rid of."

"I've never heard of this Martinez-Cisneros. Why keep a target folder on her?"

Carmen folded her right leg and massaged her foot. "Olivia was a lawyer helping peasants in Ecuador fight the oil companies trying to take their land. At the time she was small potatoes but had a lot of potential. So Olivia had to go before she became a threat."

I tried to imagine the cold stare in Goodman's eyes as he snuffed out her life.

"Olivia was shot during a robbery, and on the way to the hospital," Carmen said, "a medic administered the wrong medicine and she died. A medic, incidentally, that no one had seen before or since."

"Goodman?"

"You connect the dots. Either he killed her or planned the hit."

"If Goodman is that expert an assassin, why didn't the government sic him on Osama bin Laden or Kim Song Il?"

Carmen stretched panther-like on the bedcovers. "Using an assassin is a lot like our vampire powers. You have to be careful when you use them. Attacking a high-profile target might be too much of a risk. Even if you succeed, your target could end up becoming a martyr and even more dangerous as a symbol."

"Perhaps your scholarly pursuits can provide an insight into this." I told Carmen about Vanessa and Janice, the two missing airline passengers, and what happened in Kansas City, including the murder of Karen Beck. When I got to the part about dunking myself into the Missouri River and escaping through the sewers, Carmen was quiet for a moment. Then her calm expression broke apart and she laughed.

I didn't see myself as comic relief. "What would you have done?"

Carmen pulled the bobby pins from her hair. "Not gone into the river. I can't imagine what that would've done to my clothes. But then again, you being a guy."

"Let's stick to the case," I said. "Suppose Goodman did kill Marissa. Why?"

"That I think I can answer. I made a detour to Marissa's office in Minneapolis. She was a PI, remember? Her office had been ransacked but I did find her sister. She told me— under hypnosis, because I didn't want her to remember that I'd been there—that Marissa had been hired to find a missing woman, Naomi Peyton, and followed a lead to Key West."

"And this Naomi Peyton is connected to Goodman?"

"We don't know yet." Carmen dug her fingers under the cap of stiff hair, like she was working a shingle loose. "There are a lot of loose threads here. You said Vanessa's and Janice's bodies were missing from the morgue in the hangar. Yet the officials said they were dead, though your friend . . ." Carmen glanced at me.

"Her name was Karen Beck."

Carmen continued, "Karen said Vanessa and Janice never boarded the airliner."

All this information was a pile of facts I couldn't quite fit together.

Carmen scratched her scalp. She closed her eyes and a pensive expression settled over her face. "Goodman went to Chicago the day before the crash as a consultant with RKW for the feds. So either it's a coincidence that he was there or Goodman's a psychic or . . ." Carmen let the thought drift.

Or, or . . . what?

She wiped the flakes of dried hair gel from her fingertips. "How many people were on that commuter airliner?"

"Nineteen, including the crew of three." I remembered the pictures of the dead inside the trailer.

"Maybe," Carmen let a talon sprout from one index finger and used the point to clean her other fingernails, "what Gilbert Odin said about saving the Earth women is not about them getting killed but about something else entirely. Think about it. Vanessa and Janice are missing. As is Naomi Peyton."

"Meaning they're not dead?"

"That's what we want to find out. The mysterious aspect about Naomi was that her car went off the road, killing her husband. And she's missing."

"Sounds like a wife who got tired of her husband," I said.

"Felix, if it were that easy, why are we going in circles?" Carmen asked. "Marissa discovers a lead on Naomi that takes her to Key West and the next thing we know, she's dead from a blaster wound."

Carmen reached into her bra and pulled out a folded slip of paper. "Here's Marissa's cell phone number. Can you access her phone records?"

I took the paper and read the number. It had a 612 area code. "Consider it done."

Carmen winked. "And you didn't want me for a partner."

"That's three missing that we know of," I said. "Naomi from a car crash. Vanessa and Janice when the commuter airliner went down."

"Then where did they go?" Carmen asked. "And why would the officials lie about them? Don't forget the other plane wreck. How many of those passengers aren't dead but alive and missing?"

Trying to understand this case was like kneading a ball of hard clay. My brain started to cramp from the effort. I leaned against the bureau and rubbed my fingers against my forehead. "Was their disappearance a kidnapping? If so, could that justify the murder of all those people?"

"Maybe it's the stakes involved?" Carmen lay on the bedcover and looked at the ceiling. "Notice that Odin said 'Earth women,' not simply 'women.' And he is an alien."

"*Was* an alien," I corrected. "He's in the past tense, remember?"

"Is that the clue? That Odin was an alien? He *was* killed with a blaster."

I caught on to Carmen's reasoning. "Let's accept that Goodman was Odin's assassin. Goodman used a blaster to kill an alien. Why not shoot him with a regular pistol?"

Carmen sat up and looked at me. "Could it be that Goodman is an alien as well?" Her eyes sparkled with renewed insight.

"I don't think so. Odin referred to him as a man."

Carmen slumped her shoulders in disappointment.

I asked, "Did you ask your chalice about the ray gun?"

"I did. Under hypnosis, to keep the question a deep secret. But . . ." Carmen finished the thought by shaking her head.

"What about the 'Earth women'? Is this a plot to kidnap them?" I asked. "All of them? Or just a few?"

Carmen added another question. "And why?"

I told her about the secret annex behind the main hotel and how the GPS disabled my golf cart. I described the annex, its array of NASA-style antennas, and the arrival of a military helicopter.

"What kind of a compound is it?" Carmen asked. "If it's so secret, why build it behind the hotel?" Her aura glowed a bit warmer, the psychic equivalent of a wry smile. "Well then, Mister PI, what about this? I know why you're in this motel and not the Sapphire Grand Atlantic. Ever hear of the G8?"

I answered, "That's the Group of Eight, right? The organization of the eight richest industrialized nations."

Carmen nodded. "Depends on who you listen to, the G8 is the world leaders either discussing how to solve the world's problems or scheming how to make themselves and their cronies masters of the planet."

"What's the G8 got to do with me being in this motel?"

Carmen raised a finger. "One of the G8 study groups is holding a conference at the Grand Atlantic."

"What study group?"

"The Markov PharmacoEconomic Study Group. They

advise the G8 on medical developments and global health care."

I remembered being turned away from the resort. "Security seemed pretty tight for a bunch of eggheads meeting to talk about vaccines and Band-Aids. Would Goodman have anything to do with them?"

"I'm ahead of you, Felix." Carmen reached back into her tote bag and tossed a plastic card at me. "This is your pass for tonight's party."

The card looked like a standard-issue ID. It had my name, photo, a bar code, magnetic strip, and an iridescent stamp. "Where did this come from?"

Carmen shook her head. "Are you asking *me* that question?"

"All right. What party?"

"At the Grand Atlantic, what other?" Carmen produced a pair of envelopes in her hand, like a card trick. "You and I are guests of the G8 Markov PharmacoEconomic Study Group."

Carmen scooted back on the mattress. "Now we better get ready." She hitched her skirt and slip over her hips and peeled the stockings off her legs.

I did notice something, rather the absence of something. "What happened to your tattoo?" Carmen, always in orbit, once had a *Star Trek* insignia tattooed below her navel.

"*Star Trek* got so damned politically correct that they pissed me off. So I lasered the tattoo away in protest."

Carmen rolled across the bed and reached into her tote bag. She pulled out a pair of strappy, golden, stiletto-heeled sandals and a tiny black bundle the size of her palm.

"Let me show you what I brought for the party." Carmen shook the bundle and it unfolded into a cocktail dress. She fluffed the dress and it hung from her arm perfect and free of creases. "This is my little black number."

"It'll look stunning, Carmen."

"No. On me it'll look positively deadly."

CHAPTER
29

I KEEP AN Internet hacker on retainer. Every month I
send five hundred bucks to a private mailbox in Kalama-
zoo, Michigan. In return, he or she gives me access to almost everything wired to the information grid. I sent to an
anonymous e-mail address Marissa's cell phone number and
a request for her records. Now to wait.

Carmen and I looked up articles about missing women.
We found websites and blogs asking, Have you seen
Mommy? Daughter? Sister? Wife? One husband complained
that his wife was last seen hanging around with a mechanic
from the local Harley-Davidson dealership. I didn't think
he'd find her with Goodman. Try Sturgis.

We looked into the crash of the Cessna Caravan. It had
taken off on a chartered flight from San Diego en route to
Catalina Island. Air traffic control lost contact and, that afternoon, wreckage from the Cessna washed up near Camp

Pendleton. The victims included the pilot and six passengers: four women and two men. None of the bodies were recovered. The women were close in profile to the others: early twenties to late thirties. Nothing remarkable but suspicious, since the Araneum had alerted me about the crash.

Frustrated by how much more we learned while still remaining far from any worthwhile lead, we quit for the day, turned off the laptop, and got ready for the party.

That evening, after the sun had set, Carmen and I entered the main lobby of the Sapphire Grand Atlantic Resort. We waited in line to scan our badges under the vigilant eyes of a phalanx of sour-faced men in cheap suits.

I recognized a congressman from South Carolina, the one who looked like a wrinkled version of Harpo Marx. He stood next to the security kiosk and nodded vacantly as a man in a blazer two sizes too small and trousers that sagged under his potbelly bragged about the effectiveness of the security system.

"No one," the man in the blazer declared, his finger jousting at the scanner, "can sneak in here. This system is absolutely failsafe and foolproof."

My face appeared on the screen.

Blazer man waved me through. The congressman's gaze swiveled past me and latched onto Carmen. His eyes lit up with excitement and his wizened face turned into a giant smiling raisin.

Carmen and I stepped away from the security cordon.

I shoved my badge into an inside pocket of my jacket. "Did you notice the congressman?"

Carmen slipped her badge into her tiny purse. "Are you kidding? That eye grope of his almost left bruises. But he had better iron his birthday suit before I would even think of doing him."

We joined the crowd shuffling through the foyer and into the lobby. About two hundred people mingled around a string quartet in the center of the lobby. The racket from all the voices made normal conversation impossible; as for the musicians, it was like playing next to Niagara Falls.

Carmen and I veered to the south side of the lobby and halted between a ficus tree and a palm. We removed our contacts. I scanned right while Carmen scanned left.

The lobby was a tidal pool of red auras. Most of them bristled with excitement, but some had tendrils of anxiety looping from their penumbras, and a few party poopers simmered with a low burn of worry.

A large banner that hung from the center rafter read: WELCOME G8 MARKOV FELLOWS. The surrounding banners along the lobby ceiling mentioned various conference sponsors: both the Brookings and Hoover Institutes, the U.S. Food and Drug Administration, ConAgra, Dow Chemical, Craig Bio-Engineering, Cress Tech International, and Nestlé.

I studied the auras of the hotel staff tucked in the corners of the lobby. "See anything out of the ordinary?"

"No. Just the usual herd of blunt tooths." Carmen's gaze arced again over the crowd. "What's with all the cleavage? There are more oversized mammary glands here than at a dairy."

I motioned with my eyes to one of the overhead banners and the logo of Rizè-Blu Pharmaceutique, a DNA helix superimposed over a sunburst. I acted as if I held a pair of melons against my chest. "All it takes is a prescription and some money."

"Then they made a fortune from this gang."

Many of the women and men, all over-coiffed, kept wiping their lips.

Carmen said, "Explain the drooling."

"Side effect of NuGrumatex," I replied.

"They ought to wear spit buckets." Carmen glanced at me and did a double take. "Are you okay?"

"I feel fine. Why?"

"It's your aura. Seems a little . . . off."

I examined my hands and arms and the psychic glow outlining them. "Looks okay to me."

"Still, if I were you, I'd fang someone soon. Get a blood pick-me-up." Carmen replaced her contacts with a pair that made her irises sizzle electric blue against her orange aura. She relaxed her expression and stood straight. Her slicked-back hair was gathered into a ponytail secured with a gold lamé band that matched her purse and shoes. That little black cocktail dress was as tight as skin on a snake. "How do I look?"

"Just as you predicted, positively deadly." I put in my contacts.

She flicked a fingertip against the corners of her mouth to tidy her lip gloss. "Good. It'll keep the posers at a distance. I only want to get hit on by a man who *thinks* he can handle me."

Carmen adjusted the collar of my burgundy silk shirt and smoothed the lapel of my black jacket. "Felix, I give you a B." She glanced to my feet. "Make that a B+. I like your shoes."

We stepped from between the plants and headed into the crowd. Carmen hummed the reggae tune "Now That We Found Love."

She looped the chain strap of her purse over one shoulder and joined a clutch of elegantly dressed women, almost as regal in bearing and attractive as Carmen herself. She gave a toothy, radiant smile and must have said something witty as an introduction. Even with my vampire hearing, I couldn't pick out what she had said, because of the din. The other women laughed, and I knew Carmen was accepted as one of the girls.

A server paused with a tray of drinks and Carmen chose a flute of champagne. She sipped and said something else. The women laughed again and inched forward to soak in Carmen's charisma. If she was in a girlish mood, I'm sure Carmen would have the entire group in a sweaty, tangled pile by midnight.

I wove through the clusters of people and waited in line at the open bar. Another server circled around us with a tray of appetizers, grilled shrimp and pineapple chunks on short bamboo skewers. The shrimp looked delicious until the stench of garlic hit my nostrils. I waved her away before I barfed.

I shouted my order to the bartender. A manhattan on the rocks. Two cherries.

The bartender shook my drink in a chrome cocktail shaker for so long that I thought he was going to give himself frostbite. I raised the glass to taste the manhattan.

Someone bumped into me and I almost dropped my drink.

A man put his hand on my shoulder. His gray eyes had a self-effacing glitter. "My apologies." His left hand held the arm of a blonde in a tangerine evening gown. The top of her dress looked like a cup filled with two big helpings of firm pudding. She held a cocktail glass in one hand and a highball in the other.

He dropped the hand from my shoulder and offered a shake. "Name's William Krandall."

"Felix Gomez."

He motioned his companion forward by tugging at her arm. We huddled close.

He introduced her as Amanda Peltier, a Fulbright scholar who had worked at the FDA to fast-track the approval of Luvitmor. Judging by the way her dress barely contained her bosom, Peltier must have been an eager test subject for the drug. She gave Krandall the highball glass and shook my hand while carefully keeping her cocktail from spilling. A lemon twist floated inside.

Her eyes sparkled like stolen emeralds. "You've been to one of these before, Mr. Gomez?"

"Felix, please. This is my first time here."

"And you're with whom?" Peltier let her gaze wander to the other people.

"The G8 media committee invited us."

Her eyes locked back on me. "Us?"

I lifted my drink in Carmen's direction.

Peltier raised herself on tiptoes to better see. "The brunette with the ponytail?"

"I'll make an introduction if you'd like."

Krandall slipped an arm around Peltier's waist. She whispered into his ear. His cheeks flushed. They traded small nods. Krandall dug into a pocket of his coat and brought out a business card. "My cell number's on there. Tell your friend not to be shy."

Carmen, shy? I put the card in my coat pocket. If their plans involved a tryst with Carmen, then they better get ready for Olympic-level sexual gymnastics.

"What are you doing for the media committee?" Peltier sipped from her glass.

"We're consultants. The committee wants us to suggest new ideas for creative and collateral. Improve the messaging." My bullshit could only go so far. Better that I change the subject. "Why all the security here? Are you guys that worried about terrorists?"

Krandall waved me closer and we almost touched noses. His breath carried the odor of garlic from the grilled shrimp. I stifled a gag and tried to step back but he grasped my shoulder. "Terrorists? Of course not. It's to keep the protesters out. They're very creative about sneaking in. The pesky, tree-hugging hippie bastards. Those Luddites see a conspiracy under every rock."

"And why hold the conference here?" I thought about the antennas, the military helicopter, and the protective perimeter behind the hotel.

"You mean, why the Grand Atlantic? Take a look." Krandall swept his hand over the room. "This place is the Taj Mahal of resorts. Are you paying for any of this? If not, then don't complain."

"And what is it that *you* do?"

"I work for Rizè-Blu."

Peltier leaned toward us. "The hooters division." She chuckled and her breasts jiggled invitingly.

Krandall gave a playful elbow to her ribs. "I'm a development director in their Eden Water–Green Planet Initiative; it's a partnership between Rizè-Blu and Cress Tech."

Interesting. "What's the connection between a pharmaceutical giant and the biggest engineering company in the world?"

"Here's the corporate answer." Krandall closed his eyes and said, as if reciting from a script tattooed across the inside of his eyelids: "The Eden Water–Green Planet Initiative blends the synergy of two major global stakeholders: the engineering resources of Cress Tech International and the consumer branding and marketing expertise of Rizè-Blu." Krandall opened his eyes. "The short answer? Moola."

He pointed toward the atrium. "Let me show you."

CHAPTER
30

WE ZIGZAGGED through the drooling crowd and made our way to the atrium. Booths lined the edges of the central pathway. The riot of conversation seemed twice as loud as it bounced against the ceiling and the overhanging ledges of the mezzanine. Kiosks towered between the booths and displayed large posters emblazoned with earnest, feel-good messages. END WORLD HUNGER, sponsored by Cargill. STOP WAR, by General Dynamics (ha!). CURE DISEASE, from our friends at Rizè-Blu Pharmaceutique (that is when they were not populating the world with larger breasts).

We stopped by the Rizè-Blu booth. A monitor announced a new breakthrough in the treatment of erectile dysfunction, Rizè-Blu's new wonder boner pill: Tigernene.

Young women costumed like vintage cigarette girls in satin vests and tap pants offered samples from trays. The packets included: NuGrumatex, a translucent amber pill;

Olympicin, a tablet with a golden metallic sheen; Luvitmor, a pink tablet with a tiny button that looked like a nipple; and Tigernene, a round pill in macho yellow with black stripes.

Krandall snatched a packet of Tigernene. "This will put titanium in your pencil."

"You've used it?"

"Am using it."

"And the effects?"

Peltier perched her chin on Krandall's shoulder. "Like a stallion. Bigger *and* better."

Krandall mimicked a whinny and used a leg to act out a horse hoofing the ground.

I clasped their heads and mussed their hair. "Maybe you two need to get a private stable. And soon."

Peltier withdrew her head and frowned. She patted her hair back into place.

Krandall gave a small, embarrassed cough. "Sorry, TMI." Too much information. "Let's go meet my boss."

Krandall took Peltier's hand and used his other arm to part through a wall of people. He pointed to a portly man standing in front of the Eden Water booth. "I work for him."

The man was Daniel Gruber, the former senior advisor to the last president. Gruber held court to a small group that gathered before him, and he spoke using a brisk, rehearsed cadence.

This was the first time I'd seen Gruber in person. His head was shaped like an eggplant that had stayed in the refrigerator for too long, sagging and bottom-heavy while the top sprouted thin white wisps. Small, intense eyes shone from under his thick brow, and his gaze bore through his spectacles as if he was looking into the future for his next moves.

Gruber clicked a tiny remote in his hand. The flat monitor screen resting on the table behind him showed a graph superimposed over a couple of African children. "Once Eden

Water is established in central Africa, we can expect these levels of return from your investments."

Another click and the screen showed the line of a graph climbing to the upper right corner of the screen.

"Phase two of the Eden Water project migrates the initiative to Latin America. Here our projected returns are double those from Africa."

Another click and the screen showed the graph superimposed over a man in a primitive skiff pulling a net from the water.

Gruber's eyes focused on his audience and his attention was now firmly in the present. "Phase three implements Eden Water here at home. The challenge . . ." Gruber paused to let his gaze seize the attention of the people circled before him, ". . . will be to educate legislators that municipal control of fresh water makes as little sense as the government managing any other commodity."

An older woman asked, "What about access to safe drinking water as a right?"

Gruber's answer continued the practiced rhythm. "We live in a global economy. Rather than let arbitrary notions of rights dictate what is available to the consumer, we need to allow the mechanisms of a free market to meet the demand."

I stood beside Krandall and couldn't help but ask: "What about the right to justice? Is that also for sale?"

When he worked in the White House, Gruber had been twice indicted for perjury, and wealthy friends of the president had helped him beat both raps.

The others listening to Gruber turned their heads and glared over their shoulders. Krandall jerked on my sleeve. Did I know who I was talking to?

Gruber dismissed me with a fleeting, annoyed look. He clicked his remote again. The graph was superimposed over a girl and a boy prancing through a lawn sprinkler.

"We'll increment the adoption of the Eden Water initiative. You can see here that at milestone one, the first year return with 10 percent marginalization of the existing market—"

The woman who had spoken before asked, "Marginalization?"

Gruber smirked. "Control." The smirk gave way to a serious expression. "That 10 percent will deliver a return of 1.1 billion dollars—"

A man in the group interrupted: "You talk about investors. What's Rizè-Blu's stake?"

Gruber jabbed a finger into the air. "Excellent question." He tapped the remote. The screen showed the logo of Rizè-Blu Pharmaceutique and a pie chart. The largest slice, 87 percent of startup costs for Eden Water, belonged to Rizè-Blu. "Our recent successes with Rizè-Blu's new line of prescription actualizers—ladies, I notice that you all have at least tried Luvitmor"—(they giggled)—"has given us the resources to leverage the Green Planet project from a dream into reality."

Gruber was shilling for Rizè-Blu's idea of putting all of the world's fresh water into Eden Water's scheming corporate hands.

I raised my voice to get his attention. "What's next? Selling air?"

Gruber turned to me. His pupils dilated and shrank, as if his mind darted to another place and then back to the present. That smirk returned. "We're working on it."

Gruber shifted his attention to someone else. Krandall pulled me away. Peltier shook her head.

Krandall walked me from Gruber's booth. "What did you do that for?"

Obviously, I wanted to needle the windbag. I grasped Krandall's fingers and unwrapped them from my sleeve. "What are you getting at?"

"Don't be surprised if you never get another invitation." Krandall closed his eyes and pinched the bridge of his nose in frustration. "For guys like you and me, being at this place is all about kissing ass. Our job is to tell these guys what they want to hear. You want the attention of the most powerful men on this planet, this is where you'll find them. You won't make points by pissing them off."

"I appreciate the advice."

Krandall patted my shoulder. "Rookie mistake. By the way, where's your friend the brunette?"

"Close by, I'm sure."

A server weaved through the crowd.

Peltier set her empty cocktail glass on the tray. "What's she like?"

"Enthusiastic."

"Really?" Peltier wiped her fingers with a napkin and dropped it on the tray. "What are her plans?"

"You'll have to ask her."

Peltier gave my wrist a squeeze. "I'm sure we'll meet again."

Krandall gave me the thumbs-up. He put his arm around her waist and turned Peltier toward the Eden Water booth. Her dress swayed from her round, tight bottom.

I wondered what would happen if we did meet again.

Before then, I had to find someone else. I walked past the booths and started my search for Goodman.

CHAPTER
31

AT THE far end of the central pathway, a velvet rope blocked further passage. A placard on a lobby card-stand read: NO UNAUTHORIZED PERSONNEL BEYOND THIS POINT.

I authorized myself, unhooked one end of the rope from a floor post, and stepped through. Immediately, one of the resort guards appeared from around the corner.

"May I help you?"

"I'm looking for a restroom."

The guard pointed to the large sign behind me. Restrooms were in the main lobby.

Once in the lobby, I tried going around the concierge's desk. Again, another guard appeared as if by magic and shooed me back into the crowd.

The black plastic orbs hanging from the ceiling or jutting from the wall corners stared like unblinking eyes.

I'd better back off trying this. I was sure I had the attention of the guys watching the security monitors.

Maybe I could find something in Goodman's office. I went to the lobby entrance, passed through security, and instead of going to the garage, I went toward the golf pro shop. The golf course was closed but I could catch a hotel guest out for exercise returning through the side door.

I kept note of the security arrangements. At the corner, a black orb watched the front of the hotel. A plain video camera hung from the wall above me and pointed to the side door. I looked up the wall. There were no other cameras. I could climb between the camera and the corner of the hotel to the roof and remain unseen.

Tennis players grunted and swatted under the lights of the tennis courts. An older man, lost in thought, approached. He twirled a tennis racket and groped into the pocket of his windbreaker. I removed my contacts and slipped behind him. He fished out his hotel room card and reached to swipe it through the reader by the door.

I checked to see that we were alone. "Excuse me."

He turned around, his middle-aged face red and sweaty. His irises popped open and his aura brightened.

I took the card and opened the door. I put the card back in his hand and left him standing outside. He would think he'd just had a senior moment. I moved fast and smoothly. The security guards had dozens of monitors to watch. Unless they had been paying attention only to me, they wouldn't have noticed anything suspicious.

I walked down the hall, past the locker rooms, and toward the golf course administration. I had a hunch I'd find Goodman in his office. We'd have a long, informative talk.

I turned the corner. The glass double doors to the office were closed. The secretary's vestibule was dark. I tried the doorknobs. Locked. I didn't see any light coming from around the office doors inside. I put my ear close to the glass doors and heard only silence.

So much for hunches.

Where was Goodman?

I traced my steps back outside. Before I put my contacts back in, I scoped the grounds and looked for any suspicious auras. Nothing.

I returned to the reception and found Carmen at the bar. She leaned against the bar counter and held a fizzy drink against her temple. Sweat from the glass wet her fingertips. "I have never in my life been in such a group of pious, self-important assholes. God, they act like they're doing the world a favor dispensing this academic horse shit. Too bad they can't use it for fertilizer."

"The important question is, anything on Goodman?"

"No. You?"

I shook my head. "If he's here, the man's a ghost." I asked the bartender for a manhattan. "What about your dance card?"

Carmen took a long pull from her glass and smacked her lips. "Almost full. You know the undersecretary of state? She and her husband want to play *avec moi*." Carmen lay one hand across her breast. "Problem is, she keeps blabbing about how misunderstood the administration's policy was about Nigerian oil. The people there have to be patient, she kept saying. The wealth will come. Oh yeah? They've been waiting for thirty years and still nothing but promises."

"Politics aside, got room for two more?" I took Krandall's card from my pocket and gave it to Carmen.

I explained, "They're a younger couple. She's a Luvitmor babe and he got into the early program for Tigernene."

"Really?" Carmen's eyes widened with interest. "I'm eager to sample those results." She slid the card into her purse.

I finished my manhattan and ordered another. We wandered toward the fireplace along the northern wall and sat on the raised brickwork.

Carmen retrieved a cell phone from her purse. The phone

cover had a leopard skin print. She checked the incoming number and smiled. "It's the undersecretary. Booty duty calls. I'll give a report later." Carmen opened the phone and purred into it as she left.

I sat and drank alone. Well into my third manhattan, the cello player sat beside me. Her moist, dark hair lay in matted tangles. Perspiration darkened her collar.

The cellist was a rosy-faced woman in her late twenties. She stretched her legs, displaying a nice pair of calves that tapered to trim ankles and a pair of patent-leather Mary Janes.

"Want to do me a favor?"

"Pardon?" I didn't get the impression she was talking to me.

She put a hand on my arm. "I need a drink. A cosmopolitan would be perfect."

I did need to keep busy until Goodman showed his face, if he ever did. Why not with the cellist? We'd talk politics.

I hailed a server and ordered the drink. The cellist—her name was Sarah—told me the other musicians had been invited to a private party. She had opted out.

"I just broke up with the viola player." Sarah tasted the cosmopolitan. "If he can't hook up with someone else at the party, he'll be hitting on me again just to get laid. Asshole."

We finished our drinks, ordered another round, and talked about music. She needed to store her cello, so we walked together to the parking garage and got into an older white Dodge Carryall. We sat inside on plywood storage boxes. I needed to scout for Goodman, so I didn't plan on staying long. Sarah turned on the stereo and, being a musician, lit up a bong. I recognized the ritual. Get high then have sex. I would delay my search for Goodman.

With my new tan, I didn't have to worry about giving away my undead persona. Then I remembered how well that had worked with Belinda, the shrew who'd thrown me out.

This time I would use hypnosis, mainly to keep Sarah from going psycho on me.

She splayed her knees and cradled the bong in the hammock formed by her skirt. "You know what I like about you, Felix?"

That I'm outrageously handsome? That I make you want to fling off your panties and dive for my zipper?

"My ex only wanted one thing from me. I don't get that vibe from you at all."

You don't? I'm a vampire, my sexual vibe should be as loud as a Chinese gong. I glanced at my hands. Was this dimming of my vampire allure a symptom of the spider bite? Why wasn't Carmen affected? She had a great tan and still left a trail of erections and moist panties in her wake.

Sarah kept toking on the bong and complaining about her ex, how he was obsessed with doggie style, road head, and finger-banging her in the checkout line. "I mean," she whined as she exhaled a jet of reefer smoke, "it was so physical."

What had I done to be cast in this role of sexual confessor? Unlike a priest, I had never taken a vow of chastity.

Sarah put the bong on the floor and reached for me. Had she changed her mind? Maybe all this sex talk had made her horny?

She spilled into my lap, her arms drunkenly propping themselves on my shoulders. She smelled like the crowd at a reggae concert. I steadied her by the waist and turned her hips so that she settled on my left thigh.

She buried her warm face into the crook of my neck. "Felix, I'm glad you're here with me. I feel so comfortable. It's good that we're just friends."

Just friends? Were there two more emasculating words in the English language? I was El Macho Supernatural and she wanted to cuddle like I was an oversize puppy.

She began to snore. Apparently, I wasn't even worth a cuddle.

I leaned forward to pull her away from me. Her head lolled back and I cradled it in my hand. Her neck, deliciously firm and succulent, stretched before me.

I wouldn't take sexual advantage of a woman, but a fanging? I was a vampire, and sinking my fangs into her neck to suck her blood violated none of the rules I'd grown up with.

The undead hunger sharpened. My upper lip twitched and my incisors grew.

Carefully, hesitantly, as if I were biting a balloon and afraid to make it pop, I put my lips to her neck. I closed my eyes and felt for her pulse to guide my fangs to their mark.

I flexed my jaw, and the keen points of my teeth pierced her tender skin.

The human nectar bubbled into my mouth. Type A-negative, very nice. I forced my enzymes through the wound to deaden the pain and induce amnesia. She relaxed as if her bones had softened.

I savored her blood like it was exotic wine. I didn't drink much, only enough to make my stay here in the van worth my while.

I lapped the healing enzymes across the punctures. Sarah remained slack-jawed, her eyelids closed in lazy slumber. I wiped a kerchief across the drips of blood on her neck and laid her limp body on the carpeted floor of the van.

I sat still for a moment to enjoy the almost-orgasmic pleasure of this fresh blood meal. We hadn't had sex, but the fanging was a nice consolation prize. My *kundalini noir* made a sinuous dance that slowed as the afterglow ebbed.

The approach of a man broke the last of the spell. He wore the red vest of a parking valet and got into a Mercedes sedan a couple of spaces over. I removed my contacts and read his aura. Nothing special.

What about Goodman?

I got out of the van and checked the back of the hotel around the annex. The guards were doubled up and walked the fence. Unless I knew what I wanted in the annex, better that I wait before risking trouble.

The light of an approaching dawn brightened the sky. Time to go.

I returned to the van and used Sarah's cell phone to call Carmen. She was in her car and on the way out of the garage. I kissed Sarah's neck and quietly stepped free of the van.

Carmen drove by in her Audi sports car, saw me, and stopped. I smoothed my jacket, adjusted my belt, and put on my sunglasses. I got into the passenger seat and told her what I'd done since we split up.

"We're at the Grand Atlantic and you spent the night in a van?" Carmen shook her head. Her hair was gathered into a twist held in place with a jeweled letter opener. She wore a red leather hoodie over her dress.

I asked, "Where'd you get that?"

"I like presents." Carmen wrinkled her nose. "You smell like a frat house." She cruised through the garage. "I hope you at least got lucky."

"Lucky enough." The taste of Sarah's blood lingered on my palate.

Carmen zoomed through the exit and into the sunlight. She squinted and put on her sunglasses. "Anything on Goodman?"

"No. You?"

"Nada." She tuned the stereo and adjusted the volume. "What's the next move?"

"Infiltrate the hotel and find Goodman. I'll tell you when."

We arrived at my motel. Carmen stopped in the parking lot before the entrance.

I asked, "Where are you staying?"

"A married chalice couple owns a cozy little mortuary in Bluffton. They have the plushest caskets to nap in. You should visit."

"Later." I got out of the Audi and held the door open. "My place is comfortable enough."

Carmen slipped her sunglasses down her nose. Her eyes glowed red as lasers. "When are we going back to the Grand Atlantic?"

"Tonight. First, let me see what my hacker has found. Then we'll make a plan." I shut the door.

Carmen drove off. I passed through the entrance of the motel. When the entrance door returned with a hiss, I heard something alarming and sinister.

A faint pop . . . like the striker in an M60 fuse igniter.

CHAPTER
32

M Y REFLEXES kicked into vampire speed but too
late. I had started backtracking through the door when
the bomb exploded.

The blast came from under a magazine stand to the right.
Had I been stepping forward, the explosion would've
smashed me against the wall like a bloody sponge. Instead,
the blast hurled me backward through the door and I landed
on my ass on the asphalt parking lot.

I sat for a moment, dazed, my arms held up before me,
like a Hiroshima bomb victim. Smoke rose from my trousers and coat sleeves. Shards of glass stuck out of my clothes
like quills. My face and hands stung from the hammer blows
of the concussion.

My *kundalini noir* sputtered in confused pain. I blinked
to clear the spots from my eyes. The explosion had broken
my sunglasses and knocked my contacts out. A hundred
church bells rang in my head.

I staggered to my feet. Shattered glass lay below the gaping windows of the motel lobby. Torn blinds and window sashes jutted like torn ligaments from the blackened openings. The scarred double doors hung askew from their broken hinges at the entrance.

The ringing in my head became a loud hum. The hum softened and I heard car alarms screaming in the parking lot.

Faces blanched with terror stared from the motel windows. Red auras bobbed like bubbles. People clustered in the exits to my left.

I brushed away the glass sticking out of my body. Skin hung from my right temple and I held the flap in place. Blood oozed from the wound and the countless other cuts in my skin. The blood ran down my face and dried to brown flakes that broke apart into powder.

A wave of nausea rose in me, hot and crippling. My knees weakened.

But I couldn't rest. I had to flee. The police would be coming soon. My naked vampire eyes would give me away.

A familiar chopping sound cleaved through the hum in my head. The sound echoed over the parking lot.

A black Jet Ranger raced into view above the trees. The helicopter turned sideways and I recognized the man sitting in the open copilot's door. Goodman.

His red aura blazed like the fiery plume of an artillery rocket. He wore a headset and pointed at me.

Three black Suburbans swerved and halted on the street. Men in black uniforms sprang from the SUVs, submachine guns at the ready.

Two of the men stopped and took aim. I didn't wait for the bullets. I sprinted in the opposite direction, dove over a BMW sedan, and somersaulted onto the ground. Bullets whizzed overhead.

I took off again for the trees and bounded left and right like a hunted jackrabbit. I raced away at vampire speed, my arms and legs a blur. The faster I ran, the more intense the nausea became.

When I reached the trees, I jinked right. A dozen bullets hacked at the leaves where I would've been.

I loped through gaps in the brush. The shadows felt cool. The nausea subsided.

Overhead, the helicopter followed me. Another SUV tracked along the edge of the trees. A splash of light reflected from grass on the open ground beyond the trees. The growth of trees and brush funneled to a point in the clearing. Once out from the brush, I could break into a run but not fast enough to lose the helicopter. How long until Goodman and his thugs cornered me?

But if I stayed here, they'd surround me. So I broke from the trees and raced over the flat ground. Sunlight splashed over me, brilliant and biting, and I felt like an ant frying under a magnifying glass. The nausea returned, and I wanted to stop and heave.

But I had to keep running and escape. My skin burned hotter with every passing second. What was happening?

I held up my arms and hands. My skin faded from brown to a creamy pallor. The spot on my forearm where the spider had sunk its fangs puckered and started to ache. My body felt like acid was pumping through my veins.

The effect of the spider bite had worn off. Sunlight was now as dangerous to me as fire.

Vomit welled in my throat. My *kundalini noir* thrashed like a snake smothering under a hot rock.

The shadow of the helicopter passed over me. The darkness provided a brief second of relief. The sunlight blazed onto me again, feeling even more intense and menacing.

The SUV circled from my right and charged into the clearing. I cut left and sprinted toward a wooden fence overgrown with honeysuckle and ivy. I hurtled over the fence and raced across someone's backyard.

The air scalded me like I'd been thrown into an oven. I choked down the urge to retch.

Still I ran. I hurtled over another fence and got snagged in kudzu.

The helicopter hovered above a wall of myrtle in front of me. Goodman watched from behind mirrored sunglasses. His hands moved in animated gestures. A Suburban halted beneath him.

I tore free from the kudzu, turned left again, and raced over a wooden deck to crash through a set of French doors. A family sat at the dining room table. I leaped onto the table, my feet stomping a casserole dish and stacks of pancakes. Scrambled eggs and syrup splashed across the room. The three kids and dad screamed. The mom threw a serving spoon that bounced off my head.

I sprang from the table and bolted into the living room.

Inside the house, the nausea vanished. My skin felt as if I'd been doused with cool water. I wanted to stay and rest but the moment I stopped, Goodman and his shooters would close the trap.

I catapulted off an armchair for the front picture window and smashed through the glass.

Sunlight felt like a cauldron of lava. I tumbled over a hedge and landed on the grass. My feet pumped over the lawn and I raced onto the street. My scalded skin turned pink.

A new wave of nausea squeezed my insides and my *kundalini noir* felt like it was shoved up my throat.

My flesh was about to smolder. The pain was like getting skinned alive.

The street led to a dead end against the beach dunes. Beyond them lay the Atlantic Ocean. The helicopter flew close, keeping pace as if we were tethered by a rope. I scrambled over the dunes and through the sea oats. The blue horizon of water promised sanctuary. I pushed myself to run harder across the flat trace of sand to the surf.

The helicopter crabbed sideways toward me. Goodman brought an assault rifle to his shoulder. I hopped to my left. The spray of bullets churned the ground inches from my feet.

The sun reflected off the sand and burned my skin. My eyelids wanted to shut tight to protect my eyes and I fought to keep them open.

The roar of the helicopter sounded like a demon from hell. A second volley of bullets tore at my legs, ripping flesh and shattering bone.

I tumbled forward and smacked wet sand. I sprang up and tried to stand but my shredded left leg buckled under my weight.

The Jet Ranger slipped through the air. The shoreline waited thirty feet before me.

I couldn't make it. The agony of my burning flesh, the nausea, and now my mangled leg, overwhelmed my will to flee.

Not now, Felix. Survive. Survive. Come back and fight. I rolled upright and limped into the surf.

Two of the Suburbans raced toward me down the beach.

I hobbled into the oncoming waves, into the water that would rescue me. The surf lapped at my ankles, then my shins, and finally my knees.

Bursts of rifle fire tore into the water around me. I dove forward and clawed at the sandy bottom.

CHAPTER
33

WAVES BROKE over me, and I disappeared into the dirty foam. Gritty water stung my eyes and clouded my vision. The sunlight streaming from above cooked my back. I scrambled across the silted bottom and groped for deeper water. At last, my skin cooled. The riptide pulled me from the beach toward darker depths.

I expected the water to refresh me, but instead I felt my strength ebbing. I kept my face down and floated across the sandy bottom, limp as the sargassum clinging to my body.

My shattered left leg dragged through rocks and sand. I let out a howl of pain. My scream became lost in the cloud of bubbles blowing out of my mouth. I clutched at my leg, but moving only made it hurt worse so I let it dangle.

I was spent, down for the count.

Goodman's ambush, my wounds, and my loss of protection from the sun had sapped my will to fight. The current pulled me around the southern side of Hilton Head Island. My *kundalini noir* lay slack inside my belly.

I didn't know where the current would take me. Bermuda? The Canary Islands? I didn't care, just as long as I never came back. I only felt the now. Time lost meaning.

I was filled with a miasma of apathy. At least when you're desperate you thrash about in panic, because you think you have a chance to save yourself. But I had no chance. Hope had been crushed out of me.

I retreated over familiar emotional ground, harsh, forbidding, desolate, to a shuttered place in my past.

When I was a sergeant in Iraq, in the early months of our invasion before the war deteriorated into a complete fiasco, my platoon lost two men when their Humvee was struck by a roadside bomb. That evening, I couldn't find the words to console their team leader, my own soldiers, or myself. There wasn't anything—other than clichés—to explain the sacrifice.

Three weeks later we ambushed a family we had mistaken for insurgents. I had arrived in Iraq ready to fight against terror and injustice. Instead, what we did that night was slaughter innocent civilians. The blood of the youngest victim, an adolescent girl, stained my hands and my soul. The tragedy sent me hurling to the emotional bottom. When I hit it, it was then that an Iraqi vampire turned my remorse and desperation against me and converted me into one of the damned undead.

My mind wandered even further back. To my childhood. During one of those episodes of estrangement between my parents, my mom got tired of my dad's drinking and bullying and struck out on her own. We lived in a tiny cinderblock duplex and I know my mom fretted about money. One afternoon she got after my sisters and me to pack our things. My mom yelled at us to hurry, as if we were fleeing a fire.

We took only what we could cram into her car and then drove to my aunt's house, where we would live for a couple of months.

It rained a lot, off and on for days, and our mood remained as dark as the gray skies. When the clouds broke, I borrowed my cousin's bicycle and sweated my way across town to see what happened to all the stuff we had left behind.

Our belongings had been heaped in front of the duplex: our clothes, mattresses and bed linen, dishes, furniture, photos in broken frames. There wasn't much grass, so the days of rain had turned the tiny yard into a muddy puddle.

The wet pile stank of mildew. My mom's Formica table rested there, the chrome legs ripped loose. A dresser lay on its side, the drawers open, disemboweled, with my mom's bras, panties, and stockings strewn about in the mud. Our frayed and tattered picture books looked like the carcasses of decayed birds.

Our possessions were now garbage. Our hopes and ambitions deserved nothing better than to lie rotting in the sun. The neighbors could gawk at our shame and hopelessness. Had we stayed put, would my mom and sisters be lying out here in pieces, like broken dolls? Would I?

For a week afterward, I felt hollow, like a bottle made of fragile glass. I expected at any moment to be smashed and swept aside. My existence didn't matter.

Now I felt like that again.

Insignificant.

Impotent.

Helpless.

A failure.

Worse, others depended on me: Carmen, the Araneum, Gilbert Odin, the Earth women, and I had let them all down. I deserved nothing but oblivion.

The sun set and the sea around me turned inky black. Blurry red auras circled close, nibbled my skin, and darted away.

Something grabbed my torso. I couldn't struggle or resist.

Two hands clasped together over my chest and heaved upward. A silky head with an orange aura pressed against mine. A woman's soft lips kissed my cheek.

Together we rose from the bottom, ascending in rhythmic jerks as she scissored her legs.

We broke the surface. The clear water rinsed my eyes. Thousands of stars dotted the night sky. A breeze cooled my wet face.

I bobbed on the surface, indifferent to what happened next. My rescuer towed me by my collar. We stopped beside a motorboat floating in the gloom.

"Jack, help me lift him." It was Carmen.

A second set of hands, belonging to a big man, grasped my coat and hauled me over the gunwale. He slid me onto the deck.

I lay on my belly, too weak to move. A human with his red aura stood beside me. He had a bandanna around his neck. A chalice. Carmen climbed into the boat. She wore a cropped T-shirt and bikini bottoms. Water rained from her hair. She sat on my butt, pressed her hands against my shoulder blades, and pushed.

I puked mouthfuls of water. When I stopped coughing, Carmen rolled me onto my back and pulled my head into her lap.

She smoothed my hair and whispered, "Get a grip, Felix. You can drown later. We've got work to do."

CHAPTER
34

I BOLTED UPRIGHT, gasping, confused.

Where was I?

I sat in a coffin. I smelled formaldehyde and ethanol—embalming fluid. In the middle of the room stood a mortician's table, a white slab with a trough around the edge and a metal stand on one end to hold the deceased's head in place. Light shone through a row of frosted-glass windows high along one wall. A Porti-Boy embalming machine—it looked like a big, squat blender with a hose sticking out between the front dials—sat on a steel shelf on the opposite wall. The shelf was crowded with jugs of embalming fluid, autopsy compound, and tissue builder. Under the shelf waited a white porcelain commode for whatever was next to be flushed away. There was an interior door to my right and a wide service door to my left.

I was alone in the morgue. My clothes—a red print Hawaiian shirt and khaki cargo pants—were not mine.

I felt queasy.

I had the dim recollection of Carmen and her chalice, Jack, pulling my carcass out of the ocean. They had scrubbed me with soapy water, hosed me off, and brought me here. She had mentioned staying with a chalice couple who owned a mortuary in Bluffton. That must be where I was.

My coffin rested on a workbench. An insulated carafe stood on the table within reach. I tasted a recent blood meal. I didn't remember drinking the blood nor did I remember being dressed or falling asleep in this coffin.

My wallet, its contents, and an assortment of embalming tools—a big syringe, metal tubes of various lengths, a coil of latex hose, and forceps—lay spread across the workbench. I touched the wallet; the leather was dry. I had to have been here awhile. How long?

Bracing myself against the sides of the coffin, I started to get up. My knees were stiff and they ached, as did my lower back. I ran my hands down along my thighs to my calves. My fingers dragged across the scars where Goodman's bullets had chewed my leg.

The images and sensations from the ambush returned to torment me in a kaleidoscope of terror. First the bomb detonating, the hot blast heaving me out of the motel lobby, my face riddled with glass, smoke curling from my burned clothes.

Then the sprint through Hilton Head as Goodman and his goons hunted me, their bullets cracking the air inches past my ears.

The warming of my skin, scalding as the spider bite wore off and the sun fried my unprotected flesh.

Nausea flooded through me again. My *kundalini noir* tightened into a ball, compressing itself in a panicked spasm. I gagged, unable to do anything except fight the impulse to vomit. I clutched my throat as if trying to pull slack into a noose around my neck.

The nausea abated, replaced by an icy fear that twisted

through me. I slumped forward and rested my head against the side of the coffin, weakened and spent.

Footsteps approached beyond the door at my right. I sat up again, the nausea returned, and I waited, too crippled by my wretched condition to offer resistance if it was trouble.

The door opened. A woman asked, "Felix?"

Somehow I knew she was Leslie, Jack's wife, a chalice and co-owner of the mortuary. We must have met when I was first brought here.

Leslie stepped inside and closed the door. Her aura glowed pleasantly, like a candle behind red cellophane. She was in her early forties. A flowered blouse and jeans clothed her voluptuous meatiness—hardly a dainty woman, yet attractive in a nurturing, Earth-mother sort of way.

I felt her heat as she drew close. Her warm hand lay on mine.

"How are you?" Leslie's blue eyes had the comforting empathy of a nurse. Being among chalices meant I didn't need vampire hypnosis. I could relax.

"Not so good." My head felt unsteady and I touched my face. I had a grizzly stubble. A scab outlined a tear on my temple. "Where's Carmen?"

"With Jack. Running errands."

"How long have I been here?"

"Since last night." Leslie removed the scarf from around her neck. She pulled the tails of her blouse from her waistband and undid the buttons. Her aura brightened with a growing lust. "Would you like some fresh blood? You'll feel better."

If this was only about providing fresh blood, she could've bled herself and replenished the carafe. Chalices weren't into this exchange of fluids with the undead for charity's sake. Sex with a vampire was one of the bigger rewards for submission.

Leslie's blouse fell open and displayed her large bosom in a lacy white brassiere. Wife-husband chalices were not uncommon. They promised debauched recreation in many possible combinations. But I confined my game to females. Chalice couples brought into this arrangement their many perversions, and a favorite among the men was a cuckold fetish. I had no desire to put on a show for Jack. He would have to get his voyeuristic jollies somewhere else.

I ran my tongue across my incisors. My fangs stayed flush with my other teeth. I had no urge for fanging . . . or for sex. At least she had asked.

"Thanks," I replied. "Some other time."

What irony. When I had the tan, women were losing interest in me. Now my tan was gone and I had no interest in them.

Leslie's aura dimmed from disappointment. She smiled self-consciously and clutched the collar of her blouse. Her hands worked the buttons, top to bottom, and left the tails of the blouse outside her jeans. She tied the scarf around her neck. "You're not acting particularly vampiric."

"Let me worry about that." The queasiness clung to my throat like a greasy scum. Perhaps if I washed it down I'd feel better. "Can you get me a drink? A beer. Wine? Something hard if you've got it."

Leslie crouched beside the workbench and opened a cabinet door. She brought out a bottle of Wild Turkey, a can of Pepsi, and a pair of highball glasses, and set them on the workbench by the embalming tools.

I stared at the booze. "Do you and Jack pickle yourselves while you pickle your clients?"

"It's from our last Halloween party." She reached back into the workbench, pulled out a black paper horn, and gave it a toot.

"Cocktails and cadavers," I said, "what a theme."

Leslie put away the horn. "I'll get ice from the kitchen."

Usually it didn't take much to get me to drink but my thirst had left me too. The queasiness grew stronger and I realized why I felt this way.

Goodman had chased me to the brink of doom and I couldn't forget that. Even when I drifted in the water, already safe from Goodman, I had lost the will to resist. When the hands of my rescuer grasped me, I made no attempt to help in my own salvation. I didn't care. I surrendered to what had seemed inevitable.

I was broken.

I deserved no pleasure. I never wanted to smile again. I had no desire for liquor, or sex, or fanging. What then would be the point of being immortal? I still walked among the living but Goodman had beaten me.

As a detective, I was useless.

As a vampire, I was as good as dead.

CHAPTER
35

CARMEN AND I sat on opposite sides of a coffee table in the upstairs office of the mortuary, she in a swiveling desk chair, I in one corner of a leather sofa. She had made drinks: a cosmopolitan for herself, and a manhattan for me.

Carmen sipped from her cocktail. She smiled in an effort to push the worry from her face. "Leslie told me you're still not feeling well."

"You didn't have to ask her. I could've told you."

Carmen wore a black nylon jogging suit—sans bra—with the top unzipped to the bottom of her sternum. She put her glass down. "You look like hell. You need to shave and comb your hair. When are you going to snap out of this?"

It was a question I had asked myself and kept ignoring.

I touched my temple. The scar was almost gone, as were the wounds left by the fish nibbling on my skin. I put pressure on my left foot and felt the lingering throb where the bullets had chewed my leg. But it was remembering how the sun had cooked my skin that brought back the terror.

As vampires, our primordial fear was to be caught in the open and fried by the sun. We undead bloodsuckers have many powers, but God has damned us with one great weakness: our vulnerability to direct sunlight, the source of life on this planet.

The spider bite had fooled me. Its transient protection had made me complacent and that was what had nearly killed me. I could recover from bullet wounds but there was no undoing the memory of getting roasted by sunlight.

Carmen pushed the manhattan across the table toward me. The amber drink looked perfect, the best proof that we were civilized. Condensation frosted the outside of the beveled old-fashioned glass. Two maraschino cherries sat under the ice cubes.

I made no move for the glass. Maybe it was a good thing I wasn't drinking. If I had a thirst, then I might fill the void inside of me with hootch and wind up homeless, like Earl back in Kansas City. Vampires are immune to many human afflictions but, unfortunately, alcoholism wasn't one of them, and many vampires found themselves on skid row.

I remembered what a sip of that manhattan tasted like. Almost as refreshing as blood fanged from a neck. But I deserved neither.

Carmen reached over the table and took my left hand. "Look." She held my hand, palm-side up. "See your aura? It's milky and dim."

I shook my hand loose and withdrew my arm. I didn't need her to tell me my problems.

Carmen lifted a valise that stood on the floor beside her chair. She opened the valise and laid it on the coffee table. She withdrew a glass jelly jar and placed it between us. Inside the jar crouched a chartreuse-pine spider.

"Here," she said in a stern tone. "Time to finish your convalescence."

My skin itched where the previous spider had bitten me. My abdomen tightened at the thought of another dose of the venom.

I shook my head. "No. I'm not going through that again." The benefits of the last bite had worn off abruptly and worsened the effects of Goodman's attack, so it was pointless to try once more. "If I go outside, I'll cover myself with makeup."

"What do you mean, 'if'?" Carmen asked. "Are you going to solve Odin's case or not? Are you going to let Goodman win? What about the Araneum?"

I wanted to reply "who cares," but that would only antagonize Carmen. Better that I listen to her bark and say nothing.

Carmen stood and circled the coffee table. Her eyes stayed on me like searchlights. "Answer me. Your wounds have healed, haven't they? What the hell is wrong with you?" She clasped my shoulders.

Everything. I shrugged her off.

Carmen's aura blazed like I'd thrown gasoline on her. "Listen to me, we can't waste time. We have to go after Goodman."

"He can wait."

"What do you mean? Wait for what?" Carmen leaned over the armrest of the sofa and grabbed my collar. "You want to sulk? Go ahead. I'll get Goodman on my own."

I had underestimated Goodman and barely survived. "Don't be so sure of yourself."

Carmen shook me. "Felix, look at me."

I looked up and fixed my gaze into the vampire sheen of her eyes. What did she want?

Carmen's right hand moved in a blur. The slap was as hard and crisp as a gunshot. The blow left a lingering burn on my cheek. "See that? If you can't protect yourself from a bitch slap, how are you going to deal with Goodman? He'll destroy you."

Her words raked into me like sharp tines. The humiliating truth salted the wound.

"I'm tired of seeing you like this. Time for tough love." Her aura flared bright with incandescent fury. She balled my collar in both her fists and ripped my shirt open.

What was she up to? I reacted to fend her off but she moved at full vampire speed, much faster than I could.

Carmen lunged over the sofa armrest and toppled onto me. Her weight kept me off balance and she pushed me flat against the sofa. She seized my wrists. The hard plastic zipper of her sweat top scraped against my chest as she dragged herself across me. Her open mouth, the fangs long and fierce as daggers, approached my neck.

CHAPTER
36

CARMEN'S FANGS sank into my throat. The long teeth were like electric probes plugged directly into my spine, short-circuiting my nerves. I trembled in helpless pain. The moist ring of her open mouth worked against my neck, and her warm, wet tongue writhed across my skin.

One of her legs wrapped around my left hip and the other intertwined with my right leg. I tried to wrestle free but her grip on my wrists remained as hard as handcuffs.

Blood dribbled down my throat. Her fangs worked deeper into my flesh and it felt like burning sparks shot from her teeth deep into me. My *kundalini noir* thrashed in spastic jerks.

Her fangs withdrew. The relief was like a cool compress on a burn and left me in a dreamy state. My skin tingled all over. This was the first time I'd been fanged since becoming a vampire. Vampires don't feed from one another and the only time they fang like this is to coax *la petite mort* . . . or administer the death bite. But this was neither.

Carmen turned me onto my stomach and sat on my butt. "Felix, I'm tired of your bullshit. Any other vampire and I wouldn't care. But not you. You're too important to the undead. To me."

She used her talons to slice away what remained of my shirt.

I started to sit up when she clasped the back of my neck and pinched the top of my spine. A warm sensation flowed down my backbone. Carmen squeezed harder and her touch became hot, like melted wax dripping on my skin.

She twisted her grip. The vertebrae in my neck cracked. A second wave of luxurious heat coursed through me and I sank against the cushions.

Carmen scooted down my legs. Her hands trekked along my back and kneaded my buttocks. She ran the knife-edge of her hand along the base of my spine. "I can feel how your aura swirls around like it's tied in a knot. Your psychic force is jammed at the first chakra."

"What's this about?"

"Sex. But special sex from *The Undead Kama Sutra*." Carmen reached under the sofa and slapped a thick manuscript on the coffee table.

Sex with Carmen? I'd always turned away her advances, thinking that she would screw like a machine. But she had sex with humans and they came back for more.

The truth about my reluctance to mix it up with Carmen? Blame my ego. What if Carmen did me and found me wanting, especially when compared to her human lovers? That humiliation would scar me to the bone.

"I've made progress with my research." Carmen thumbed the pages of the manuscript. "If we do this right, I should be able to help you by manipulating our psychic states during sex. I read the color of our auras. Yellow indicates the next psychic plane. If our auras go from orange to yellow, then bingo. But that won't happen unless," Carmen whapped the center of my back, "whatever crap is in here goes away."

"You make it sound like we need a plumber."

"I'll work you over with a plunger if I have to, Felix."

"Let's stick with your *Kama Sutra*."

Carmen lifted from me and yanked off my trousers and briefs. She piled my clothes on the floor, followed by the rustle of her garments joining them. "But it will take more than a massage to heal you."

Carmen pulled my hips from the sofa until I was on my hands and knees. "We'll start with the pose on page 24, 'Tending Limp Fruit.'"

When my fruit was no longer limp, we moved to "Lapping Frog with Two Backs." From that to "Horse Pushing Plow." Carmen recited the name of each new pose like she was a tour guide in the garden of sensual delights.

I didn't feel any shift in my psychic balance. But Carmen's demanding and precise touch, and the tug of her hands and the pressure of her ankles on my shoulders, stoked a growing fire within me.

The wound from her bite on my neck throbbed, reminding me of her fangs tapping my jugular.

I had thought sex with Carmen would've had the grace of a free-style wrestling match complete with folding chairs smashed over each other's heads. Instead, the touch of her body was like being drawn into a sea of pleasure that we both shared. Carmen's eyes fluttered in sublime release. Her aura undulated with waves of ecstasy.

We switched to "Flood of Apple Blossoms," followed by an enthusiastic "Springtime Menagerie."

The fire inside me grew brighter and hotter. The heat centered at the bottom of my spine, the first chakra, then percolated to my second chakra. The warmth in my lower abdomen shot rays of energy through my body.

Carmen flipped onto her back and clasped me with her legs. We held hands and she rocked her hips against mine.

Our auras fused. Her mouth opened and exposed the tips of her fangs.

My *kundalini noir* relaxed and uncoiled. It seemed to straighten along my spinal column and anchor itself to my chakras.

Flecks of yellow dotted our auras.

Carmen squeezed my fingers. "Almost, Felix," she gasped. "Almost."

The energy rising through me sputtered inside my belly and hovered between the second and third chakras. Suddenly, my *kundalini noir* relaxed and coiled into a loose ball. Our auras faded and became solid orange.

Carmen let go of my hands and closed her eyes. Her complexion flushed, a first for a vampire. I sat on my heels and rested between her legs. The meaty aroma of fresh, hot sex scented the air between us.

Psychic energy circulated freely within me. I felt strong.

Powerful.

Dangerous.

This *Kama Sutra* was more than sexual calisthenics. I stroked her knee. "Wow. You're on to something."

Carmen shushed me and lay still.

"You okay?"

She gave a long, satisfied sigh. "That was fucking great."

"We didn't reach the third chakra."

"Got close." Carmen rubbed one foot against my belly. The familiar glint of lust returned to her eyes. "Reason enough to do more research."

"You get off?"

Carmen brought her legs from around me. "I lost count. You?"

"Almost." I sat next to her.

Carmen brushed hair from her face. The color receded from her cheeks. "We'll have to fix that." She slid off the sofa and knelt on the floor.

I asked, "What exotic position of your *Kama Sutra* is this?"

"One of my favorites."

"What's it called?"

Carmen pushed my knees apart. She ran the tip of her tongue across her lips to moisten them. " 'The All-American Blow Job.' "

CHAPTER
37

CARMEN LEFT the office to shower. I lay against the sofa and closed my eyes, and before I knew it, I fell asleep.

I dreamed of walking through the familiar hills of northern New Mexico, the air fragrant with sage and piñon. A sudden nervousness fell over me. My steps sped up into a jog, then a fast trot. The nervousness tightened into fear. The hills turned into the condos of Hilton Head and I found myself running desperately across the beach, terror-stricken, splashing into the surf, as giant, many-headed dogs chased me.

I awoke with a start. My talons clutched the shredded sofa upholstery where I had ripped it during my dream spasms. I sat upright, my sixth sense buzzing. My *kundalini noir* coiled inside me, tense as a rattlesnake.

I let my fangs and talons retract. After brushing tufts of

sofa lining from my body, I slipped my underwear and pants back on.

Carmen returned, wearing a short bathrobe. Her hair was wrapped in a towel and her face looked freshly scrubbed.

She surveyed the torn sofa and the bits of upholstery littering the floor. "What the hell happened? If you were in the mood for rough sex, you didn't have to go at it solo."

"Nightmare," I muttered, embarrassed.

"How do you feel now?"

I tightened my fists and flexed my arms. An athletic energy pounded through me. "Better." I wanted to run, to jump, to smash things. I wanted to fight.

One name came to mind. Goodman. *Your hours are numbered.*

Carmen smiled. "Felix, your aura is so bright it could spark an explosion."

I clasped her neck. "Speaking of explosions."

She pulled away. "Don't have the time. Remember that couple at the Markov PharmacoEconomic party?"

"Which couple? There were dozens."

"Krandall and Peltier. You gave me their card."

I nodded in recognition. That blonde Peltier had two nice big reasons why I couldn't forget her.

Carmen undid the towel around her head and rubbed her scalp. "They called me just now. Want to get together."

"Fun and games?" I knew the answer. A touch of jealousy brushed over me. Carmen and I had finally had sex and it was pretty damn good. But we vampires knew that sex was just another language that existed between the undead. Undead friends with undead benefits. I could no more be jealous of Carmen screwing around than I could be of her talking or dining with others. We could get attached to humans, and hell, I still had a soft spot—in the place where my heart used to beat—for a forest sprite who had come and gone through my undead life like a breeze.

Carmen laid the towel around her shoulders. "More than

fun and games. I'll see what they know about Goodman, aliens, and the missing women."

"Be careful."

"With those two?" Carmen stifled a laugh. "They try anything funny and I'll stuff their remains in mason jars."

Carmen bent over to pick up her discarded jogging suit. She looked at me from between her legs. "Felix, if you get down, you can see right up my bathrobe. And that, in case you can't tell, is an invitation for a quickie."

CHAPTER
38

I T WAS my turn to get cleaned up. I took a long, hot shower and shaved. As the water pounded my back and shoulders, I scolded myself for slipping into despair. How had I let Goodman do that to me?

Then I remembered floating in the Atlantic, my flesh torn and my will shattered. One's psyche can be mangled as deeply as one's tissue. In my arrogance, I had thought that as a vampire I was invincible. I kept forgetting that I was not.

The spider bite had disappeared. No blemish. No scar. Only bad memories.

When I got out of the shower, Carmen was gone. I went to the kitchen. The chalices had left coffee brewing and a carafe of their mixed blood. Hers was B-positive, his O-negative. A nice, complementary blend, but I wanted something fresh.

Jack and Leslie were out. A note on the refrigerator wipe

board said they were tending their boat. I went to the morgue and gathered my things from the workbench.

The front door opened. Leslie's footsteps approached and she appeared in the morgue door. "Good morning. Carmen tells me you're feeling better."

"I am. And thanks for your hospitality."

Leslie walked over to the mortician's table. "I noticed you didn't touch the carafe we'd left for you."

"Is that a problem?"

"Maybe not." She gave a tempting smile that I was familiar with. My tan was gone but my sexual prowess was back, thanks to Carmen.

"You do look better," Leslie said. "Could I ask a favor?"

"Depends, but I'll probably say yes."

"I'm glad you didn't drink from the carafe." Leslie undid her scarf. "I'd rather you snack from me."

"I can do that."

Leslie unbuttoned her blouse and hopped on the mortician's table. She peeled loose her jeans and panties, and let them drop.

"Where's Jack?" I asked.

"On the boat. He'll be there all day."

With her large breasts, thick thighs, and wide hips, there was nothing little about Leslie. I approached her, my smile matching hers, my fangs growing long. She pulled her bra up and let those big puppies out for air. She scooted back on the table and propped her head on the steel headrest.

Made sense that she wanted to screw here in the morgue, on the mortician's table. For the same reason office workers sneaked into their cubicles and boinked at their workstations. I knew chalices who owned a ranch, and they liked to screw in the barn, surrounded by the smell of alfalfa and horse shit.

I am a vampire. I've had sex in a coffin—albeit with a skinny chalice—and in crypts. But always with the living. I'd no sooner screw a corpse than eat soup from a toilet bowl.

I undressed and climbed on top of her, excited to have my power back. Leslie's arms and legs clamped around me. I eased into her, enjoying the sensation of her moist warmth. She smelled of lilac soap with traces of bilge water, creosote, and gasoline. Leslie was a hands-on woman.

My fangs found her jugular. Her warm blood spurted into my mouth, deliriously tasty and satisfying. I pumped my hips and reached climax. As a reward to her, I lapped a good dose of pleasure enzymes into the wound of her throat. Leslie gasped. She reached up and grasped the edge of the table. Her legs squeezed tight and her body trembled under mine.

Her eyes remaining closed, she relaxed. Sweat dotted her forehead and puddled in the hollow between her breasts. I got off her and lapped the drops of blood clinging to my fangs.

Leslie's chest heaved. She brought her legs up and hugged them as if to prolong the afterglow.

Rather than settle my nerves, all this sex sharpened the knives within me. My arms flexed and I worked my fists.

I wanted Goodman.

Now.

Leslie got dressed, then helped me apply sunblock and makeup. I put my clothes back on and went to the front room to look outside. A bright Carolina sun bore upon us. For a second I felt the fear but relaxed, as I knew the sunblock protected me.

I knew what to do. Go back to the resort and tear it apart looking for Goodman. I called Carmen from the house phone and left a message: I'm going after Goodman. Meet me when you can.

I told Leslie I needed a ride to Hilton Head, and she dropped me off two blocks from the first guardhouse of the resort. Sneaking in proved easy. I levitated across a slough onto the resort property, zapped a couple of golfers, and left them inside a clump of palmettos while I took their cart.

I thought about all the pain Goodman was in for. I would

enjoy interrogating him. As a human, he could keep no secrets from my hypnosis.

Considering that only days ago armed guards and a helicopter had chased me off this island, the resort seemed sanguine and inviting.

I followed the curving asphalt trail of the cart path, turned the corner, and spotted a man teeing off by himself. His build and stature looked familiar.

Goodman.

I stopped the cart and slipped my sunglasses down to read his aura. It was red and simmered with impatience and anxiety. Whatever bothered him was about to get worse.

He was alone. He was mine. This was too easy. It was about time the breaks fell my way in this case.

I adjusted my sunglasses, got out of the cart, and marched directly toward him.

Goodman stopped his club in mid-swing. He stared at me and relaxed.

When I was seventy-five yards away, he cocked his body in my direction, readied his club, and swung.

The ball cracked from the tee and zoomed right at my face, like he'd shot it from an antitank rifle.

I snatched the ball before it hit me between the eyes.

I kept walking toward Goodman. He lowered the club and waited. A straw fedora shaded his face. His gray eyes were the color of lead bullets. Both of his hands worked the grip of the club like he was trying to choke it. His mouth chewed these words: "You're harder to kill than a fucking roach in a woodpile."

Ten feet from him, I snapped my wrist and flung the golf ball too fast for him to react. The ball thwacked his forehead and bounced aside.

Goodman flinched in pain and sank to his knees. He rubbed his forehead and steadied himself by leaning on his club.

"You son of a bitch," he said, standing. The ball left a red welt the size of a quarter.

I stepped toward him. "I'm just getting started. The next thing I'm going to do is shove that club up your ass."

"Not so fast, you freakish fuck."

"You and your mouth need some manners." I got closer.

He held his hand up and dug into his pocket. He tossed something at me.

A cell phone. I caught it. The phone had a leopard skin cover, like Carmen's.

My ears and fingertips tingled in alarm.

I opened the phone and recognized the photo on the screen—Carmen blowing herself a kiss.

It was Carmen's phone. How did Goodman get it? The tingling turned into an electric shock.

"The last message in her voice mail was from you, Felix." Goodman rubbed the knot on his forehead and winced. His frown changed into a smile. "Behave yourself, and you might see her again."

CHAPTER
39

CARMEN CAPTURED?

My mouth went dry. My fingers started to tremble and I forced them to keep still. "This is a trick."

A dozen men in black uniforms appeared from behind the trees and bushes. They pointed submachine guns and assault rifles. My fingers trembled again. I'd come here thinking I was the tough guy and instead I stumbled into their trap.

My thoughts careened into one another.

Everything in this case had been about the darkest of conspiracies and the confluence of cold-blooded human cunning and alien murder. What was the Araneum warning? That I not allow one of us vampires to get compromised.

But I had. Worse, it was a good friend, someone who had saved me.

The trail leading here began with the death of one alien,

so were other aliens involved in her capture? I didn't know, but how else could Goodman have managed to snag Carmen?

Another golf cart rounded the corner past a stand of live oaks and palms. The cart drew closer and I saw Krandall driving, Peltier by his side. Both wore matching dark uniforms and equipment harnesses. At the party, these two looked like pampered yuppies; now they had the menacing presence of wolverines. An HK submachine gun with a silencer rested on Peltier's lap. Make that armed wolverines.

Carmen had gone to see them for a session of casual sex. So these two had set her up. How? They and Goodman had to know more about us than I could imagine. What device—alien or otherwise—had they used to capture her? Carmen? Mice subduing a tiger made more sense. My *kundalini noir* tightened in confusion.

Goodman would tell me. Quick as a thunderbolt, I seized him by the neck. I whirled him around to use as a shield. If the guards opened fire, Goodman would be the first to die. Movement rippled through the security detail as they steadied their weapons to shoot.

Goodman waved his arms. He coughed twice and pulled at my fingers. "I'm okay."

Peltier and Krandall cupped their earpieces and shouted into the microphones clipped to their harnesses. "Check fire. Check fire."

My talons pressed into his throat. "Where is Carmen?"

Goodman squirmed from the pain. He turned to look at me. The arrogant smile of his was long gone, replaced by a grim, hateful stare. "You're one of them, aren't you?"

"One of them, who?"

"The alien Gilbert Odin."

Goodman knew about aliens and had me mistaken for one of them. A little bit of good news.

Unfortunately, I was surrounded by bad news. If the guards opened fire, I would kill Goodman first and then leap at Krandall and Peltier and slash their throats. After that?

"Easy now," Goodman said. "Don't forget about your friend."

He didn't need to repeat the threat. What were my options? Only one.

"I'm not leaving without Carmen."

More armed men crept out from the surrounding trees and brush.

"I knew you'd say that." Goodman couldn't keep from gloating.

I gave him a fresh taste of my talons. "If you think you'll survive this, think again. I'm going to tear that smile off your face before this is over."

Goodman's face turned red from the pain. He gasped, "You want Carmen? Then let up and you'll find out what I want from you."

What could he possibly want? I relaxed my hold.

Goodman's color faded and he stumbled and coughed. He turned his attention toward Krandall and Peltier. "Tell everyone to stay cool. We're going inside. Pass the word."

"Inside where?" I poked my talons into Goodman's neck.

He winced and grabbed my wrist. The guards steadied their aim.

"Somebody wants to talk to you."

"Who?" My *kundalini noir* coiled in alarm.

"Mr. Big."

"You've lost me." I gave Goodman's neck another squeeze.

He choked and clutched at my fingers. "You want to talk to the one in charge, let's go."

My *kundalini noir* coiled tighter.

That arrogant glint hovered in Goodman's eyes. "You don't have a choice. Carmen, remember?"

I thought I had come here to bully Goodman. Instead I was the one with my back against the wall.

Goodman clasped my hand. "Mr. Big wants to talk. He's got questions about you and your friend."

"Who is this Mr. Big?"

"Does it matter? You don't think you can handle him? I thought you wanted your friend back. No? Then stay out here and pick your nose." He gestured toward the guards. "They need something to do."

I had Goodman by the neck but he had me by the balls. I let go. "What kind of questions?"

"That's between you and him."

I looked back at Krandall and Peltier. She was touching her earpiece.

I warned them: "There isn't a bullet fast enough to kill me before I can rip the heart out of your boss. Either one of you want to bet that I couldn't kill you now?"

I expected Peltier to flinch in horror. Instead she put a hand on her submachine gun and flicked the safety to the fire position.

I pushed Goodman into his golf cart. "You drive. Don't want to keep your Mr. Big waiting."

He got behind the wheel and I sat next to him. I rested my hand on his shoulder. "Goodman, if I detect anything suspicious . . ."

Goodman massaged the red marks I'd left on his neck. "You mean more suspicious than being escorted by a platoon of armed guards through a golf course?"

Good point. "Despite what you think," I replied, "the odds aren't in your favor."

"Don't get too cocky, my weird friend." Goodman's demeanor frosted. "I've made a career of beating the odds."

"So have I."

Goodman pursed his lips in contempt before giving a rude smile. He pressed the accelerator pedal and the cart rolled forward. He drove on the asphalt cart path toward the hotel. I counted more than thirty guards along the way. Hotel guests gathered a safe distance from the display of firepower and gawked at the spectacle.

My sixth sense buzzed constantly, from what, specifically, I couldn't tell. Despite the fact that he was but one short second from decapitation, Goodman seemed at ease; then again, he was a professional assassin. A squad of snipers could be aiming for my head, or the cushion under me could be hiding a Claymore mine.

I thought about what got me started on this case. "You murdered Odin, didn't you?"

Goodman sneered. "You can only murder humans."

"What about Marissa? She was human."

"I had to."

"Why?"

Goodman kept quiet.

I poked a talon against his ribs. "You don't have to talk. You don't have to live, either."

Goodman said, "Sure you want to do that? It would make your job harder."

"Why would you care? You'll be dead."

Goodman must have thought about that, because he offered, "The nosy bitch knew too much."

"About whom?" I asked. "Naomi Peyton?"

The color receded from Goodman's ruddy cheeks. "You know too much."

"Not enough. What about Vanessa Tico and Janice Wyndersook? Where are they? Or did you kill them too?"

"They're still alive."

Where? Why? Are they with Carmen? "Why are you telling me this?"

"To make you aware of the stakes involved. You make a wrong move and it'll be more than your friend Carmen who gets popped for good."

I snatched Goodman by the throat. He grunted like he was passing a stone. "Don't put their murders on my head." Droplets of my spit sprayed into his face.

The cart shuffled to a halt. I wanted to squeeze his neck until his eyeballs popped out.

"You caused their commuter plane to crash, didn't you? And murdered seventeen more innocent people."

"It's called collateral damage."

Collateral damage? "What about Karen Beck? More collateral damage?"

Luminous red spots the size of peas floated on my arms. A couple of the dots hovered on my nose and dazzled my eyes. The guards were painting me with the laser pointers on their rifles.

Goodman's eyes traced the laser dots dancing on my face. "Go ahead and play the angry macho man. See where that gets you."

It would finish me off and Carmen would remain a prisoner. I let go. The laser dots disappeared.

Goodman took a deep breath. "I did what I had to do."

"What you've done is mass murder," I said. "And you're admitting it?"

"What are you going to do about it? Tell the world? You're a fucking alien."

Alien? By using the word, Goodman admitted he knew about the extraterrestrials. I wanted to shout my questions at him, then pick him up by the ankles to shake the answers loose. But if I asked him, then I'd be giving away what I knew or didn't know. Let him think I was an alien.

"What do you care?" he said.

I grabbed his collar. "I care about Carmen. Why did you do it? Why did you murder all those people? To cover up the kidnapping of Tico and Wyndersook? To kidnap Carmen?"

Goodman tensed his arms as he put a death grip on the steering wheel. His knuckles turned white. "Ever try making people disappear? Pretty soon the numbers add up and the goddamn noise about what happened to all these broads can get fucking deafening."

"You like being a murderer on the government's payroll?"

Goodman stared, and his expression grew ever more hateful. "Do me a goddamn favor, Felix. Don't patronize me. I know I'm a henchman for this kleptocracy we call a democratic republic. I've always been a soldier. I still am. They give me my orders and I say, yes sir, three bags full."

"Only following orders? You sound like a Nazi."

Goodman stepped on the accelerator. The cart lurched forward. "Read your history books." Goodman added a dismissive look. "We didn't beat the Nazis by being pussies."

"These are innocent women, not Nazis."

"Orders are orders."

"If you ever met Mother Teresa," I said, "I'm sure she'd shoot you."

"Not if I shot her first."

"What happened to the blaster you used on Marissa and Odin?"

"I gave it back to Mr. Big."

Was Mr. Big an alien? Why had he ordered the hit on Gilbert Odin? What did Mr. Big have to do with the disappearance of the women? Was this the threat the Araneum wanted me to investigate? Every question was like a box with another question inside.

We passed through a cordon of guards. Goodman nodded at them and they nodded back.

"Think you've seen everything?"

"Why do you ask?" I replied.

"Because if you think you've seen everything, guess again, wise guy." Goodman smirked. "Compared to what's coming up, you haven't seen shit."

CHAPTER
40

GOODMAN TOOK a left and followed the fence around the service area. We rolled behind the maintenance shed and the Dumpsters and continued past the parking garage.

I'd come here to rescue Carmen and instead I was letting my enemies take me deeper into their lair. The guilt of failing to protect her weighed on me. My hidden ace was that Goodman assumed I was an alien and had no idea that I was a vampire. When the time came, I hoped my supernatural powers were enough to help me find and free Carmen and for both of us to escape.

Krandall and Peltier trailed behind us with three more carts and a Gator after them. Each of those carts carried three armed guards, the Gator four. To complete our little circus parade all we needed was a brass band and a bear riding a tricycle.

Our convoy went beyond the back of the hotel and halted at the gate in the chain-link fence around the enclosure of the annex building.

Two guards wearing sunglasses and cradling submachine guns waited for us. An electric motor retracted the gate.

Goodman drove the cart over the threshold and into the grassy enclosure the size of a baseball infield. A concrete pad with a yellow H occupied the middle of the enclosure. This was where I'd seen the military helicopter land before.

The annex, a featureless three-story box with the antenna farm on the roof, stood to our right.

The gate closed behind us. The guards and the other carts remained outside the enclosure. As far as I could tell, Goodman and I were alone, though I was sure we were being watched.

I didn't notice an entrance into the annex until Goodman headed toward a concrete driveway that inclined into the ground under the wall. We proceeded down the incline. A metal door scrolled open and we entered an underground corridor.

My *kundalini noir* tightened with apprehension. I put my hand on Goodman's leg above the knee and pressed my talons into his thigh. If this was an ambush, I'd pull him apart like a wishbone.

Goodman didn't slow the golf cart as we drove onto the linoleum floor and under the fluorescent lights. The whine of the cart's motor echoed in the hall. The corridor continued straight down a long tunnel that must connect the annex to the main hotel building. A second hallway opened to our right. Placards on the doors of wall compartments indicated access to power and water conduits. We made a right turn at this second hall and stopped at a set of elevator doors. They pinged open and waited for us. We were being watched, for sure.

Goodman halted in front of the doors. I locked my fingers around his arm. We got out of the cart and walked into the elevator. I turned Goodman toward the video camera in the upper left corner. I grasped his chin and lifted his face to the camera. I scratched his neck with a talon to make him wince. "There's more of that, if your friends are not careful."

The doors closed and the elevator rose. I got ready for anything and held Goodman by the back of his collar. If the floor dropped, I'd leap through the ceiling. If a flamethrower sprayed fire, I'd use Goodman for cover.

The elevator stopped on the second floor. In the moment before the door opened, I listened carefully. I detected no rustle of clothing, no muffled click of a weapon's safety moved into the firing position, nothing that threatened me.

When the door opened, I pushed Goodman in front of me into a deserted foyer. A simple steel door stood across from us. A red light glowed above the access lever. The light went off and a green one lit up.

Goodman grasped the lever. He paused and glanced over his shoulder at me. Did his look telegraph a warning?

"Think twice before you try to surprise me, Goodman," I warned.

"You're going to be surprised all right, hero boy."

The door swung open. We entered a large sitting room decorated with high-end wood furnishings. Pistachio-green floor mats, table linen, and tapestries accented the room. Fresh flowers—red alpinias and camellias, purple and white pansies, and yellow trumpet flowers—stood in crystal vases on a console table and a credenza. Despite the blossoms, the room smelled like a humidor.

A fabric screen of shiny green material partitioned the floor. Past the left side of the screen I could see the door of what looked like a freight elevator. What did that transport?

In front of the screen sat an emerald-green velvet love seat and a leather cigar chair. This place was right off the cover of *Better Homes and Gardens*.

Something stirred behind the partition. Mr. Big? My sixth sense tingled.

CHAPTER
41

"C OLONEL GOODMAN, you are dismissed." The voice
was high-pitched yet sounded male, like a teenage boy
breathing helium.

Goodman tugged against my grip.

I held firm. "You and I are in this for the duration."

"We have your friend," the voice behind the screen reminded.

Goodman gave a dirty grin, like he'd wiped a booger on
my sleeve and there was nothing I could do about it.

I let go. Goodman straightened his rumpled collar. He
backed out the door and it snapped closed. A light beside the
door lock went from green to red.

Who lurked behind the screen? I knew it wasn't the Wiz-
ard of Oz. I was sure it was an alien and hoped it didn't
come out with Carmen's head in one hand and a blaster in
the other. My *kundalini noir* knotted into a tight ball, like a
fist ready to strike.

I removed my sunglasses and surveyed the room again, looking for any obvious threat. I could trust nothing and expected the worst.

"Have a seat, please," the voice said from behind the screen.

I walked to the love seat and cigar chair. Both pieces of furniture looked normal enough. A step of polished heavy wood had been pushed against the front of the chair. Why the step? Was Mr. Big a midget?

An end table, in a finish matching the step, separated the chair and love seat. On the table sat a heavy crystal ashtray and a shallow glass bowl with a red cactus blossom floating in water.

The step indicated that the chair was reserved, so I stood beside the love seat and waited. I remained very still, to let my sixth sense absorb every nuance. My muscles remained primed to react to anything.

Whatever was behind the screen moved into view: a short bipedal creature with skin the texture and color of tarnished green leather. A yellow aura surrounded him like he stood inside a burning torch.

Yellow aura. Extraterrestrial.

I stood in stunned disbelief. This little goblin was Mr. Big?

Beside being called "mister," it was the smooth head and masculine form that made me assume this thing was male. His head had the shape of an egg—the narrow end formed his chin—and was the size of a basketball. His almond-shaped black eyes were as large and glossy as billiard balls. I couldn't discern any features within the obsidian orbs, no separate pupil or iris.

Twin nostrils the shape and size of coin slots occupied the blank space between his eyes and lipless mouth. A pair of tiny, bud-like ears sprouted on opposite sides of the crown of his bald head.

His skinny ankles were attached to dumbbell-shaped feet that had wide circular pads for "toes" and "heels."

As a vampire, I was used to the grotesque, but this repulsive dwarf belonged in a freak show from hell.

Is this what Odin looked like in his natural state? Or was this alien a different species altogether?

He appeared similar to another alien I'd seen, a corpse recovered from the wreckage of the Roswell UFO. I learned that during my investigation for Gilbert Odin, when he had used me for his own devious ends.

I gave the alien a vampire glare. He took no notice of my naked eyes. When first I tried to zap Gilbert Odin, nothing happened either.

I had also experienced this before with one human. She not only proved invulnerable to vampire hypnosis but used her knowledge of the supernatural to manipulate us—the undead. Didn't do her much good, ultimately, because another human killed her.

Neither she nor Odin could see my aura and, hopefully, this alien couldn't either. I still had that advantage.

Yet, when his gaze turned upon me, I sensed a confidence and a paternal charisma, like he was used to being in charge.

He wore a simple gray suit buttoned up the front to a high Mandarin collar. The material looked like satin. The alien carried an unlit cigar. As he walked closer, I was struck by how short he was, maybe four foot six.

He motioned to the love seat with his free hand. He had three digits: two fingers and a thumb. All were thin and sinuous, like tentacles, and ended in flat disks. His mouth curved into a pandering smile that meant "please."

He climbed on the step and turned around. We sat simultaneously—I, slowly and cautiously.

He planted those weird feet of his on the step, the toe pads drooping over the front. He relaxed and crossed his legs.

I said nothing and waited for him. My sixth sense made the hairs on my arms bristle.

Unlike Odin, this freaky creation had no cabbage odor; in

fact, I couldn't smell anything except for the flowers and tobacco. But the stink of sleaze was as tangible to me as was his aura. I hadn't come all this way only to stare at his ugly face. Time for Q and A about the only reason I was here. "Where is Carmen?"

His lipless mouth moved again, but it took a second for the words to come out, as if he were being dubbed. "Safe."

"Not as long as you have her." I clenched my fist. *Careful.* At the moment, I couldn't afford to antagonize this little green spaceman. Goodman and the security complex deferred to this Mr. Big, meaning he was numero uno. I relaxed my hand.

The alien noticed this and nodded once, pleased that I acknowledged the situation. He lifted the cigar and stared at it. "My name is Clayborn." He repeated his name, as if amused by the sound. "Clayborn."

I wasn't surprised that he spoke English, but his squeaky voice threw me off. Was he the one who ordered Gilbert Odin's assassination? Clayborn, or whatever the hell his moniker was, possessed a gangster's arrogance, so I didn't doubt it. I'd find out why he murdered Odin, and why Goodman and our government protected his ET ass. But first, I had to rescue Carmen.

Clayborn swung that black gaze to me. "Goodman told me that he'd found another one of us. But you're not, are you?"

They knew I wasn't human, and so assumed I was not of this earth. Good enough. It didn't matter what they thought I was as long as they didn't know I was a vampire. "You didn't answer my question. Where is Carmen?"

"And you didn't answer mine. I don't recognize you as any of the species in the Galactic Union." Clayborn pointed upward with the cigar.

"Okay, I'm not one of you. There's your answer."

"Where are you from?"

"Colorado."

Clayborn nodded again, his manner less amused than irritated. "What's your business here?"

"To get my friend Carmen. Let her go and then we'll chat over tea and cookies. Where is she? Why did you take her?"

He rolled the cigar between his fingers. "That concerns my business."

"Which is what?"

Clayborn blinked. When his eyes closed, both wrinkled eyelids looked like the butt ends of overripe avocados. That creepy smile deepened. He pressed the cigar against his nose slits and inhaled. "You smoke?"

"No."

"Pity. This is a *Bolivar Belicosos Fino*." For a guy from a million miles away from here, Clayborn's Spanish pronunciation was pretty good. Clayborn shifted and slid his free hand into a side pocket of his coat.

I flexed my legs. If he took out anything other than something to light his cigar with, he'd end up with a stump.

He produced a cigar clipper. After trimming the pointed end of the cigar, he put the cigar nub and clipper into his pocket and retrieved a cheap plastic lighter. He brought the cigar to his face. The flesh around his mouth extended to grasp the cigar. He sparked the lighter, bellowed his cheeks, and lit the cigar.

Puffs of spicy, aromatic smoke clouded the air between us. Magicians smoked to distract their audiences. What tricks did this alien joker plan?

"You're here on business, right?" I asked. "Then what do you want for my friend?"

Clayborn lifted his chin. His eyes narrowed to ebony slits. "Ah, a deal? What have you got?"

I'd give anything to guarantee Carmen's release. I offered Clayborn my most prized possession:

"Me."

CHAPTER
42

AFTER A moment, the smoke lost its pleasant notes and the smell became heavy and stale. Clayborn kept puffing on the cigar and fouling the air. A fan clicked on and the smoke swirled upward through a vent in the ceiling.

Clayborn removed the cigar from his mouth and examined it. "I can't do that."

"Why not?" I curled my hands into fists to hide my extending talons.

"Because your friend is worth more to me than you are."

"How so?" I fought to keep my fangs from sprouting from under my lip. I wanted to attack Clayborn and make him suffer, but I knew this intergalactic mafioso wouldn't have allowed me here without a scheme to keep me at bay. If I wanted Carmen back, I had to behave myself.

"Let me put this in a context you'll understand." Clayborn put the cigar in his lipless mouth and talked around it.

"Among my 'people,' " he made quote marks with his hands, "the name for this planet is Harnaz, which means 'the forbidden jewel.' We have myths of heroes risking everything for Harnaz, often tragically."

"I can help you get to the tragic part and it won't be a myth."

Clayborn pulled the cigar out. He paused and let smoke linger in his open mouth before puffing it out. "Since you're from 'Colorado,' " he made more quote marks in the air, "you're not much of a space traveler, are you? If you were, you'd realize what a treasure this planet is."

He brought the cigar before his face. "Take this for example. Such an aroma. Exquisite. Reminds me of the Luzee, the inhabitants of Quark-42. They consume these extravagant feasts and then emit wonderful olfactory melodies through their various orifices."

"Let me eat some beans and I'll fart you a symphony."

Clayborn stuck the cigar back into his mouth. He snorted, "Ha. Ha. Ha." Little balls of smoke jetted from his ears.

"What's this got to do with Carmen?" I asked.

Clayborn tapped an ember from the cigar into the ashtray. "You know about the psychic world?"

"You mean Tarot cards and Ouija boards?"

"I'm talking about the many dimensions of the universe. Coincidences are more than random chance," Clayborn replied. "Living creatures have psychic energy fields that bind them together. Me. You. Carmen."

"I only know about the here and now," I said. "That's all."

Clayborn appeared disappointed by my answer, like he was hoping I'd join him on common ground. He kept tapping his cigar. The tiny bumps undulating across his aura formed larger nodules in the energy sheath.

It was good that I made him uncomfortable. "And this interest in the psychic world is what brought you to Earth?"

"Some of my colleagues died testing an invention, the

psychotronic device." Clayborn took a puff. "The infamous Roswell crash. You've heard of it?"

I shrugged. But I did know about Roswell and the psychotronic device. That was the reason Odin wanted me to infiltrate government security at Rocky Flats, to recover the psychotronic device from the UFO. When I learned that the device was designed to control humans by manipulating their psychic energy, I destroyed it. We vampires weren't sharing our humans with any aliens.

"The psychotronic device proved to be a dead end," Clayborn said. "For now. Manipulating psychic energy is a frustrating challenge. How then can we control humans?"

"Why do you want to control them?"

"Humans are the most violent and treacherous of all creatures. If we want to do business here, we'll need every advantage." Clayborn stared at me, as if trying to peer straight through my skull and into my brain.

I matched his gaze until he looked away. Never try a staring contest with a vampire.

"We've studied humans for a long time. Even with our superior technology, we know from their stories that they'd fight a military conquest. I've read *War of the Worlds*." Clayborn looked back at me. "The ability to wage war is the most developed of their society's traits. We'd be playing to their strongest suit."

Given the centuries of art and literature, it was telling that the aliens considered war-mongering humanity's greatest achievement.

"The situation here requires a delicate hand." Clayborn's fingers undulated like snakes.

"Of course it does, considering the quarantine." I couldn't help but smile. "Gilbert Odin told me about it. You and he are not supposed to be here."

I wanted this extraterrestrial scumbag to realize I knew of his part in this murderous game. "Why did you kill him?"

Clayborn withdrew the cigar, looked at it, then at me, and

frowned, as if the cigar had lost its flavor and I was to blame. "How does that concern you?"

"Because now it concerns Carmen."

Clayborn pointed one of those tentacled fingers at me. "Only because you got involved."

I wanted to twist that finger off his hand. "You're right. Where do we go from here?" I pressed the argument. "The U.S. government has invested a lot in protecting you. Why?"

"Power." Clayborn rubbed his fingertips together. "Money. We learned that humans are as greedy as they are violent. Why fight them? Why not make it in their interest to give us what we want? We'd approach those in power, the leaders of the largest governments and businesses, and offer to sell our technology."

"What technology?"

"The easiest to deliver and the most profitable. What we'd appeal to is human vanity. Sell to the emotion, the intangible. Their culture is obsessed with appearances and the trappings of sexuality."

Appearances and sexuality? "I don't follow you."

"You've heard of the actualizers of Rizè-Blu?" Clayborn smirked, the kind of smirk I'd expect from a frog after it devoured its insect prey. "I brought them here."

What would it take for a vampire to let his jaw drop in astonishment? This news. The months of relentless hype on every venue: billboards, television, radio, print, Internet, podcasts, text-message blasts, even urinal cakes. Take our pills. Grow your hair. Lose your hair. Get bigger breasts. A harder erection. Rizè-Blu was making billions and the campaign was only a few months old. And aliens were behind it all?

I closed my mouth, coughed in embarrassment, and sat up to regain my composure. "Interesting scenario except for one problem. Don't underestimate the humans. What's to keep them from copying the formulas and cutting you out of the picture?"

Clayborn nodded, pleased by my question. "The molecular structure is designed to break down after a few weeks. That means that Rizè-Blu must continually update the formula and renew our franchise agreements."

Clever. "I'm confused about something. Since you come from space, what good would money do?"

"What do you mean?"

"Do you wire the money to an account on Jupiter? What's the exchange rate between dollars and your outer-space *pesos*?"

Clayborn studied the smoldering tip of his cigar. "We don't take cash. Instead, Earth has commodities that demand a high price among members of my social circles."

"Social circles? You mean your fellow crooks?"

Clayborn didn't challenge the slur. "No, they're similar to the humans who run the show here on Earth. The politicians and corporate leaders."

Of course. Crooks. The universe was full of them. "You said commodities? The quarantine means no contact or trade so it must be contraband. You guys violating the quarantine means that whatever you've come for must be worth the risk."

"They are." Clayborn blew on the cigar tip and the ember glowed. "These cigars for example. One box pays for a trip here."

"Give me another example. I'm not convinced you've traveled all this way for stogies. You mentioned trading your technology for contraband. There's got to be more to your visit than shilling hair products and filling larger bras. What about intergalactic communicators? Stellar-drive engines? Blasters?"

"Don't be stupid. We give humans blaster and space-drive technology and within a century they'll do to the Galactic Union what the Europeans did to the Indians."

Smart thinking. The alien's regard for human treachery rivaled mine. "What is this commodity?"

"This planet has two great treasures. Water and women." Clayborn relaxed, his aura smoothing with confidence. "They can keep the water."

I stayed quiet, to absorb this revelation. Odin had said the reason for his murder had to do with saving the Earth women. I never dreamed it would be from alien gangsters. But what did the aliens want with the women? Why and where were they taking them? And what about Carmen? I forced myself to remain calm. "How so? Earth women have a completely different anatomy from yours. Try as you might, good intentions will only get you so far."

"So what? Despite our physical differences, your females are remarkably alluring."

"Meaning everyone likes Earth pussy. It's quite a compliment."

"We don't have to mate with them to enjoy their company."

"Then you're missing out on the best part. What kind of outer-space geniuses are you guys anyway?"

Clayborn's laugh came out more as an annoyed chuckle. "Quit thinking with your gonads. Earth women possess an intuitive sense much more developed than the males. They have an awareness for the psychic world that we didn't expect from such primitive thinkers as the human race. Because of that, Earth women make great companions."

Companions? "I don't understand."

"Think nice collars. Lots of pampering."

Collars? Pampering? "You mean like pets? You're trading your advanced technology for Earth women and turning them into pets?"

"You say that like it's a problem."

"Of course, it's a problem. A huge problem. A crime."

Clayborn gave a gloating laugh. "Crime? According to whom?"

"Me."

"Why do you care?" Clayborn asked. "The women will be well taken care of."

"But pets? You said 'collars'? What about leashes? Are you going to make them do tricks?"

"That's up to the owners."

"Owners?"

Clayborn gave a confused look, as if I didn't understand the meaning. "This is a business."

The revulsion made me sick and dizzy. What other plans lurked in the fine print of their pact? How long before the aliens figured out what I was, and then what? The extermination of us, the undead?

I asked, "Do the women know of this arrangement?"

"Their government does and that's all that matters. They've weighed the moral concerns versus the material gain to society and decided it's worth the cost."

Those bastards. Selling out their fellow humans to the aliens. "Guess it's easier to count the profits when someone else's sister is sold into slavery."

"How is this slavery? The women will do no work. They'll live in undreamed-of luxury. Only the wealthiest among us can afford them."

"You can't buy human beings. It's wrong."

"Too late for that. We already have. The U.S. government, acting as an agent to its corporate sponsors, sold them to us. I can show you the bill of lading."

"But the government doesn't own the women to sell."

Clayborn raised his hands in a sly, innocent gesture. "That is a domestic matter. Out of my control completely."

"You're forgetting murder. Not just Gilbert Odin's. What about Marissa Albert and Karen Beck? What about all the passengers on the commuter plane killed to hide the disappearance of Vanessa Tico and Janice Wyndersook? And there are other missing women. Did you abduct them all?"

"The logistics of this operation are," Clayborn rubbed the ends of his fingers together, "sticky."

Sticky as blood. "How do you choose which women to kidnap?"

"I have a profiling list and I give the names to Colonel

Goodman. He and his team have been resourceful and thorough. If their government doesn't have a problem with this, why should I?"

His logic made me dizzy. "How many women do you plan on taking?"

"Whatever the market will bear."

I wanted to puke. I couldn't hide my disgust with him and his human partners in this gruesome conspiracy.

"Don't look so upset." Clayborn uncrossed his legs. "I'm an expert in homo sapiens behavior. They can rationalize anything. Take war. They'll bankrupt their economies, sacrifice the best of their young, unleash a bloodbath that impresses even me, at the expense of providing shelter, food, and medicine for their own people. Compared to that, the sale of a few women is trivial."

"Unless you're one of those being sold. I don't trust you, Clayborn. There's more to this than taking Earth women and cigars." I grew quiet and thought about what he really wanted.

"When I said we wanted to *control* humans, perhaps that was the wrong word." Clayborn's mouth curved slowly into a reptilian smile. "I should've said 'domesticate.'"

I immediately saw rows of humans tagged and warehoused in pens. "Like animals? You're crazy. Impossible."

"Not at all. We give the humans what they want and they line up so we can milk them like contented cows. They hand over their women and in return they make more money." Clayborn leaned forward from his chair. "We've already got Cress Tech and their Ivy League patrons in the National Security Agency mooing for more."

The very people who were supposed to protect us have sold us out. There hasn't been a betrayal this deep since Judas. "Clayborn, you've been doing a lot of talking. What for?"

The alien set his hands on his knees and leaned even closer. "Good point. That brings us to your friend Carmen."

My anger snapped back into focus.

"She's a special prize. I don't blame you for wanting her back. At auction, she brought an astronomical sum."

Carmen sold at auction? My *kundalini noir* rose within me, a cobra readying to strike. I boiled with rage. Clayborn must have surely been blind to psychic auras, or else he would've seen mine light up like an exploding bomb.

"What makes her so special is that she's one of you. Her psychic energy field is exceptionally strong. What is she? What are you, Felix?"

Vampire. I wanted to flash my fangs and talons. I wanted to revel in his gore as I ripped that leather hide off his alien bones.

My sixth sense made my ears ring and my fingers hurt, they tingled so hard. *Careful. He's baiting you.*

My mind stepped back to distance myself from my emotions. How could I regain the advantage? What did Clayborn not expect me to know?

I smiled. "Where's Goodman's blaster? The one he used to kill Marissa?"

Clayborn nodded. "I have it."

I kept my smile. "Odin had a blaster of his own."

Clayborn's aura flared. His fingers clutched, as if snatching something from the air. He caught himself, relaxed, and smoothed his trousers. "I wasn't aware of that. Where is it?"

"Before he died, Odin asked me to dump his body in the gulf. A spaceship took his corpse and the blaster. Don't suppose they were friends of yours?"

Clayborn's penumbra tightened around his form. He snubbed his cigar and left it in the ashtray. "Are you sure you're not with the Union? You ask a lot of questions."

"I'm a curious guy."

"What's the expression? Curiosity killed the cat."

"A cat's got nine lives."

"How many have you used up?"

"I'm keeping track, don't you worry. Give me Carmen. I'm not leaving here without her."

Clayborn swiveled his big head toward me. His eyes were as cold as ice. "You shouldn't have said that. Because it means you're not leaving."

A wall of white light shone between Clayborn and me.

Time to strike. I sprang to my feet.

He smiled from behind the translucent haze.

I didn't know what that light was. I snatched the ashtray from the end table and threw it against the light. The ashtray exploded.

Clayborn's smile widened. A force field protected him. He retreated behind the partition.

An alarm went off. The red light on the entrance flashed.

I ran to the closest wall to break through and escape. I scraped my talons against the surface. Concrete. Same for the floor and the ceiling. It would take time for me to claw my way out, time I didn't have.

CHAPTER
43

T HE LIGHT beside the door went from red to green.
The lock snapped open.

I ran beside the door and got ready to attack.

Two men carrying submachine guns rushed in. I swept
my foot along their ankles and bowled them over. Their
heads smacked the floor and their auras dimmed as they lost
consciousness. I leaped into the foyer and slammed the door
shut behind me.

The elevator doors were open. Red lights blinked in the
hallway. An alarm blared, its horn screeching and echoing.

I didn't see any stairs or another way out, other than the
elevator. The exits out of the building were below me, and
the guards would assume that the only way to escape would
be down.

The elevator was all I had and I got in, trap or no trap.
Cameras stared at me from opposite upper corners in the

compartment. I swung my fists and knocked the cameras from their mounts. Let the guards work to find me.

I jumped and hooked my talons into the elevator ceiling. I tore at the ceiling panels and made a hole big enough to slide through.

Standing atop the elevator, I saw that I was on the second floor. I grasped the girders supporting the elevator and climbed to the third floor.

I set my toes and hands against the doors for the elevator and clung with supernatural sticky force. I ran my fingers between the doors and pulled them apart.

I faced an empty hall and paused for a second to get my bearings. No alarm sounded on this floor, but I could still hear the one shrieking downstairs.

Men shouted to my left.

I dodged right down the hall, turned the corner, and came face-to-face with a human guard armed with a shotgun. He stood before a metal door that looked like the hatch on a ship.

His eyes gaped at me. I didn't have time to zap the guard; instead I knocked him out with a punch across the jaw.

The door was milled from thick steel and fastened to the wall with heavy bolts. The door lock had a slot for swiping a badge.

The guard carried an ID badge clipped to a shirt pocket. I took the badge and swiped it through the lock.

A screen above the lock flashed: BEGIN RETINAL SCAN.

What now?

An arrow on the screen pointed to a lens above the door lock.

I lifted the guard by his hair and pulled his left eyelid open. I wasn't sure if this would work.

I pressed his face against the wall with his eye centered over the lens.

The screen showed an image of the guard's retina. A line scrolled top to bottom across the screen.

The screen flashed: RETINAL SCAN COMPLETE.

A light on the door lock pulsed from red to green, and a latch inside the door clicked.

I dropped the guard and turned the handle of the door. I stepped over the threshold into a long, darkened room.

The only illumination in the room came from small desk lamps and the blank faces of computer monitors. I could see well enough.

I pushed the door closed. All the outside noise hushed. I spun the door handle until it stopped, then gave it an extra twist to jam the mechanism.

The room took up most of this floor, about fifty feet wide and a hundred and twenty feet to the far wall. Computer servers sat in bookcases, blinking spasmodically, sharing shelf space with stacks of notebooks and binders. A laboratory of some type?

Two rows of strange metal cylinders, each with a soft, bluish luster and big enough to hold a coffin, rested on wheeled dollies in the middle of the room. Each row had four cylinders, for a total of eight.

Four more cylinders stood along the circumference of a pedestal in the middle of the floor. The circular pedestal was about fifteen feet wide and rose above the floor about a step's height. Two more rows of cylinders lay on dollies on the opposite side of the room.

The door of a freight elevator stood on the north side of the wall, directly above a door similar to that I'd seen in Clayborn's suite. This elevator must be how they moved the cylinders from floor to floor in the annex.

I approached the closest cylinder. It held a large glass capsule. Inside the capsule lay a woman in a white medical gown, resting on her back against a white cushion, hands to her sides, her expression serene, as if in peaceful sleep. This woman's complexion was the color of milk chocolate. Given her skin tone, her nose, and the oval shape of her face, she looked like the photo I'd seen before of Vanessa Tico. I turned to the next cylinder.

Inside rested a blonde. Janice Wyndersook, Vanessa's fellow passenger on the doomed flight.

I dashed between the rows of cylinders, hoping that I'd find Carmen. Another woman, whom I didn't recognize, lay in one of the cylinders. The rest were empty.

I approached the pedestal. Each of these cylinders stood on parallel grooves that pointed to an indentation in the center of the pedestal. The glass capsules of the cylinders faced the indentation.

Hesitantly, I put a foot on the pedestal—it looked made of polished steel—and stepped up to see inside the cylinders.

The first one contained Carmen.

The joy at finding her ran through me like electricity. I got close to the cylinder and placed my hands against the cool glass.

Restraining bands across her torso, middle, and arms held her upright. Like the other women, Carmen wore white. Her eyes were closed.

Her aura shimmered softly, the visual equivalent of a soft hum. She was in a deep sleep.

How had they captured her? Drugs? A paralysis ray? A mechanical restraint?

I had to get her out of the capsule. I raked my talons across the glass. Didn't even scratch it.

I tore the metal leg from a nearby table. I smacked the capsule again and again. Carmen remained in her slumber.

A circular contraption the diameter of the pedestal hung from the ceiling directly over us. The contraption was a concave disk dimpled with ridges radiating from a thick glass rod pointing to the indentation of the pedestal.

The capsules must be slid down the tracks to the indentation, and then what? Was this a scanner? To measure psychic energy? A diagnostic tool? What?

In any case, it didn't look good.

I beat my hands against the glass and shouted: "Carmen.

Carmen." I wanted her to wake up and shine her *tapetum lucidum*.

Desperation choked me. I roiled with anger. I tried to tear the cylinder from the tracks but it remained fixed in place.

Okay, acting like a gorilla wouldn't solve anything. I calmed myself and examined the outside of the cylinder. There had to be a way of opening these things. I found a rectangular indentation on the right side beyond the glass front. The indentation was at hip height, low for me but right for someone of Clayborn's stature.

The indentation protected a series of slots and female connectors. This was where external devices or cables were attached. What devices? What cables?

Heavy steps rushed to the door.

Hurry, Felix.

I looked around for anything that would seem to fit the connections. A collection of devices, small boxes with cables, sat on the closest desk. I ran to the desk, scooped all the devices in my arms, and hustled back to the cylinder.

The front door began to squeal as if it was being twisted apart. The guards would soon make their way in.

I grabbed one device, ran my fingers over the cable to the end plug, and hunted for the correct connection. I turned the plug until it seated square, and pressed it tight.

The device, a blue plastic rectangle the size of a wallet, suddenly flashed a row of blinking lights. I fumbled with the device, trying to make it work. Nothing.

I dropped the device and picked up another. Its plug fit into a slot. This device, the size of a paperback book, had a screen that lit up. I tapped, then pounded on the buttons along its side. Again, nothing.

The front door clicked, the sound of metal snapping.

I rested my cheek against the cold metal of the cylinder. Carmen, I was so close. *Please hear me.*

Suddenly, there was silence. The guards in the hall had quit moving.

They were about to charge in. I had no choice but to escape. I couldn't fight them forever. With every passing moment, the guards would gather more reinforcements and greater firepower.

I felt like a coward abandoning Carmen, but if I stayed I'd be overwhelmed and either dead or inside one of these cylinders myself. In a final gesture of desperation, I kicked the pile of devices and cables and scattered them across the floor.

I pressed my hands against the glass. "Carmen, I'll come back and get you." I wanted her eyes to flutter, her mouth to twitch, anything, but her expression remained distant and serene.

Escape. That's what mattered now.

I chose an empty cylinder closest to the door the guards tried to open. I tripped the brake on the dolly. I wheeled the cylinder to point one end toward the door.

The door opened with a groan.

I shoved the cylinder and raced behind it.

Ramming speed.

Gunfire started and bullets pinged off the cylinder in front of me.

Men shouted, "Get back."

The cylinder rolled to the doorway and smashed into the center of the group. Two men tumbled past me. A half dozen more scrambled to get away. I leaped over the cylinder toward the open door of a stairwell beyond. I levitated over the steps and was out of sight before the guards could yell a warning.

At the bottom of the stairwell, six more men stood, barking orders into their radios. They jumped in astonishment and clutched their weapons.

I ran through the center of the group. I grasped the largest guy by his equipment harness and swung him in a circle to knock the others down like nine pins.

I let him go and sprinted at vampire speed down the corridor. A steel blast door lowered and I dove under it, sprang to my feet, and raced out the basement door, up the incline, and out onto the grass.

Guards on the roof shouted and opened fire. The silencers on their weapons muffled the gunshots to *fft, fft, fft*.

I dodged left and right. I hurtled over the chain-link fence and landed beyond the hedge. I turned south and raced through the trees of the golf course.

A white SUV, lights flashing and siren blaring, charged onto the golf cart path after me.

I reached the resort boundary and vaulted a fence into the garden behind a row of condos. I kept going into the street. A panel truck pulled up to a stop sign.

I slid under the truck. Down here it smelled of hot metal and grease. I hooked my hands and feet into the frame and hugged the drive shaft. The truck rolled forward. The universal joint of the shaft spun inches from my crotch. I hoped the driver took it real slow over the speed bumps.

A quarter of a mile down the street, the truck halted. From this angle I couldn't see much, except for the bottom halves of cars and the legs and shoes of people.

The baggy black trousers and boots of a guard came up to the driver's side of the truck.

"We're looking for a fugitive. About this tall, black hair. He's wearing a red shirt."

"Haven't seen anything," the driver replied.

"Get out anyway. We need to search your truck."

The driver stepped out. He and the guard went to the back of the truck. The latch snapped open and the rear panels rattled.

"Nothing but furniture. Wanna look? Be my guest."

The man in black climbed inside. His boots scuffed the floor above my face, and it sounded like boxes were being shoved around. He hopped out. The driver rattled the rear doors closed.

"If you see anything suspicious, call this number."

"Why not 911?"

"No. It'll be easier if you call the number on the card."

So the hunt for me wasn't about law enforcement. Surprise, surprise.

The driver got back in the truck. The guard returned to the SUV. The truck started up again and we drove to Highway 278, over the bridge, and into Bluffton. The odor of exhaust, especially the accumulated fart smell of catalytic converters, made me gag.

The truck passed a golf course and made a left off the highway. I craned my neck to see that no one followed. When the truck slowed at a corner to make another turn, I let go and dropped to the road. I kept myself as flat as possible, to let the differential pass and not conk me on the forehead.

The truck pulled away and the bright sunlight hit me full in the face. I jumped off the asphalt and hustled into the shade of an oak.

I was in an older residential section, mostly cottages with sagging fences and kudzu choking everything. The highway was to the north. The chalices' mortuary should be south, between here and Buck Point.

I dug into my pocket for my contacts, which I put in. Goodman and that extraterrestrial hoodlum Clayborn were on to me. They had Carmen and they knew I'd be back to get her. Plus they knew I wasn't human. Both of them assumed that I was another species of alien, which was fine. As long as they didn't realize the truth, that the undead walked among them.

I had to get Carmen soon, as I didn't know what plans Clayborn had for her. The familiar clammy hand of panic gripped me. I had to act.

Down the street I saw a *carnecia* and a shopping center catering to area Latinos. Piñatas dangled from the awning. Signs advertising phone cards and music CDs decorated the windows of a *mercado*. A truck from May River Commercial Laundry sat in the corner of the parking lot. I'd seen this truck before, at the Grand Atlantic.

A banner hung over the side of the truck facing the road: BUSCAMOS TRABAJADORES. PAGAMOS POR LA SEMANO. Looking for workers. We pay by the week.

A rescue plan started to gel. I'd return to the resort and I'd get in right under their noses. And I wouldn't be alone.

CHAPTER
44

THE SOUND of a big motorcycle engine chugged in front of the mortuary. Gravel crunched under the weight of the machine. The engine quit. They were here.

I fed a stack of e-mail printouts through a shredder in the kitchen. They were the replies my hacker had sent, Marissa Albert's cell phone records from the day she had arrived at Key West. Her last calls had been with her home office voice mail, her sister, Carmen's resort, and a listing for RKW. Who else could that have been but Goodman. He had set her up.

Heavy steps pounded up the wooden stairs onto the porch. I'd left the door unlocked because I knew they'd barge in.

The clock on the wall said 9:45 P.M. Less than six hours since I'd called.

Jolie shoved the door open. Her expression looked like she'd swallowed nitroglycerine and was about to explode.

Her aura blazed as hot as the jet from a flamethrower. A raccoon mask outlined with grime set off her eyes. Goggles rested on her forehead, across a green do-rag cinched over her scalp. Her muscular, freckled arms jutted from a sleeveless denim vest. Grease-splattered cowboy boots showed under jeans and a pair of black leather chaps.

Antoine clomped in behind her. His aura undulated with alarm. He lifted the goggles from his face and the clean skin around his eyes made the rest of his grimy and bug-plastered face look gray by comparison. He brushed dirt from his goatee. "That's from doing five hundred and forty miles in under six hours."

"Big fucking deal," Jolie replied. "We'd've been here sooner but the goddamn bike wouldn't go any faster."

Antoine peeled the leather helmet off his head. "Serves me right for not getting my helicopter fixed. That's the last time I ride on the back of your bike."

Jolie wore fingerless gloves and clasped and unclasped her hands. "Felix, what's your plan to rescue Carmen? Mine would be to kamikaze my bike right down Goodman's throat."

"I feel the same way," I said.

"So what's the plan?"

I led Jolie and Antoine to the morgue. We gathered around the work table holding my coffin. I sat and readied my pen over maps that I'd drawn on a yellow writing pad.

The chalices, Leslie and Jack, came to the door.

I turned to Jolie and Antoine. "How about a bite to eat? It'll get your mind right."

Jolie eyed the chalices and shook her head. "No thanks. I'm too worked up. Put me close to a neck and I'm likely to do more than feed."

"Antoine?"

He went to the sink and ran the water, holding his hand under the spout as he adjusted the temperature. "Sure. With coffee. I'll hold off using my fangs for the serious work."

Antoine splashed water onto his face and scrubbed with a bar of soap.

I said to the chalices, "Coffee then. If you don't mind, we have private business to discuss."

"Of course," Leslie replied. She and Jack left and closed the door.

Jolie paced about the room, still opening and closing her fists. "So what's the plan?"

Antoine wiped his face and hands with a towel. He balled the towel and tossed it to Jolie. "Here, wash up. It'll help you cool off."

Jolie caught the towel and threw it back to Antoine. "I don't want to cool off."

"You need to. We all need to be thinking clearly."

Jolie kept pacing. "I can think clearly enough."

Earlier, I'd told Jolie what I knew about Carmen's capture, Goodman, and Clayborn. I was sure she'd shared that with Antoine.

"Just get to the plan." Jolie kept pacing.

Antoine pulled a chair and sat at the table beside me. I pointed to the map with the layout of the resort, the hotel, and the annex. "We sneak in."

"Why?" Jolie's aura burned with so much anger that if it were fire, the house would've gone up in flames. "I'd hit them hard in the gullet and plow through their defenses. We'd be in and out before they finished shitting their pants."

"I like the way you think, Jolie," I said. "But if we did that, we wouldn't get close to Carmen, much less rescue her. They have a lot of firepower."

I pointed to the maps. "My plan is that we sneak inside."

Jolie clenched her teeth. "I don't want to sneak."

"Hear the man out." Antoine clasped Jolie's wrist. "After we get Carmen, then you can settle whatever scores you want."

I nodded to Antoine, thanking him for helping calm Jolie.

I smiled at her. "Don't think of it as sneaking. We're infil-trating."

She pulled her arm free and went back to pacing by the table.

"When we trip the alarm, I want us to be here," I tapped my pen against the drawing of the annex, "instead of here on the perimeter. That will buy us time. I'd rather that we infiltrate in and then fight our way out."

Jolie stepped close and moved my pen to study the map. "Yeah, makes sense. That way we can recon their defenses on the way in. Plus their attention would be on keeping us out. When we have Carmen, we'll be attacking security from their rear. That's always a good tactic."

"We'll meet here." I noted a place between the northwest corner of the hotel and the side entrance, where there were no security cameras. "We'll climb to the hotel roof. From there we'll make our way to the annex. I'll get in through the top. You two go through the basement entrance." I showed them the door that Goodman had driven the golf cart through. "You'll find the electrical conduits here. Disable the power. Look for the backup and disable that as well. We'll use the dark."

"Dark?" Antoine asked. "When are we going?"

"Tonight. As soon as we're ready."

Jolie nodded again but didn't smile.

I showed them another map; this one had the layouts of the basement, second, and third floors as best as I could re-member them. I drew asterisks where the electrical panels would be. I traced my pen over the stairs and elevators. "There is a freight elevator on the north side. That must be how they move the cylinders."

Jolie stopped her pacing. "Like the one holding Car-men?"

"Yeah."

"Okay, we're in the annex," Jolie said. "Then what?"

"We go after Clayborn on the second floor."

"Why? This plan is to rescue Carmen."

"I need him to open Carmen's cylinder."

"What if Clayborn's not there?" Antoine asked.

"If, if, this plan is riddled with ifs." I raised my voice in irritation. "If Clayborn is not there, then we either break Carmen out or we find a way of escaping with the cylinder."

Antoine pressed on, "We spring Carmen, we capture this Clayborn alien, what's next?"

"We should be here, back in the basement of the annex. As to getting off the resort, that's the iffy part of my plan," I confessed. "We'll have to play it by ear."

"Playing it by ear, huh?" Antoine rubbed his chin. "Well, me being a musician, I don't like this tune." He sorted through my drawings and took my pen. Antoine hunched over the table. "How about a suggestion? You and Jolie get in the annex on your own." He drew another rectangle. "This is the roof of the annex." He marked an X on the rectangle. "After you get Carmen and Clayborn, wait for me here."

"You lost me, Antoine."

"Go back a bit. While you and Jolie go to the resort, I'll make a detour to Hunter Army Airfield and borrow a helicopter."

Hunter Army Airfield lay southwest of Savannah, a two-hour drive from Hilton Head. The airfield was the home of the aviation brigades for nearby Fort Stewart.

"And this makes my plan less iffy?"

"Considerably. Once Jolie, Carmen, and you get on the roof, I'll swoop down and scoop you up."

"In a helicopter?"

"That's what they got at the airfield."

I studied the sketch. His idea gave us more of a chance than mine did. "What kind of helicopter?"

"Yeah," chimed in Jolie, "I don't want nothing like that piece of crap you got back on the island."

Antoine scratched his temple. "Depends on what I can get

my hands on. Maybe a Blackhawk. A Huey. A big Chinook. That would be fun."

"You know how to fly a Chinook?"

"Nope. I've never been in a Blackhawk either but I'm a quick study. I have confidence in myself."

"The army's not going to let you fly off with one of their helicopters."

Antoine chuckled. "Like I haven't thought of that already. You take care of your part of the rescue and I'll worry about getting you off the roof."

I said, "Timing's going to be critical."

"I'm ahead of you. Helicopters carry two-hours-plus worth of fuel. Call my cell phone when you start to move in. I'll give you an hour. That will leave another hour's worth of gas to get away."

"Away to where?"

"That's the iffy part of *my* plan. By the time you call me, I'll have it figured out. I do well in pinch situations."

I thought about my getting past security, our attack into the annex, the reaction of the guards, and us being ready just as Antoine swooped to pluck us off the roof. This rescue was a real lash-up job. Rube Goldberg wouldn't lend his name to this rickety disaster-in-waiting.

CHAPTER
45

JOLIE SHUFFLED the drawings. "Is this going to work?"

"It has to," I replied.

"What if you run into Goodman?"

"I hope I do. Because then he dies."

There was a knock on the door and Leslie announced herself. I answered. She brought in a tray with a carafe and three heavy mugs. She set the tray on the table next to the writing pad.

Antoine took the carafe and filled a mug. The steamy aroma told us it was Peruvian Andean Gold and type B-positive.

"Is the blood fresh?" he asked.

Leslie rolled her right sleeve and showed us the new bandage on the inside of her forearm. "Any fresher and you'd need to fang me."

Antoine nodded appreciatively and sipped his coffee.

I poured the blend into the other two mugs.

"Do you need anything else?" Leslie unrolled her sleeve and covered her arm again.

Antoine shook his head. Jolie acted as if she hadn't heard. I thanked the chalice and dismissed her.

Antoine snagged a chair with his foot. "Jolie, sit already. You acting this nervous is going to curdle the blood in my coffee."

Jolie stopped and stared at him. Her aura slowly dimmed, like she had turned down the burner on a stove. Grabbing another chair, she spun it around to sit astride it. She crossed her arms and propped them on the top of the chair's back. I gave her a cup, which she sipped. Her aura dimmed a little more. Good.

Jolie said what all of us knew but none of us wanted to say: "You know that if we can't rescue Carmen we'll have to kill her."

Her tone was heavy and ominous, but she was right. The protocol set by the Araneum was that no vampire could be detained under conditions that could expose the existence of the undead world. Spending the night in a drunk tank was one exception. Either the vampire was freed or, if that was not possible, the vampire would be annihilated along with evidence of its existence.

Antoine rubbed the creases growing on his forehead. "Does the Araneum know about this?"

"I haven't said anything to them," I replied.

"When will we tell them?" Jolie asked.

"If we fail to get Carmen out."

Jolie stared at me. "Or destroy her."

We all had the same question. *How do you kill a friend?*

"We fail and it's shit creek," Jolie continued. "Felix, it's vampires like you and me that the Araneum would dispatch to handle a situation like this." Jolie put her hand on Antoine's knee. "No offense big guy, but you're not the kind of muscle they'd call for this."

Antoine waved her off. "None taken. The less I hear from the Araneum, the better."

His aura percolated with worry. He was an artist, not a fighter. Conversion to the undead doesn't change one's basic nature. A crook is still a crook, a liar remains a liar, a decent musical guy, well, he's still musical and decent, if you overlook the penchant for occasionally biting people on the neck and sucking their blood.

Antoine flipped through the writing pad and found a likeness I'd drawn of Clayborn. "Is this the alien?"

"Yeah."

Antoine took the pad, studied the drawing, and passed it to Jolie.

She grunted dismissively and laid the pad back on the table. "That's one ugly motherfucker. Probably got chased off his home planet for scaring the neighborhood kids."

"Where is this Clayborn from?" Antoine asked.

Jolie chuffed. "What? You're going to send this troll a Christmas card?"

Antoine let the sarcasm slide. "How was Carmen captured?"

"I don't know," I answered uncomfortably. "She went to meet a couple, boyfriend and girlfriend, for fun. You know Carmen. Turns out it was a trap."

Jolie rose from her chair. "You know this couple?"

"I do. In fact I introduced them to Carmen." Saying this made me feel like a dumb ass.

"Are they still at the hotel?"

"Probably."

Jolie's talons extended into spikes. "Good."

Antoine downed the last of his coffee and blood. He stood from the table. "I better get going. Hunter Army Airfield is not close."

"Either of the chalices will take you there," I said.

Antoine returned my pen. "How exactly are you going to get in the hotel?"

Jolie unsnapped her denim vest and arched her back to stretch the tank top across her breasts. "I know men. Some stupid bastard won't know what hit him."

"And you, Felix?" Antoine asked. "They'll be expecting you to come back for Carmen. They've certainly got your name and face on some watch list. How do you plan to get in? Transform into a wolf?"

"Nope. Nothing that complicated." I slipped the pen back into my pocket. "I'll be coming right through the service door."

CHAPTER
46

I CLIMBED INTO the middle seat of the Chevy van. Leslie the chalice had used her mortuary makeup magic and fixed me up with a mustache, soul patch, and a wig. The rug gave me a disheveled look, like I hadn't found my way to a barber's chair since I'd crossed the border from Mexico.

Another Mexican climbed in behind me, so I was squeezed in the middle next to Pablo from Nicaragua.

Angelo Sosa, the foreman, handed us Styrofoam cups of coffee and said in Spanish, "Here's so you sleepyheads are awake when we get to the hotel. Don't spill anything on your uniforms, you clumsy *tarugos*."

We were the night maintenance crew for the Grand Atlantic. That a bunch of immigrants were let onto a secure site should surprise no one. Back in Colorado, the newspapers had discovered that undocumented workers, most of them from Mexico (where else?), were tending the landscaping and cleaning toilets inside the perimeter of the satellite complex at Buckley Air Force Base. Weeds and dirty toilets don't take care of themselves.

I had zapped Angelo earlier and made him forge identity papers for my application and assign me to this crew.

He looked inside the van and counted heads. He lingered for a moment on my face, his expression perturbed. My post–hypnosis control wasn't perfect but was still good enough. I smiled at him. He smiled back and slammed the door shut.

The van pulled away from the curb and followed a panel truck loaded with clean laundry. Our headlights cut a swath through the darkness. The driver turned up the stereo and sang along to a ballad in Spanish.

We drove out of Bluffton and over the bridge onto Hilton Head Island. Traffic was light. I pretended to sip from my cup. Even with premium blood, this frog water wouldn't have been drinkable.

How was Carmen? My *kundalini noir* curled anxiously. How had they captured her? What was it like being in that capsule? She had looked okay, even peaceful.

Whom was I kidding? She was on her way to a kennel on another planet.

How many other women had Goodman pimped for the aliens? And at what price? In what other evil plans was our government in cahoots with Clayborn?

The fingers of my right hand closed as if gripping the edge of Carmen's cylinder. Before daybreak, she'd be free.

Step one was getting on this van.

Step two was getting past the guard. We made the final turn toward the resort. The headlights made the guard in a black SWAT uniform stand in relief against his shadow cast on the wall of the guardhouse.

The driver turned the stereo down. He asked, "What's with the guard's getup? Why all the guns?"

Pablo replied, "You know how it is. Somebody skips on

their hotel tab and they blame us. Good thing we work in this country. The rich gringos have someone to blame for their troubles."

The panel truck halted at the striped traffic bar blocking the road. The guard went to the driver's window and shined a flashlight. He was handed a paper, which he scanned by the beam of the flashlight and then stuck his head through the driver's window.

The guard stood away from the truck and waved. The traffic bar pivoted upward.

"Okay, *desgraciados*," our driver said, "make sure eagle-eyes can read your badges."

Everybody in the van opened their nylon jackets and flipped out the badges clipped to our neck lanyards.

The van pulled up to the guard and scrolled down the window.

"Good morning, sir," the driver said.

The guard shined a flashlight into the driver's face. He turned the interior lights on. The guard read from the paper the panel truck driver had given him, and counted faces.

I followed everyone's example and avoided eye contact.

The guard pointed the flashlight at me. "You. Are you new?"

I glanced at him, then at the driver. I raised my eyebrows and feigned ignorance. "*¿Que?*" What?

The driver turned in his seat. Damn, what if he had tried looking for me in the mirror?

"The guard wants to know if you're new," the driver said.

"It's my first time here, so of course I'm new," I replied in Spanish. I looked at the guard, nodded, and gave him my most simple-minded grin.

The guard stepped back and waved us through.

We turned left where the road forked, and passed the front of the hotel. I saw guards paired up and on patrol. On the roof of the hotel two more guards watched us drive by.

The van continued to the service area and parked. The panel truck backed up to an open bay.

The driver got out. "Everybody inside. The dollar is calling."

Step one. Check.

Step two. Check.

Now for step three.

CHAPTER
47

MY CREW and I pushed laundry carts filled with fresh linen and towels out of the panel truck. We arranged the carts on the right side of the service bay. The left side of the bay had rows of carts piled with soiled laundry. We hustled those carts into the truck. I had the privilege of pushing a cart heaped with damp towels that reeked of stale perfume and the nastiest body odor I had ever imagined possible from a living human. If rich people thought their money made them smell better than the rest of us, then they ought to get a whiff of this.

Pablo joined two other workers pushing a train of carts with clean laundry out of the bay through the swinging doors into the hotel. I ran up to him and helped shove the last of the carts. We guided the carts down the hall to a storage room and sorted the towels and bed linen onto shelves.

Angelo came by and put me to work running a vacuum cleaner in one of the conference rooms.

I kept reading my watch. Finally it said two A.M. Time to move.

I pushed the vacuum cleaner down the hall close to the side exit where I would meet Jolie. I hid the vacuum in a closet and went out the door.

At this time of the morning, anyone moving on the grounds would look suspicious. The guards watching the monitors would be bored and certainly notice me. But in this uniform, I was just another of the workers tending the property.

Outside, I stopped in the blind spot between the video camera and the corner. Where was Jolie?

A Gator drove up the road toward the guardhouse. I took out my contacts and scanned for auras. Other than the two guards in the Gator, nothing.

I stripped out of my uniform and disguise. Underneath I wore black sweats. I rolled the uniform and wig into a ball and stashed it behind a hedge.

Two fifteen. Antoine should be on the way. What about Jolie? She was supposed to be here. Knowing her, I should expect an entrance. Like a meteor crashing. I told her this operation had to be stealthy. We'd get plenty of fireworks before the night was done.

I couldn't waste more time. I had to get on the roof and scope the grounds. Two guards waited up there. I wouldn't have a problem dealing with them.

I set my fingers and the toes of my shoes against the wall. I looked up and around again. A light illuminated the side door and another the front corner of the building. The path on the wall above me was in shadow.

I climbed up, as sure-footed as a spider. I stopped short of the roof and listened.

I expected to hear footsteps or conversation. Where were the guards? Why were they so quiet?

CHAPTER
48

I COULDN'T BE too careful. What if the instant I poked my head over the wall, a searchlight nailed me and volleys of machine gun bullets clawed my body to pieces?

I raised my head and looked.

Jolie sat on the prone bodies of the guards piled on top of each other. "Hey there. In another minute I was about to do my nails." Her aura glowed with triumph. "It's showtime." She stood, her lean body clothed in a trim black jogging outfit. She showed me her cell phone and tucked it back into a pocket. "Antoine's on the way. We got a half hour."

We surveyed the grounds. Sprinklers on the fairway to the right whooshed. Something heavy splashed in one of the ponds, probably an alligator lunging for its prey. A minute later, the sprinklers to the right fell quiet and the sprinklers on the left whooshed on. The red auras of tiny, nervous animals flitted underneath the brush.

Jolie and I walked across the roof toward the corner overlooking the annex. We levitated so that our feet barely scraped across the surface.

A video camera was fixed to the corner and swiveled to pan the annex and surrounding area.

"This has to go." Jolie knelt behind the camera. She grasped the cable and yanked it from the camera housing.

We waited for a moment, to see what happened. The gate to the annex enclosure opened. A golf cart with two guards rolled through.

"That's your cue," I whispered. "They will. be going through the basement entrance."

Jolie stepped to the edge of the wall. She dropped and glided down, silent as an owl.

She landed on the grass between the hotel and the annex, where the guards couldn't see her.

The cart rumbled toward the access ramp. As they turned to drive down the ramp, Jolie bolted around the corner and jumped into the cart behind the guards.

The cart disappeared from view. The door rattled open, then rattled again to close. Jolie was inside. My turn.

The annex roof had two lattice microwave antennas, five dishes pointed upward, and half a dozen whips arranged around a circular dish mounted flush with the roof. This dish sat right over the pedestal in the floor below. What was the purpose of this dish? It didn't look like a hatch. Was it an antenna? Did it have something to do with the cylinders inside?

I spotted a large square hatch. From its position along the center of the northern wall I knew it lay over the freight elevator that connected the lab to the lower floors. This was my way inside.

I flexed my legs and leaped for the annex. I spun my arms to keep the momentum. As I approached the roof, I summoned my powers of levitation so that I landed on the roof as softly as a pair of women's silk panties falling against a carpet.

I continued to levitate, and my feet barely touched the roof as I walked to the hatch.

It was made of steel, with two big hinges and a simple handle. No lock was visible. The hatch must be secured from the inside and rigged to the alarm. I knew the moment I pried the hatch open the circus would start.

Voices carried across the hotel roof. A guard called out: "Tom? Jerry? Why aren't you guys answering the radio?"

Tom and Jerry? Who else was up there? Woody Woodpecker?

From this angle I couldn't see the guard, but I could hear his boots creep across the roof.

I grasped the handle of the hatch.

He whispered, "Uh-oh." Then he shouted, "Command Group, two guards down on the roof. Code 116."

An electronic horn sounded and red lights flashed throughout the compound.

They know we're here.

I gave the hatch a mighty tug. The handle bent. I pulled again. Something inside snapped and the hatch swung open.

A red light flashed in my face. The alarm shrieked. The hatch opened to a shaft that dropped to the basement four stories below. A wire dangled from inside the hatch. The guards would know I had come through here.

I floated down the shaft and landed on the edge of the elevator door to the third floor, to plan my next move.

I looked across the shaft and stared into the lens of a video camera. The elevator doors opened behind me. A hand emerged and dropped a grenade.

CHAPTER
49

NICE MOVE, if I were human. I swatted the grenade
back through the door and slid it closed.

The voices on the other side yelped in terror.

Anticipating the explosion, I braced myself against the
jamb of the door and rode out the blast.

The plan had been to get Clayborn first and then come
back to this floor and free Carmen from the cylinder. But the
guards knew about me and that I was after Carmen. I had to
see if she was okay.

I slid the door open and sprang inside. Acrid smoke from
the explosion billowed around me. Peltier and Krandall
stumbled about, their faces ashen, and dust settled on their
black SWAT garb. Surprise and pain rippled through their
auras.

I snatched Krandall's submachine gun from his hands. I
squeezed a burst into his neck and torso. He flopped onto his

back. I fired two shots into Peltier and she fell. Krandall had no psychic cloud around his supine body. Peltier's aura quivered like the flame of a pilot light struggling to stay lit. These two got off lucky, compared to what I could've done vampire-style.

A third man wearing SWAT gear stumbled backward from me. He clutched his throat and coughed. I knew the man.

Goodman. He was as good as dead.

The overhead lights flickered, then went dim. The sudden darkness worked in my favor. I had the advantage of night vision, and the loss of power would have also disabled the security system. A couple of seconds later, an electronic hum reverberated through the annex and the lights flicked on again. A generator must have switched on. So much for that advantage.

The humming stopped and the lights went out again. Excellent. Jolie had disabled the annex's power.

The emergency lights above the door flickered on. I aimed the submachine gun and blasted the lights. Let's keep it dark.

Goodman stumbled like a drunk. His aura sizzled with confusion and pain. Blood dotted his face. He crashed against a desk and knocked a stack of notebooks to the floor.

Peltier's aura brightened as she rallied against her wounds. She fumbled for the submachine gun that lay by her side. She lifted her head toward me and struggled to aim the weapon. The laser pointer illuminated and the thin red light slashed through the smoke.

Stubborn, murdering bitch. Taunt the bull and expect the horns. I leveled my submachine gun and squeezed the trigger. The bullets tore the fabric of Peltier's chest armor and then chewed her pretty face apart.

Goodman's head jerked from left to right in confusion. Blood clotted his eyes.

The magazine empty, I tossed the submachine gun aside. "In case you're wondering, your matched set of killers is dead."

His expression darkened when he recognized my voice. He snatched a Glock pistol from his thigh holster. "You again."

"Expecting someone else?"

His aura signaled surprise but not fear. Goodman remained cold as steel.

He panned the Glock in my direction.

"Don't bother," I said.

Goodman fired anyway. Blinded, he was only wasting ammunition. The bullet punched into the wall.

I crept toward him, moving as silently as a shadow.

Goodman's breath escaped from his mouth in ragged gasps. His pistol trembled. He wiped the blood from his eyes and squinted at where I'd been.

I smiled at the futility of his efforts. "I'm right here."

Goodman swung the pistol at me, fired, and missed again.

I slapped the Glock from his hand. My talons sliced his fingers, and the pistol clattered across the floor.

Goodman retracted his wounded hand, cradling it against his chest, and slid against the desk away from me.

I stared into his eyes, the irises gray and dull, the whites bloodshot. They registered nothing.

Blinded, Goodman posed no threat. I would finish him later. My priority was to rescue Carmen from the cylinder.

The computer monitors presented their blank faces. Without power, the machines lay dormant.

The twenty capsules were still here, sixteen on the floor and four on the pedestal. But I didn't see any auras. My *kundalini noir* stiffened in alarm. I rushed to the closest capsule and looked inside. The padding showed the form where a human would be. It was empty.

I dashed down the rows. All were empty. I bounded onto

the pedestal and checked out the rest of the cylinders. They were all empty. I pressed my face to the glass and looked up and down, as if there was another place in the capsule to hide a body.

Despairing and then enraged, I grabbed the sides of the capsule. It remained fixed in place. I might as well have tried shaking a mountain.

I turned toward Goodman and shouted: "Where is she?"

Goodman's aura brightened with defiance. "You mean your friend, the other freak?"

"Where is she?" I grabbed a desk and flung it at Goodman. The desk whirled through the air, the drawers opening and spilling pens and papers. The desk crashed against the wall beside Goodman.

His aura flashed with fright. He jumped, lost his balance on the floor debris, and staggered back to his feet. His aura dimmed to a fearful glow. Good, the bastard needed to be afraid of me.

His face searched for me. "Clayborn took her. And the others."

"Where?"

"Away from here."

"Goodman, I'm way beyond pissed off. Give me a straight answer. Now."

"Clayborn sent the women up there." He pointed to the sky with his thumb.

"You mean outer space?" The hairs stood on my arms. I didn't want to know the answer.

Goodman replied, "Of course."

The aliens. This had grown worse beyond belief. "When?"

"Yesterday. Right after you got away from us."

"How?"

"Using more of that alien hocus-pocus."

"What does that mean?"

"It means, you stupid fucking bastard, that I don't know

and I don't care. Clayborn doesn't share everything with us. I don't trust him but that's not my job. I only follow orders, like I've done my entire life."

"How do I get Carmen back?"

"My guess is that you hitch a ride to Pluto and start there." Goodman straightened and squared his shoulders. He chuckled. "In other words, Felix, go back to your home planet and fuck yourself."

I stepped in front of Goodman. I grasped his upper arms and held him tight. He squirmed to escape but my grip was like iron.

"Goodman, listen to me. I got news for you. I am on my home planet." I stared into his eyes, the whites now gray and marred with clots of red. His irises dilated in the effort to focus on me. I gave him an ultra dose of hypnosis, and still nothing.

"I'm no alien. In fact, I'm a veteran and every month I collect a disability check for what happened to me in Iraq."

He squirmed again.

"Goodman, do you believe in the supernatural? You should."

"What the hell do you want from me?"

"I want you to die knowing the truth. I am a vampire."

Goodman shook and howled. His spit splattered on my face. "Vampire. Alien. I don't give a shit."

I wrapped my arms around him and nudged his head aside with mine. He smelled of burned ammunition and explosive, sweat, and my favorite, raw fear. My fangs rasped against the nubby beard growing from his throat.

I sank my fangs into his flesh. His blood spurted into my mouth, a delicious male nectar flavored with testosterone and adrenaline from his terror.

I pumped enzymes to hasten the healing process and hide my marks. Then I stopped the other enzymes that deadened pain. I'd kill him the way Carmen would have, al dente.

Goodman howled in agony. He wrestled to get free. His

face and neck became livid and red. The tendons pressed against the inside of his throat. His hands clutched my side and his boots thumped against my shins.

I let him go and he crumbled to the floor, grasping his throat. He retched and convulsed. Drool seeped between his teeth, over his lower lip, and down his chin. Pain surged through his aura, the penumbra becoming as turbulent as waves in a storm.

He dropped to his side, still retching. His eyes bugged out from their sockets, big as peeled eggs. Blood dribbled from his ears and tear ducts. His legs kicked and his back arched. His aura flashed and dimmed, fading until it disappeared. His corpse lay with his limbs splayed in a death dance.

Goodman was dead, yet I felt empty, unsatisfied. Another death on my slate and what had I accomplished? My friend Carmen was still on her way to another solar system.

I grabbed a desk and hurled it against the computers.

"Where is she?" I screamed at no one. I seized another desk and continued my rampage through the lab, wrecking as much as I could to vent my fury.

CHAPTER
50

I WAS WASTING time. I returned to the freight elevator
and looked down to the floor below, where Clayborn
lived. I'd go there and interrogate him, provided Jolie hadn't
ripped him to pieces already.

I smelled a different odor from the burned explosive in
the lab. This smell came from below. Was the annex on
fire?

I leaned forward and caught the elevator cables. I shimmied down one floor to the next door. The smell grew stronger. I swung from the cable and balanced on the ledge below
the elevator door.

I felt heat coming from the metal door. There was a fire. I
had to find Clayborn.

I jabbed my talons through the door. Smoke jetted past
my fingers. I sawed a gap wide enough for me to use both
hands and tear the door in two.

Heat and smoke rolled over me. I started to panic. I had to act fast or I'd lose any way of ever finding Carmen. I dropped to the floor, where the air was clearer.

I shouted, "Jolie."

"Felix," she answered from inside the smoke-filled room, "he's coming your way. Get him."

Before I could think to ask whom, Clayborn rushed from the smoke, bent over in a stooped sprint, those big clown feet of his propelling him with amazing speed. He clasped a ray gun in his right hand.

I pushed from the floor and clotheslined him. His neck folded over my arm and those Bozo feet of his arced through the air. The gun clattered across the floor and down the elevator shaft. Clayborn landed on his back, and his head smacked the hard floor.

Jolie appeared through the smoke and crouched beside Clayborn. "The little fucker shot at me with the ray gun, missed, and started the fire. Now that we've got him, let's rescue Carmen."

I didn't move.

Jolie looked at me. "What's the matter?"

It was hard to admit my failure. "Carmen's gone."

Jolie remained stone-faced. "What do you mean?"

The next admission was even harder. "She's been taken from Earth. She's in outer space somewhere."

Jolie's aura blazed as bright as hot, glowing metal. She wrapped her talons around Clayborn's neck. "Where is she? Tell me or I'll gut you like a fish."

Clayborn struggled for breath. He gasped. "There's nothing you can do for her now."

Jolie tightened her grip. "You better hope not."

The fire gained on us. We didn't have much time.

I peeled her fingers loose. "We better get moving."

"What about him?"

"We'll take him with us. He wouldn't let himself get stranded here without a way to get home."

Jolie jumped and tore a light fixture from the ceiling. She grasped the wire dangling from the hole and cut a length of about six feet using her talons.

"Here, bind him with this." Jolie handed the wire to me.

Clayborn remained dazed and docile from the blow against the concrete floor. His black eyes bulged from their sockets. A corona of pain flared around his yellow aura.

I looped one end of the copper wire around his skinny neck and twisted the wire tight. I wrapped the rest of the wire around his torso, cinching his arms against his chest, and trussed him like a pot roast. I picked Clayborn up and tucked him under my arm. He weighed the same as a medium-sized dog.

I returned to the elevator, paused at the threshold, and planned my jump.

Clayborn started to moan.

"Shut up," Jolie hissed. She tore a swatch from his pants cuff and stuffed the cloth into his mouth.

Flames roared in the room behind us.

I bounded against the opposite wall and zigzagged up the elevator structure to the access hatch I'd torn loose.

We emerged on the roof through the column of smoke pumping out the elevator shaft. Jolie and I coughed to clear our throats. Clayborn gagged and squirmed against me.

Jolie punched him in the head. "I told you to shut up."

We stepped away from the smoke and crouched on the roof.

Guards shouted in a frenzied chorus. Red and amber lights flashed across the resort. Alarms and claxons blared like wounded animals. Trucks and carts raced over the grounds in carnival-like pandemonium.

"Felix, if your intent was to confuse them, good job." Jolie dug a cell phone from her hip pocket. She glanced at the phone briefly. "That was Antoine. He's almost here."

Jolie lifted her head toward the west. The chopping noise of rotor blades approached.

CHAPTER
51

L OW ABOVE the trees raced the dark, humpbacked silhouette of a Blackhawk helicopter, showing no lights and with an orange aura behind the controls. Antoine.

"He's not going to stop." Jolie rubbed her hands together and flexed her legs.

I noticed the radio masts behind us. I'd forgotten to mention that hazard. Hopefully, Antoine had spotted them.

The helicopter roared over the resort like a specter. I got ready.

"You go left, I'll go right," Jolie ordered.

The Blackhawk rocked and altered its course for us. I aimed my jump for one of the main wheels hanging from the struts on either side of the fuselage.

The helicopter lifted its nose to decelerate. I adjusted my hold on Clayborn and kept him tight under my right arm. The helicopter rushed for us, as big and noisy as a locomotive tumbling off its tracks.

The wheel swung toward me. My legs snapped straight and propelled me through the air.

The tire slammed against my chest, and for an instant I panicked and thought I was going to bounce off. My left hand grasped the oleo strut and I swung my leg to sit on top of the tire. Jolie clung safely to the other wheel.

Clipped radio masts and a couple of dish antennas went whirling below us. I guess Antoine hadn't seen them.

The helicopter dipped its nose and sped toward the Atlantic. We banked north over the sheen of the metallic water. Behind us we left the resort in shambles and chaos. Flames and smoke swirled from the annex. Dozens of flashing emergency lights clustered around the hotel. Spotlights knifed across the grounds and the walls of the buildings.

Jolie squatted in the cargo hold of the helicopter, her hair tangled by the wind. She shouted over the deafening racket: "Let me take Clayborn."

I handed the alien to her and I climbed in.

I expected the Spartan interior of a military helicopter. This one had the upholstered seats of a limousine. I kept the cargo doors open to air out the smoke. I took the center seat behind the cockpit and strapped in.

Jolie climbed over the center console and slid into the copilot's seat. She put on a headset.

Antoine peered over one shoulder back at Clayborn and me. He shouted, "Who is that ugly bastard? And where's Carmen?"

I shouted, "She's gone." Saying those words brought the loss back and rekindled my guilt.

Antoine's aura brightened with shock. "Where?"

"Where we can't reach her." Someone had to pay for the way I felt and I tightened the wire around Clayborn's neck. "How can we get Carmen back?"

He gagged and managed, "What?"

I shouted louder, "How can we get Carmen back?"

Clayborn twisted his neck and turned one of his little ears toward me. "What?"

"You want to play deaf? We'd get to the questions later and I won't be so polite." I shoved Clayborn against the floor and used him as a footrest.

The helicopter kept close to the water and banked for the coastline. The inside of the Blackhawk was darker than the night. Antoine flew without needing the instrument lights.

He pointed to another headset hanging from the compartment ceiling. I pulled the headset on and the snug ear cups muffled the noise. I adjusted the intercom switch.

"Hear me okay?" Antoine asked, turning his face to me again. Jolie handled the controls. His voice crackled through the headset and his eyes glowed like red embers.

I answered yes and explained how we'd lost Carmen.

"Damn," Antoine replied. "I stole this helicopter just for her. This plush ride belongs to the Department of Homeland Security."

"She would've appreciated that."

"So what do we do?"

I stomped Clayborn across his back. "We grill our stow-away."

Jolie piped in, "I'll supply the lighter fluid."

Antoine clicked his intercom twice and turned around. He took over the controls and made a small adjustment to our course.

Lights dotted the shoreline. I guessed it was Parris Island, north of Hilton Head.

"Where're we going?"

"I had this all figured out," he answered. "I have a vampire friend in Green Pond. Runs an artists' colony. The plan was to ditch the helicopter close by and then lie low for a while."

"Good idea. We'll do that then until Clayborn comes to his senses and tells us what we need to hear."

Antoine announced that we were cruising up St. Helena

Sound. The cool air swirled around us with the humid scent of swampy water. We flew across the ragged shore and over the black Carolina landscape. The moonlight glistened across the surf and the marshes. We flew for another minute. Below us the ground was mottled with the deep black of the woods against the pewter gray of the grasses.

Suddenly the instrument panel lit up. Static rushed through the headset and became quiet. The engines surged, then quit, and the roar of the helicopter was replaced by a foreboding silence. The helicopter yawed to the left. Antoine adjusted the controls and the Blackhawk settled into a flat glide. All the instrument lights went dark again.

CHAPTER
52

ANTOINE'S HAND danced over switches and fumbled with the overhead circuit breakers. He started to shout, then realized how quiet it was. "We've lost power," he said.

I didn't need to hear that. Every setback put us further and further from saving Carmen.

"No shit, Orville Wright. What happened?" Jolie asked. Tendrils of worry whipped from her penumbra.

"You tell me."

"Now what?"

"I pick a nice place to land and autorotate, baby." Antoine shifted in his seat to peer down over the nose of the Black-hawk.

"Autorotate?" I asked.

Jolie answered, "Means gliding this helicopter to earth by windmilling the rotors."

Somehow, gliding and helicopter didn't belong in the same sentence. "You've done this before?"

"Not at night. And never in a Blackhawk." Antoine hunched over the controls. "Hold tight kiddos, and enjoy the ride."

Jolie cinched her harness and glanced at me. Her aura erupted with alarm.

Fear pulsed through Clayborn's aura. He wiggled to get free. I kicked him in the ass to settle him down.

"There's a road cutting through the marsh," Antoine announced. "I'll put us there."

As we *glided* down, the serrated tree line rose to meet us.

The helicopter pitched upward and the whirling rotor blades bit the air with a *whoosh, whoosh*. A cloud of sand bellowed around us and swirled into the helicopter. My stomach sank against the bottom of my belly.

The tail wheel snagged the ground and the helicopter whipped forward. The main wheels slammed the ground. I knocked my head against my seat. Clayborn bounced against the floor.

For a moment, all of us, even Clayborn, remained still. I wiped the dust from my face and hands.

Antoine released his harness belts and flung them aside. "Safe." He took off his headset and dropped it on the center console.

He and Jolie climbed out of the cockpit and came around to my side of the helicopter.

"What happened?" I asked.

"Hell if I know. I'm not going to fix the damn thing." Antoine panned the sky as if to renew his bearings. "Hope you guys are up for a hike 'cause we're freaking miles from Green Pond."

"Why not call for a ride?" Jolie dug her cell phone from her pocket. Her expression blanched in surprise. "My phone's dead."

Antoine pulled his phone out and flipped it open. "Mine's dead too."

I noticed that the second hand on my watch had stopped. I pressed the stem to illuminate the face and it remained dark. This was too suspicious.

Clayborn wormed into a sitting position. His aura undulated in a low boil of despair. Tendrils of anxiety lashed from the penumbra.

Jolie grabbed a loose section of wire and used it to drag him out of the helicopter. Clayborn tipped over the edge of the cargo compartment and fell headfirst onto the ground. He balanced on his big head for an instant, then landed on his back, faceup in the dirt, and those dumbbell feet splayed apart. His pained expression screamed, man, that hurt.

Jolie reached down and jerked Clayborn to his feet. "Ask that little fucker what the hell's going on."

I unwound the wire but kept it cinched around his neck. I looped the free end around my wrist to keep him tethered.

Clayborn pulled the cloth gag from his mouth and tossed it on the ground. He stayed quiet.

I tapped my watch to see if it would start working again. It didn't. "Seems all the electronics are toast."

Antoine looked up the engine cowling. The rotor blades spun lazily as they slowed. "Could be from an EMP."

"A what?" Jolie asked.

"Electromagnetic Pulse."

"Where would that come from?"

"Usually, a nuclear blast," I answered.

"I would've seen that," she replied.

Clayborn's big eyes turned upward to the twinkling stars. I gave the leash a tug. "What are you looking for? Your friends?"

Clayborn's aura sputtered like the fuse on dynamite. His black eyes fixed me with a glare of hatred. His toothless gape curled into a snarl. He mouthed the words "You'd better kill me because I'll never forgive this."

I brought my face close to his. "I don't remember asking for forgiveness. What I want to know is, how do we get Carmen back?"

Clayborn narrowed his dark, wrinkled eyelids. "Then consider me dead because you can't. Carmen and the others are gone for good."

Rage pounded through me. I fought not to kill Clayborn. I froze my grip to keep my talons from ripping him apart. "How'd you move them?"

"Teleportation."

Teleportation? "Like *Star Trek*?"

Clayborn smirked. "Please."

I wrapped both hands around his skinny neck and throttled him. "From where?"

He clutched my wrists. "The lab in the annex. That pedestal? It's the transmitter. We transported them to an orbiting ship."

" 'We'?"

"My comrades on the ship." A veneer of triumphant smugness smoothed Clayborn's aura. "The payment's been made. You'll be lucky to find where your friend Carmen will end up. Make it easy on yourself and forget trying to get her back."

I punched his ugly face. "That's not an option."

Clayborn dropped to a knee.

A low hum echoed through the darkness. Clayborn struggled to his feet and his aura blazed with terror. He shrank toward the helicopter.

Jolie and Antoine gazed about. Their auras surged with confusion and alarm.

"I've heard that noise before." My skin tingled with dread. "When another flying saucer came to take Odin's body."

"Flying saucer?" yelped Antoine. "Shit, first the power goes out on everything, then a flying saucer? Whenever one of those shows up in the movies, it's never good news."

"The last time they didn't do anything to me," I replied.

"Well pardon me if I don't share your confidence." Antoine's aura and face lit up with distress.

Jolie pointed. "There it is."

A black shape—a disk bisecting a spherical body—

floated into view above the trees. This flying saucer was a smaller version of the one that had taken Odin's body and the blaster.

Antoine backed away in the opposite direction. When his feet stepped off the sandy road and squished into the marsh, he bolted from us. His feet spanked the mud and his orange aura bounced over the saw grass like a burning ball.

Jolie shouted after him. "You goddamn coward, don't you want to see what happens?"

"Post it on your blog." Antoine's voice ripped through the darkness.

CHAPTER
53

T HE SAUCER glided close and hovered a hundred feet
from us, right on the edge of the marsh. The hum felt
like an electric tickle. The hairs rose on the back of my
neck. My *kundalini noir* writhed in alarm.

Clayborn's aura burned incandescent yellow with terror.

"They're not here to rescue you, are they?"

Clayborn stood beside me, quiet as a condemned man.

I gave the leash a tug. "Didn't think so."

Three struts extended from the belly of the saucer. It settled into the marsh, the struts flattening the grass and sinking into the mud.

A hatch the size of a car door opened and a ramp extended to the ground.

Clayborn squirmed. Jolie took a step from me.

"Where are you going?" I whispered to her.

"No sense bunching up, in case they open fire."

Clayborn tried stepping away.

"Not you." I jerked the leash and put my arm around his shoulders. "Who are they?"

Tendrils of despair snaked from Clayborn's aura. "I don't know."

"Then why are you so worried? Are they fellow crooks you cheated? Or are they the law?"

The tendrils twisted like burning snakes. Either way, Clayborn was in deep intergalactic doo-doo.

But before I gave Clayborn up, his captors would have to help me find Carmen.

A yellow aura filled the hatch of the saucer. One alien emerged, squatting through the hatch and climbing onto the ramp. He had a humanoid shape and unfolded his legs to walk upright down the ramp. A second alien followed him, then a third. Their auras signaled caution, and they each advanced with one arm extended and holding a blaster pistol.

They were identical triplets and looked exactly like Gilbert Odin: mustaches, short-sleeve shirts, and wrinkled khaki trousers—the kind of cheap clothes a civil servant like Odin would wear.

At the bottom of the ramp, the first alien tripped and fell splashing into the marsh. His aura blazed with surprise. The other two aliens rushed beside him, all three tromping in the mud and struggling to get the first alien to his feet.

"So much for an awe-inspiring close encounter," Jolie whispered.

Finally, the three aliens marched toward us, the mud-splattered one leading. A clip-on tie dangled from his collar. His aura simmered with embarrassment. They halted ten feet from me.

The alien at the left nudged the leader. "Go on."

Alien number one pointed his blaster at me. His aura brightened with confidence. "Surrender your prisoner."

A glop of mud fell from the tip of the pistol barrel. Another wave of embarrassment surged through his aura.

Jolie coughed.

The auras of all three aliens flashed like camera bulbs. They whirled and aimed their blasters at her.

I coughed.

Another flash from their auras and they whirled toward me.

I raised my free hand. "Easy now, guys. Someone could get hurt. We don't want trouble."

Alien leader lowered his pistol. The other two took his cue and lowered theirs as well.

"Who are you?" I asked.

"Deputies," said the alien on the right.

"Marshals," said the deputy on the left.

Alien leader flexed his jaw in irritation.

"You're cops?" I asked.

Alien leader nodded. "Cops. From the Galactic Union."

"You got any ID?"

"Yeah, sure." Alien on the right reached into his back pocket.

More embarrassment flared through the leader's aura. He elbowed the other alien. Leader raised his blaster. "Here's all the ID I need. Now give us Fugitive 187."

"Fugitive?" I gave the leash a tug. "I knew Clayborn here wasn't on the up-and-up. You got a warrant?"

Leader steadied the blaster. "Don't push it."

Jolie took careful steps toward Clayborn and me. "What's he wanted for?"

"Class 2 crimes against the Union Code of Order. Violation of the quarantine. Interplanetary racketeering. Smuggling exotic contraband. Social contamination of a primitive species."

"What primitive species?" I asked.

"You."

Jolie stood behind Clayborn. "Anything else?"

"Class 1 crimes. Murder. Conspiracy to commit murder. He's been sentenced to death in absentia. We're to bring him back, dead or alive."

I patted Clayborn's head. "Is there a reward?"

"Yes. We leave you two alone." Alien leader swung his pistol from me to Jolie.

"How did you find him?" I asked.

"We were patrolling near your planet Neptune when we picked up the power surge of a transporter dematerializer orbiting Earth. By the time we got here . . ."

By the time they got here? How many millions of miles away was Neptune? The teleportation happened yesterday, so they must have hauled serious space ass to get here.

Leader continued, ". . . the ship with the transporter was gone. But we got a fix on Fugitive 187. I didn't know how we'd get him from the compound on Hilton Head but when you escaped with 187 in the helicopter, it was easy as cake."

"You mean pie," Jolie corrected.

"Pie, cake, doughnut, whatever."

"My friend was teleported," Jolie said. "Where to? Is she okay? I need to get her."

Alien leader raised an eyebrow. He fixed his attention on Clayborn. "So it's abetting the illegal transport of a native species? That's a Class 4 offense."

"If we turn Clayborn over," Jolie asked, "can you get him to tell us where my friend has gone?"

"There is no if." The alien on the left motioned with his blaster at me. "Fugitive 187 must answer for the Class 1 crimes."

Jolie circled her hands around Clayborn's neck. Spots of intrigue formed and floated in her aura. "Then give us a day, a few hours, to get him to talk."

The leader snorted. "Don't bother. Show her, 187."

Clayborn slowly raised a hand and splayed his tentacle fingers across his right eye. The tips of his fingers squeezed around the eyeball and entered the socket. He winced and the eyeball popped out with a wet slurp. A wire bundle, like an optic nerve, extended from the eyeball into the socket.

As a vampire, I've seen all kinds of creepy shit. This ranked near the top.

He offered the eye to Jolie. She shook her head.

"It's a prosthetic," the leader said. "Your Mr. Clayborn embezzled from his fellow gangsters. They kidnapped and tortured him to find out what he'd done with the money. Besides taking his eye, they roasted his wives and children in front of him. And still he wouldn't talk."

Clayborn licked the eyeball to moisten it and screwed it back into the socket. "I remain true to my principles."

Alien on the right nodded. "So you see, it would be pointless to question him."

Jolie massaged Clayborn's neck. "Then you'll help us find Carmen. I can't abandon my friend." Her aura brightened with anger.

"Our friend," I added.

The leader answered, "Like I mentioned, that was a Class 4 violation. We have the Class 1s and 2s to investigate first."

"Too bad for your friend," said alien on the left. "We have our orders."

"Meaning Clayborn keeps his secrets."

"Probably." The leader beckoned that I turn Clayborn over to him. "We need to take him."

Jolie's aura raged with defiance. "You said dead or alive?" Her talons extended quick as hornets' stingers. With a move that would've been invisible to mortal eyes, Jolie's talons scissored Clayborn's neck. One second she was standing behind him, clasping his neck. An instant later she backed away, her hands held up. "Then take him."

Clayborn wobbled in place. His knees buckled, his body sagged, and his head tipped forward. Purple blood gushed from the neck toward the alien cop trio.

They recoiled in horror. By the time they gathered themselves, Clayborn had plopped dead between them. His head plunked facedown into the sand. I held the empty hoop of wire.

The leader paced forward and examined the corpse. He sighed with disappointment.

I extended my talons and readied myself for the attack. "Don't try to take us."

The leader shook his head. "Earthlings are outside my jurisdiction. I'm pissed because you just cost me a bonus." He shoved the pistol into a holster. He waved to his comrades. "Grab his arms and legs." The leader picked up Clayborn's head and jammed his fingers into the nostrils and mouth. He held the head like a bowling ball and at an angle, to keep the still dripping stump from soiling him with purple blood.

"What about Carmen?" Jolie asked.

"Can't help you."

"How can we find her?"

"Know any detectives?"

Jolie pointed at me.

The leader stopped and gave me the once-over. "Good luck, lady."

He followed the others up the ramp but slipped and caught himself before falling again. "I'll be glad to get home," he muttered. "This isn't worth the overtime."

The ramp retracted into the hatch, which then closed. The hum started once more. The saucer lifted and the three landing struts folded flush with the belly. The saucer rose into the sky, going faster and faster, and became a black circle that shrank into the void of night.

I stared into the spot where I'd last seen the saucer disappear. Jolie sat on the bottom lip of the helicopter cargo door. Her aura tightened and waves of despair pulsed through it. Her shoulders quaked and she rubbed her eyes. "Damn it, I wish I could cry."

She turned her vampire eyes to me. This was the first time I'd ever seen *tapetum lucidum* clouded with grief. "Where is Carmen? How can we get her back?"

She might as well have asked me to shit rocket fuel.

I looked back to the stars. Carmen was among them, not in a spiritual sense but for real. In a UFO, like she'd always wished for, but not under these circumstances. All my life I'd looked up at the night sky and wondered when and if it were possible to cruise among them. Now I knew it was not only possible but that I had to. How? And when?

"Call me a coward?" Antoine's voice carried across the marsh. He marched toward us, splashing through the muck, his orange aura signaling a fight.

"You're late for the festivities," I told him.

"Late hell." He pointed to the sky. "They left early." Antoine hefted a two-by-four with a big nail sticking out one end. "I needed something to even the odds. Took me forever to find this."

"Antoine, I can't even give you credit for trying. They had blasters and God knows what else. A board with a nail in it wouldn't have done much."

Antoine swung the two-by-four like a ball bat. "Let me hit you and then you tell me." He turned to Jolie. "What's up, babe?"

She started to explain. Antoine walked up to her and they hugged. A moment later, Antoine tore himself from her and flung the two-by-four into the sky. "Useless bastards." The board whirled and splashed into the marsh a hundred meters away.

Jolie checked her phone. "It's still dead."

Antoine leaned into the pilot's side of the cockpit and flicked switches. "Same here."

I said, "We better get moving before the government comes looking for their helicopter. Antoine, you lead the way."

He tugged at Jolie's hand. She pulled free, straightened up, and marched alongside him up the sandy road. I followed right behind.

Antoine began to trot. Jolie and I took up the pace.

"What about you, Felix?" He quickened the trot into a run. "How do you plan on bringing Carmen back?"

What was my answer? I glanced back to the sky and the stars. Carmen was a long distance away, even for a vampire.

CHAPTER
54

I HEADED BACK to Colorado on I-10. I drove straight
through, stopping only to gas my Cadillac and to hide in
the restroom of a Houston diner while I waited for the sunrise to pass. Some big, bad vampire I was, loitering in the
stall of a men's room. Times like these made me wish for
another spider bite . . . almost.

Afterward I sat at the counter and ordered a large coffee
and a breakfast burrito to go. Outside, I dumped half of the
coffee from the Styrofoam cup. Back in my car I set the coffee in a console cup holder and unwrapped the burrito, which
I lay on my lap. From the console I pulled out a plastic squirt
bottle of type A-negative. I filled the cup so the mixture was
fifty-fifty blood and coffee. I took a sip and added a little
more blood. I pumped a couple of squirts of blood into the
burrito. Mmmm, egg, jalapeño, and type A.

I didn't want to think about what had happened in the last

two weeks, I only wanted to get home. The enormity of the loss of Carmen overwhelmed me. This was worse than her being dead for good. In this case, the great sea of space and getting Carmen back seemed as impossible as me plucking a star from the heavens.

I couldn't do anything about it, and worrying didn't do anything except leave me frazzled and feeling helpless.

Something rapped against my car. I looked up. A crow peeked over the upper left corner of the windshield.

A crow? This meant the Araneum wanted something.

The bird's claws scratched across the roof of the Cadillac. The little black head appeared over my side window and tapped again, this time impatiently.

I felt a queasy hollowness and I knew I was in trouble. I had failed in my mission. I found out about the alien threat but the cost had been losing Carmen.

My appetite vanished and I put the burrito and coffee away. I scrolled the window down. The crow perched on the windowsill, facing me. A filigreed capsule the size of my little finger was clipped to the crow's right leg.

I caressed the crow's warm, soft head. The beady eyes expressed no emotion. With my other hand, I slipped the capsule from its leg.

I spread my knees and held the capsule low between my legs to keep it in shadow. I unscrewed the jeweled ruby cap from the platinum-and-gold capsule. The familiar and ran-cid smell of flayed vampire skin wafted upward. I used my little finger to pull out a roll of parchment.

I unrolled the tissue-thin paper and read this note.

We've been texting you. Check your cell phone.
Araneum

So the Araneum had gone snippy on me. I had a new cell phone but no car charger, so I had left the phone off to con-serve the battery. I turned the phone on and got an alert that

I had several voice mails and a text message waiting.

I checked the text message first.

FELIX
BE AT THE MOTHER CABRINI SHRINE THIS WEDNESDAY
AT 3 P.M.
ARANEUM

Sounded like a trip to the woodshed. Not good. I erased the message.

The Cabrini Shrine stood west of Denver on I-70. An unlikely place for a meeting.

I balled the parchment and tossed it out my window. When the parchment flew out of the shadow of my car and into the sunlight, the note immediately flared into a burst of fire that darkened into a puff of black smoke.

The crow stared at the vanishing smoke and blinked its eyes. Then it turned around on the windowsill and tapped against the capsule in my hand. I screwed the cap back on and fit the capsule on the bird's leg.

I tried to shoo the bird, resentful of the news it had brought. When it didn't move, I scrolled the window up. The crow jumped away, startled by the glass pane rising against its tail feathers. It flew to the hood of my Cadillac.

I honked the horn to shoo it again. The crow wouldn't scram.

I checked my voice mail. Jolie left a message wishing me a safe journey and telling me that she missed Carmen.

She signed off: "Call me."

There was a lot of sadness in her voice. I could wait for that conversation.

The other calls were from human clients asking when I'd return to my office. *When I got there.*

I started the car. The crow hadn't moved. When I got to the highway, the crow centered itself on the front of my car and faced ahead like a hood ornament. I accelerated to ninety miles an hour. The crow hunkered down and squinted into the slipstream.

Was this bird going to freeload a ride all the way to Denver? Fat chance.

I slammed on the brakes. The crow shot from my car like it'd been catapulted from an aircraft carrier.

Hasta la vista, you little feathered bastard.

The crow sailed over the concrete lane for a hundred feet. It spread its wings and wheeled upward to arc over my car.

Bird poop splattered on my windshield.

The crow gave a laughing caw. *Hasta la vista,* back at you.

CHAPTER
55

I WAITED AT the Shrine of the Sacred Heart, better known locally as the Mother Cabrini Shrine. The Catholic Church built the shrine to commemorate the first American saint, Maria Francesca Cabrini, Patroness of Immigrants. Her twenty-two-foot-tall statue stood on a commanding hill overlooking the Colorado plains to the north and the town of Golden straight east. Close by, I-70 snaked westward through the foothills into the Rocky Mountains and over the Continental Divide.

If anyone believed the myth that the Christian cross was as feared as garlic by us vampires, then a stroll to this shrine would destroy that fiction.

The Stations of the Cross bordered the concrete steps leading to the shrine. The dozens of crucifixes here—imbued with Resurrection juju, no less, should've been enough to incinerate any undead bloodsucker. But the only way to hurt a vampire with a cross would be to either bonk him on the head or sharpen one end and stab him through the chest.

Here I stood, at the top of the shrine, waiting for the Araneum. I didn't know their agenda. I was only told to show up. I'm sure they were pissed over what happened to Carmen. So was I. I'd be surprised if I didn't get a major ass-chewing . . . or worse. The worse part unsettled me. I didn't want my skin used for undead Post-it notes.

The sun warmed me and I touched up my sunblock with a tube I pulled from my pocket.

Mother Nature had given the Front Range one final arctic blast as a going-away present. Smudges of snow lingered in the shadows. Cirrus clouds traced across the distant sky like scrawls of chalk against cerulean blue. A brown haze ringed the horizon.

Two women in their mid-thirties, both wearing fleece vests over black jogging tights, leaned forward against the base of the shrine and stretched their legs. They chatted about tax law and money, so I guessed they were lawyers or accountants playing hooky from the office.

I peeked over my sunglasses to study their auras. Neither seemed interested in me. Good. I didn't want to be so far down on the vampire pecking order that the Araneum sent *humans* to interview me.

The two women turned from the shrine and bounded down the steps.

Coming in the opposite direction, another woman jogged up the stairs. Her skin was the color of a roasted coffee bean and she had short, black, nappy hair under a red head-warmer band. She held the leash of a large dog, some mutt with a blue-gray coat with yellow tufts around its neck and down its long, skinny legs.

I read her aura.

Orange.

Vampire.

The time was three on the dot.

An uneasy feeling ran through me. My *kundalini noir* shifted like it wanted to relieve a sudden kink.

Her aura had the even glow of a bulb filament, not betraying any hint of emotional turbulence. The Araneum had sent a real composed one to interrogate me.

The vampire crested the top of the stairs and halted. She stood a bit over five feet and wore sunglasses with rhinestones and a green jacket over a navy blue jogging suit. She carried a messenger bag over one shoulder. In human years, she looked in her early forties.

The dog had a red aura, so I knew it wasn't a supernatural in disguise. With its tail wagging and ears perked, the dog lunged playfully for me. It was a cross between a blue heeler and a golden retriever, hence the unusual coat. The vampire pulled the dog back, patted its head, and unclipped the leash. The dog bolted for me, sniffed my crotch, and turned away to explore the garden around the shrine.

The vampire wound the leash around one wrist. "Felix, good to meet you." She kept her distance, about six feet away, and didn't bother to extend her free hand to thaw her frosty greeting. "Phyllis." All business, she was. No point in asking her favorite color or taste in music.

I didn't recognize her face or name. "I know most of the vampires in the Denver *nidus* but not you. Where are you from?"

"You have a way of contacting Carmen Arellano?" Phyllis didn't waste time with prolonged introductions.

I didn't want to discuss Carmen but I knew we would. Thinking about her only uncovered the loss and deepened the scar.

I started with my story, beginning with my acquaintance of the alien impostor Gilbert Odin.

Phyllis raised a hand to stop me. "I've read Jolie's report."

How should I handle confessing my failure to protect

Carmen? What fate awaited me? Was the Araneum going to tear off my skin? The Araneum should have shared more information, preparing me to better deal with Goodman and Clayborn. Still, the fault was mine. Anything I had to say in my defense remained clotted in my throat.

"Sorry to hear what happened to Carmen," Phyllis said. Her admission surprised me.

"We would have told you more," she continued, "but we were afraid that you might get captured and talk. You didn't fail, considering the circumstances."

The words didn't make me feel any better. I was supposed to prevail regardless.

"What we want to know is, is there a way to get Carmen back?"

The question seemed absurdly simplistic. "If I knew where she was and if I had a flying saucer. You got one handy?"

Phyllis's stony smile meant of course not.

"I know the rules," I said. "No vampire can be held prisoner in a situation that threatens the Great Secret." The existence of the supernatural world. "If we couldn't rescue Carmen, we'd have to destroy any and all evidence of her existence. Jolie and I were ready to do that."

"I don't doubt you, Felix. But the situation has reintroduced a level of tension within the Araneum."

"What kind of tension?"

"There's a small but vocal minority within the high council who wants greater control over the vampire community. The majority, the status quo, says we continue with our laissez-faire approach. Only when a vampire threatens the Great Secret do we act. Outside of that, we're each on our own."

"You mentioned 'reintroduced,' meaning this tension has existed before."

Her blue heeler began sniffing one of the memorials in the garden. Phyllis whistled. The dog lowered its leg, gave an open-mouth dog grin, and trotted away.

"It's always been under the surface but not this pronounced," Phyllis replied, "not recently anyway. The flip side to control is who determines what control is? What is acceptable, what is not, and how are the rules enforced?"

"Not recently? There's a history to this?"

Phyllis's aura dimmed and nodules of discomfort budded along the penumbra. Considering how cool she'd been before, this must be some bad news.

"Civil war. It happened in the thirteenth century, about a hundred years after the Araneum was formed in reaction to the growing threat of the Knights Templar. The vampire leaders turned on each other, followed by assassinations, then more violence, and eventually an undead bloodbath. We almost exterminated ourselves."

"What saved us?"

"It wasn't because we came to our collective senses. All trust in the leaders collapsed and the violence lost its momentum. Basically, we got tired of killing one another."

"Interesting lesson. I've heard about our past troubles but I didn't know of a war among us."

"It's not a moment we're proud of. The war proved we are more human than we want to admit, despite what we say and how we act. The human lurking inside of us does more than nag our conscience with the need for compassion and the yearning for love. It also nurtures the irrational lust for mass violence and destruction."

"And Carmen's kidnapping by the aliens has rekindled this argument?"

"More than rekindled. And it's more than about Carmen. Or you. The aliens are a new threat and we have to decide how to deal with them. They'll be back and they'll want more. We have to be ready. We've learned the humans are willing to sell themselves for petty material gain."

"That a surprise?"

"'Course not. Heaven help us if we get in the way."

I hadn't realized any of this. I was worried about getting

my ears boxed by the Araneum, while the problem was way beyond that.

Phyllis continued. "The aliens have a psychotronic device, right?"

"That's correct."

"Meaning they have a primitive understanding of psychic energy but the point is, they know. This time they used money and the illusion of power to control humans. The next time they might have a more advanced version of the psychotronic device, something that can directly manipulate humans, or even us."

"Where does this leave me?"

Phyllis extended an index finger and touched the tip with her other hand. "Right here. At the vanguard. You're the point man in our negotiations with the aliens. They come back, you'll talk to them."

"And if I find a way to rescue Carmen?"

"Consult with the Araneum before you do anything. We'll help in whatever way we can."

"You sound like you know something I don't."

"We're not keeping anything from you, Felix." Her aura stayed calm. Still, Phyllis represented authority and those in charge always take liberties with your fate. If you object, it's because you can't "appreciate" the big picture.

"What about Goodman?" I asked. "He's dead but the people he worked for know a lot about Carmen and me."

"The government has a vested interest in keeping what happened quiet. We have family and chalices in place who can arrange that."

She opened the messenger bag and pulled out a small glass bottle with a chartreuse-pine spider inside. "You know about this?"

"I do. Wouldn't recommend it."

"Why?"

I told her my experience with the spider bite and that it had left me worse off.

She stuck the bottle back into her bag and slipped out pages from *The Undead Kama Sutra*. "And this?"

"Carmen about had it figured out."

"So it works?"

"She was close."

Phyllis nodded, allowing herself a fleeting expression of regret. She put the pages back in the bag. She pursed her lips and whistled. The dog perked its ears and loped back to her. She clipped the leash to its collar.

"Later, Felix. Try and stay out of trouble." Her aura pulsed and she smiled. "For as long as you can."

CHAPTER
56

I SAT WHERE my adventures usually began. In my office on the second floor of the Oriental Theater in Denver, Colorado.

I flipped from website to website on my laptop. The owners of the Grand Atlantic Resort blamed a foiled robbery for the shootout week before last. The hotel canceled all reservations and conferences, citing security concerns and structural damage. Two days later the resort was sold to Cress Tech International, and the next morning, the assault ship USS *Bonhomme Richard* arrived off the shore of Hilton Head Island. Helicopters ferried a battalion of marines, who formed a perimeter around the hotel complex. Landing craft shuttled Seabees and their heavy equipment from the ship to the beach. The sailors quickly demolished the hotel and surrounding buildings. They hauled the debris to the beach, where a dredging crane clawed through the piles and dumped them onto a barge guarded by patrol boats. By the time the sun had set the next day, all that remained of the Grand Atlantic was a shallow hole littered with concrete, broken glass, and twisted lengths of rebar.

The Beaufort County citizens' coalition threatened to sue the federal government and Cress Tech for violating scores of environmental and economic impact laws. The Hilton Head Association of Retirees also threatened to sue, because the noise from the demolition had ruined their golfing "experience."

No mention of aliens or kidnapped women. A link on one of the websites told about a helicopter from the Department of Homeland Security, recovered from a marsh inland of the Carolina coast. A spokesman from Homeland Security didn't say if the incident was related to what happened at the Grand Atlantic.

Rizè-Blu announced that it was temporarily suspending production of its cosmetic actualizers Olympicin, NuGrumatex, Luvitmor, and Tigernene, citing problems with quality control. The price of Rizè-Blu shares fell, and a Swiss spokes-blonde stated that the drop in production had nothing to do with the sudden cancellation of all the Eden Water–Green Planet projects, Rizè-Blu's partnership with Cress Tech.

Of course, I knew the truth. Clayborn had told me that without updating the formula, the actualizers would be useless. Without the profits of the actualizers, Rizè-Blu and Cress Tech couldn't afford their scheme to take over the Earth's fresh water using Eden Water–Green Planet.

I never found out the number of women kidnapped or the number of innocent people killed as "collateral damage." Vanessa Tico and Janice Wyndersook remained listed as dead in the plane crash.

I turned off and shut my laptop.

Where did this leave me? And the aliens?

I thought about the characters I'd met during this adventure. The ones I'd killed—Goodman, Krandall, and Peltier. The one who paid the ultimate price for helping me—Karen Beck. The one who had saved me—the homeless drunk Earl in Kansas City. I still owed him. Plus the fiery Jolie and her chum Antoine. I knew I'd see them again. As I would Phyllis from the Araneum. That was a meeting I hoped would never take place, since it would mean the aliens were back.

And then there was Carmen.

I collected the pages of her unfinished manuscript for *The Undead Kama Sutra*. I shuffled them and pulled a page at random.

Title: "Maid Churning Butter." The drawing showed a female vampire astride a mortal man. Her feet were on top of his face and her hands on his hips. She pumped herself by flicking her wrists. Obviously, she needed either exceptionally strong wrists or the power of levitation to make this position work.

The eroticism escaped me. I didn't see two lovers flailing in passion. I instead saw Carmen taking notes and trying to fathom the spiritual undertow as would a hydrographer studying the ocean currents.

I slipped the page back and thumbed the manuscript. The drawings flashed by in a shifting kaleidoscope of carnal contortions.

Carmen was on to something, something deep and spiritual beyond the ken of the undead.

Where was she? How could I find her? What were they—whoever, or whatever, they were—doing to her? I fought to keep my imagination from running amok with gruesome images.

I blamed myself for what happened to Carmen. She was a victim of my hubris. We should've been more careful. It wasn't the alien gangster Clayborn who had captured her, it had been his human accomplices. Fortunately, if there was an untarnished spot anywhere in this fiasco, it was that Clayborn and the humans remained convinced that we vampires were a rival alien species. For now, the secrets of the undead realm remained safe.

I could keep Gilbert Odin's money (the original fake Odin) in good conscience. *Good conscience.* There I go again. What kind of a vampire was I?

As for any hope of rescuing Carmen, I could only wait until the improbable happened again.

My desk phone rang. I set the manuscript down and picked up the phone's receiver. "Felix Gomez speaking."

A man replied, his voice husky and eager. "Mr. Gomez, private detective?"

The timing of the call seemed too coincidental. My *kundalini noir* stirred. My fingertips tingled. I clumsily sketched a UFO on my desk blotter. "Yes."

"Good. I'd like an appointment. I have uh . . . a delicate situation to discuss."

It's always a delicate situation. "Your name, sir?"

"Charles Mancinelli."

"Does this situation involve extraterrestrials, Mr. Mancinelli?"

"Extraterrestrials? You mean like aliens? Hell, no. This is something legitimate."

"Sorry, I had to ask." My *kundalini noir* calmed. My fingertips stilled. I drew a line through the UFO, crossing it out. "Please continue."

"Yeah, I imagine a man in your line of work gets a lot of nut jobs. Extraterrestrials. Aliens." Mancinelli laughed. "Little green men. Go figure."

I didn't feel like laughing. "Let's get to your case."

"You're a serious guy, aren't you?"

"You want to hire a clown, check the *Yellow Pages.*"

"Okay, let me tell you about my case. Hold on. It'll astound you."

I doubted it.

**Flip the page to check out
the next declassified installment
from Mario Acevedo,**

JAILBAIT ZOMBIE

Coming March 2009

"FELIX, DROP your pants."

The last time I heard those words, they were from a topless stripper.

Tonight was different. Mel said them, but the wound on my leg hurt too much for me to protest.

Mel was the acting head of the local *nidus*, Latin for nest, in this case the community of Denver vampires. Tendrils of anxiety writhed from his orange aura, a bright contrast against the gloom of an autumn night. With a greasy gray mane combed back to his shoulders and scraggly white muttonchops, Mel projected none of the glamour associated with Hollywood vampires.

We were on a deserted construction site in Aurora, a suburb east of Denver. Though Aurora's the second largest city in Colorado, it's the Fresno of the Front Range: square mile after square mile of strip malls and cheap rents that run together to create an asphalt grid of nothing.

I rested against the foreman's trailer, unbuckled my trousers, and slid them to my knees. Smoke and blood trickled from the teeth marks on the inside of my left thigh.

"Smoke?" Mel asked, astonished. "That damn zombie must have left silver fillings when he bit you."

Silver. No wonder this hurt so much.

Mel's right index fingernail extended into a talon. "Hold still."

I gripped the muscle around the wound to distend the punctures. Mel crouched and slid the razor-sharp nail into an opening where the smoke puffed out. A fresh jolt of pain coursed up my spine and out my arms. He flicked his wrist and a tiny piece of smoking goo spun to the dirt.

He spit into his palm and pressed it over the wound. "This is as close to a hand job you'll get from me. Doesn't mean we're in love or anything. In fact, please don't call me in the morning."

I massaged the injured muscle. "How about a card on Valentine's?" The vampire enzymes in his saliva dulled the pain and accelerated my supernatural healing. By this time tomorrow, all I'd have is another battle scar to add to my collection.

I put weight on the leg and it finally felt like I wouldn't collapse from the pain. I fastened my trousers and limped to the edge of a hole excavated for the basement of a large building. Concrete slabs formed two sides of the hole but the rest was still packed dirt.

The zombie shambled within the hole where we'd chased it. He—obviously once a man—cradled his head under one arm and used his other to grope along the concrete. His mottled, waxy complexion and the clumps of trash stuck to his grimy clothes made it look like he'd been rotting in a shallow grave for a week.

I had removed the special contacts that masked my *tapetum lucidem*, the mirror-like retinas at the back of my eyes. The contacts were part of my cover to hide from humans, but wearing them kept me from using night vision or seeing psychic auras.

I didn't know if zombies had night vision; I had no idea of any of their powers other than they were supposed to be hard as hell to destroy. Tonight I had discovered an important fact, they had no auras, which made them a bitch to track in the dark.

The zombie clawed a dirt wall, climbing up a foot before stumbling backwards. He dropped his head. It plopped against the dirt and rolled like a lopsided melon. The animated corpse sank to its knees and crawled along the ground, one arm searching in a wide arc.

The head worked its mouth and turned onto its face, where it used its nose and chin to inch toward the body. I was more disgusted than fascinated. Yes, zombies are undead, as we vampires are. But comparing them to us was like comparing turds to eagles.

The *Araneum*, the world-wide network of vampires has one standing order: *Destroy all zombies.*

The reason?

We must ruthlessly protect the Great Secret—the existence of the supernatural world—from humans. Their disbelief of the supernatural was what kept us vampires safe.

We've seen what humans have done to each other.

War.

Genocide.

Wal-Mart.

Against their growing technical prowess and corporate savagery, what chance did we the undead have? Our best hope for survival was to remain cloaked by superstition and fable.

Zombies have no regard for keeping the Great Secret. They materialize (From where? I don't know.) and begin their rampage for mortal flesh, literally mindless of the consequences. Vampires have been able to disguise zombie attacks as examples of deranged cannibals—Jeffery Dahmer copy-cats. But zombies may make one attack too obvious and then humans would be on to all of us supernatural creatures. After that, we can expect the methodical obliteration of the undead.

Therefore, all zombies must be exterminated.

Protecting the Great Secret is what I do for the Araneum. My day job is private detective. My real job is the pro bono work I do as a vampire enforcer.

"This your first zombie?" Mel asked.

"Yeah."

"How'd he get the drop on you?"

"I was stupid," I replied. "After I laid him out with a shovel, I was going through his pockets."

"Why didn't you decapitate him?"

"I did. Right after that he shot from the ground, head in hands, and clamped onto me. Don't let that walking corpse routine fool you, he's got moves."

The zombie found his head, picked it up, and stood. Strands of muddy drool hung from the lips and the neck stump. The dull eyes swiveled left and right and fixed upon a wooden surveyor's stake pounded into the dirt. The zombie approached the stake and yanked it free. He worked the square end of the stake into the raw meat of the neck opening in his torso. Using both hands, he fit his head over the sharp end of the stake. He gave himself a rap on the top of his skull and the head squished tight into the collar of his shirt.

Looking at this repugnant creature was like watching an abscess ooze pus.

Where did the zombie come from?

Who made it?

And why?

Mel propped himself against a length of pipe that he'd used to club the zombie. He handed me a wallet. "Your zombie dropped this."

The wallet looked—and smelled—like it had been recov-

ered from a Bourbon Street gutter. I opened the wallet and
sorted through a Colorado driver's license, supermarket
cards, and a debit card. The money bills and business cards
were scraps of wet, dirty pulp.

I read aloud, "Name on the driver's license is Barrett
Chambers. From Morada." That was in the San Luis Valley,
over two hundred miles away. How did he get here?

I slid the wallet and cards into my coat pocket. I brushed
my hands across my trousers to wipe away the slime.

The zombie made noises like he was gargling sludge. The
smell hit us. Make that sewer sludge.

"This guy doesn't seem much for conversation," Mel said.
"Wouldn't do any good to question him."

A young vampire named Dagger appeared from behind
an excavator and walked to the edge of the hole. Mel had
brought Dagger because the newbie bloodsucker wanted to
prove himself as an undead terror.

Trouble was, Dagger was a high school dropout and a
punk. Once undead, he changed his name from Bartho-
lomew, said it lacked vampiric *panache*. Must've taken him
all day to find that word in the dictionary.

Dagger carried a metal garden sprayer. He set the sprayer
between his feet. "I filled this with super unleaded. It's
gonna make one hell of a flame thrower." He waved the
sprayer nozzle at the zombie. "Hey smelly boy, feeling cold
dressed in those rags? Let me warm you up."

The zombie turned toward Dagger. He stopped at the bottom of the wall, raised his arms, and emitted a guttural
moan.

Dagger laughed, kicked dirt into the zombie's face, and
aimed the nozzle. Gasoline splattered on the zombie's head
and soaked his clothes. He waved his arms to block the
spray.

Dagger took a cigarette from his shirt pocket and set the
butt between his lips. He dug a plastic lighter from his pocket
and held it to the cigarette.

"I wouldn't do that," I warned.

Dagger dismissed me with a fanged sneer. "Hey, I got it, pops. Anything happens, I got my vampire reflexes." He bobbed side to side.

I wanted to find the vampire who had turned Dagger and slap her. She hadn't done our bloodsucking tribe any favors by converting this arrogant dumb ass.

Dagger thumbed the lighter. It sparked and the gas fumes went *whoosh*. His clothes on fire, Dagger screamed and tripped over the sprayer, tumbling him and the sprayer on top of the zombie. They tangled together, their flailing bodies sandwiching the sprayer. Flames jetted from the pile, followed by a roaring fireball that mushroomed into a column of black smoke.

The heat slapped Mel and me and we were surrounded by the stink of burning compost. We stepped back. Mel covered his sideburns and said, "Awesome. I would've paid good money to see this."

The charred bodies settled in a burning heap.

We experienced vampires have a mandate to protect the newly turned, to protect them against everything except their own stupidity.

"That Dagger," Mel said, "what a dumb ass."

"At least he took one with him. What now?"

Mel ambled toward the excavator and climbed over the caterpillar treads to get into the cab. "Gotta make sure the zombie is a goner." He fumbled in the cab and tossed a padlock to the ground. A minute later the diesel engine grunted to life. The excavator boom lurched up and jerked left and right.

I hobbled out of the way.

The bucket on the end of the boom swiveled outward until its claws pointed down. The boom dropped and the bucket cleaved the bodies. Mel raised the boom and the bodies fell apart in halves. Smoking embers of flesh and clothes fluttered to the ground. He lifted and dropped the boom again and again, hacking the bodies into smoldering pieces. He yelled out the cab. "Hey, I oughta get a job at Benihana."

After Mel had chopped Dagger and the zombie into hash, he pulled the boom up and away. He climbed down from the excavator and stood beside me.

The pile of dirt looked like a lumpy mass of rancid bread dough. "Good job Mel, but we can't leave evidence."

"No problem. I'll make some calls."

This wasn't all we had to worry about. "There's a more pressing issue, I'm afraid."

"What's that?" Mel asked.

"Where did this zombie come from?"